# ULTRA

Also by Tim Sebastian

SPECIAL RELATIONS
WAR DANCE

# Tim Sebastian

# ULTRA

ORION

The right of Tim Sebastian to be identified as the author
of this work has been asserted by him in accordance with
the Copyright, Designs and Patents Act 1988.

First published in Great Britain in 1997 by
Orion
An imprint of Orion Books Ltd
Orion House, 5 Upper St Martin's Lane,
London WC2H 9EA

A CIP catalogue record for this book
is available from the British Library

ISBN 0 75280 792 7

Typeset by Deltatype Ltd, Birkenhead, Merseyside
Printed in Great Britain by
Clays Ltd, St Ives plc

For my mother and father

June 9 1969

House Committee on Appropriations, Washington DC. Subcommittee on Department of Defence Appropriations. Part Six.

Witness: Dr Donald M. Macarthur, Deputy Director, Research and Technology, US Department of Defence.

Dr Macarthur: Eminent biologists believe that within a period of five to ten years it would be possible to produce a synthetic biological agent, for which no natural immunity could have been acquired.

Committee: Are we doing any work in that field?

Dr Macarthur: We are not.

Committee: Why not? Lack of interest or lack of money?

Dr Macarthur: Certainly not lack of interest . . . It is a highly controversial issue. [But] without the sure scientific knowledge that such a weapon is possible . . . there is little that can be done to devise defensive measures. Should an enemy develop it, there is little doubt that this is an important area of potential military inferiority . . .

Committee: We would not want to have in the record anything that would be damaging to the security of the United States, but otherwise we feel that the Congress and the American public are entitled to know all the basic facts.

Dr Macarthur: A research programme to explore the feasibility of this could be completed in approximately five years at a total cost of $10 million. It is a highly controversial issue and there are many who believe such research should not be undertaken lest it lead to yet another method of massive killing of large populations. On the other hand, without the sure scientific knowledge that such a weapon is possible . . .

there is little that can be done to devise defensive measures.

What you have just read is fact. The date is real, so is the event, as well as the record of what was said.
What you are about to read is by no means simply fiction.

# Prologue

26 February 1991

Sixteen of them lay sprawled out in the back of the aircraft that night, eyes half closed, consciences left behind in another country This time, as every time, there were maximum levels of discomfort. Seats you wouldn't give to a dog, noise all the way to hell and back again. And then the jolts and jarrings of the Hercules that could shake your innermost convictions. 'Plane without Mercy', they used to call it, carrying killers and their toys on trips around the world – and then bringing somewhat fewer of them home.

They would joke that the in-flight service was off that day, like every day – and all they'd been promised was an endless, roundabout journey to get them somewhere they weren't supposed to be, with no unwelcome attention. Flight plans were filed, then de-filed, then finally torn into pieces in the wind. They were just another blip on a radar screen in a crowded corridor. Everyone was flying the same route.

Five hours out of the US Special Forces Headquarters at Hurlburt Field in Florida and they were over the Atlantic at no more than three thousand feet. With a moon out and a bit of imagination one or two fancied they could see every curl of the waves, every ship, every living thing out there in the maritime wastes. But Harden didn't do that. Imagining, he would say, only distracted him from the fucking awful things he had to do later.

He stared round the cabin, aware that most of the others had gone into that state of semi-sleep reserved for soldiers and the criminally insane. There were no markings on the fatigues. And that in itself said plenty. Heading into a war zone with no identification, no dog tags, just some weapons, a map reference and some very specific orders. And back home there were, as ever, no records, no paperwork, nothing to show they had ever left the US. The journey would never happen, had never happened. No one would go – and no one would die. And day was night, just as night was day.

'Land of make-believe,' Harden whispered to himself. All in the mind.

Some time, on that first day, Cyprus came out to meet them. So did Israel. And then it was clear they were on the final leg. Each knew it was the Gulf – and that something had gone badly wrong there. There could be no other reason to send them in. The war was in its closing stages. The Iraqis were about to concede defeat. Time for the US to pack up its bags and its bodies and take them home. Not send in a bunch of the Army's most secret units to do what they always ended up doing. Killing.

As the plane sank on to the desert runway and the propellers whipped up the sand, Harden screwed the silencer to a matt black stick of steel. He looked across at the men and gave a grin of reassurance he didn't feel. He had a few teeth left but not many.

And then there was no more time for thinking. Even as they came out into the sunlight, the Apache helicopters were landing about a thousand yards away, in their desert camouflage, angry and pointed, and built very much in the tradition of that kinder, gentler country that Washington likes to boast about.

They could have fitted in two machines, but you take three for back-up.

And only now, Harden observes, is the blood beginning to pump. Only now is the system engaging. This is the part where you don't look back and you don't wonder. You come in smooth and practised, and you answer the call.

Jerking now, as the machine pulls away from the ground, up through the dust and into a cloudless sky.

Weapons check. Just one more time. Like all the other times.

And it's always the last. However you sell it, whether it's an ad in a tiny paper or an Army recruitment poster, killing is temporary employment.

Twenty minutes gone and they came into the south of the encampment, counting the trucks and tents and personnel, seeing the men on the ground waving and jumping in the air. Reading the expressions of relief on their faces. They'd been waiting for this since they sent the message. The foot soldiers in the desert. Waiting for support from their allies in the coalition force. Waiting for the US Army to help them out.

And now the US had arrived.

Get among them, thought Harden. Let them come in close. But keep the engines running.

A dozen swarm in around the helicopters. Another ten emerging sleepy from the tents – Czechs and Norwegians – split away from the main battle group. Keep coming. Come one, come all . . .

And now they're shaking hands out there in the middle of nowhere, laughing, nodding, and a few start pointing to the thing that's brought the little party together.

The pallets, the containers, about a hundred yards away, with letters and numbers on them, and they never should have seen them, never should have approached.

Without appearing to move, Harden steps back, forming an unseen line in the desert, sun behind his men, sun blazing in the eyes of the Czechs, a few of the faces looking puzzled now. Little question marks. And then one of them has it: 'Oh my God,' he shouts and pulls at his pistol.

But Harden and the others are a thousand years too quick for him and before he's unfastened the clip on his belt the bullets are on their way to his skull. And then they're all firing. Weapons kicking and pumping at them, aiming mostly at their backs as they turn and run, falling, turning, falling again, face down in the sand. Ally killing ally.

Over so quickly, as Harden walks among them, sorting, finishing, taking the tags, flinging them all into a plastic container.

Fresh dead in the desert.

'What about the canisters, Harden?' A twenty-year-old, from Poughkeepsie, New York, gun in his hand.

'You leave 'em where they are, boy.'

'I thought we came to get 'em.'

'We've done what we came for.' He goes over to the stockpile. 'Hasn't been touched. That's all we needed to know. Nobody touched it.' He directs the others to turn over the containers, checking the undersides, the seals, the markings. No cause for concern because it's all in order. Nothing got out.

Nothing. No one. And only the sun has seen them.

Fast back into the helicopters now, rising as one. And it's not until they're at five hundred feet that they see the two armoured cars, heading east, and fast, if the dust around them is anything to go by.

'Fuck!'

Harden is right beside the pilot and fear is breaking out on his forehead. Tiny droplets rolling towards his eyes.

He taps the pilot on the shoulder and points, ordering him down.

The pilot shakes his head. 'Coalition aircraft coming up from the south. Saudi F16s. We have to get out of here.'

'The orders are to finish it.'

'Then finish it from the Hercules.'

Harden turns to look at the men. 'Fucking bastards!'

Harden remembered those minutes passing, like an illness. Jagged minutes. Some slow, some fast. He remembered telling his mind not to think any more. Not to replay. Only to go forward to a dark, quiet room, where he'd persuade himself none of this had ever happened.

Piling now into the Hercules, only one more piece of business to settle. One more thing to keep the clients happy and finish the contract.

'It's a detour, guys,' said Harden. And they all knew what he meant. The canister at the back of the plane was already being stripped of its tarpaulin, stuck on the chute, made ready to go. They would fly back east, over the area they'd just visited. And then the back of the plane would open on its hydraulic levers and they would kiss a little portion of the world goodbye.

It must have been twenty minutes' flying time – no more – before the orders were given. The pilots had scanned the skies. Nothing else was in sight and the so-called fuel air weapon was ready to go.

He remembered shutting his eyes, so he didn't see it run off the back, out into a cloudless sky over the thousand miles of desert. Didn't see it open up to begin spraying the atmosphere with petrol. Didn't see it ignite in a fireball, across hundreds of acres, sucking the oxygen from anything that lived, destroying all trace of men and machines and chemicals.

And because he didn't see it, it was easier to tell himself it had never happened.

Right from the outset, when they had gotten the call in Florida, he had known the details. The Czech decontamination unit had gone prowling off into the sand where it had no business to be. The location was an Iraqi speck in the sand called Al Samit, a hundred miles east of the Saudi border, just north of the 31st parallel. And way out in the wilderness, buffeted by the desert winds, they had stumbled over something that shouldn't have been there: a hundred canisters of a biological agent, so new and so secret that it didn't even have a name. On their radios, the Czechs had begun screaming their heads off in broken English, yelling and accusing, and the boys at Centcom had been unable to understand more than one word in ten. And then, in the middle of a sandstorm, their communications had gone down and the radios and satellite systems were useless. They were stuck in the desert with one of the most lethal substances on the planet – and no one to tell.

Only, without ever knowing it, they had told enough. Seven thousand miles away, by a six-lane highway in California, the giant radio dishes of the National Security Agency had plucked their message out of the sky, clarified it, and set off alarms right across America. Because the NSA was only too aware of what the Czechs had found, and who had put it there. The biological agents had come from a consignment tested out there in the Gulf War on a tiny remote town that no one would ever care about, because no one knew it was there. It was a huge success: most of the victims had died outright and the others were dying more slowly. Bonus cheques all round, cases of California champagne. Until the Czechs had discovered the spare supplies: a hundred of the most lethal canisters in the world. Made in the West and left by some God-almighty stupid bastard in the middle of the desert.

Small wonder Harden had received the call.

Bury it, they'd told him. Destroy all traces. And now he had.

Three months later, back at the Special Forces base in Florida, Commander-in-Chief, Gulf Land Forces, leads Harden out of the mess and into the darkness, like a dog on a leash. They had served four tours together. Killed and cried together. There is no ceremony between them.

'I've had a piss, sir, let's go back in.'

Lovett ignores him. 'That stuff in the Gulf, Vic. Get it out of your mind. It's over.'

'How do you know?'

'I've been given assurances.'

'Bullshit assurances.'

'Highest levels.'

'That's where they lie best, sir. You know that. You of all people should know it. Look at the record. Agent Orange, radiation, all the agencies they set up that Congress never knew existed.'

'This time it's different. The research has ended, the stockpiles are being destroyed. It's all over, Vic. Believe it.'

'You're a prick, sir. It's never over.'

Harden remembered shaking his head and walking away, hoping he'd never see or hear from Lovett again.

# Part one

# Chapter one

The edges of the buildings were jagged ice and the sky was unending grey. It was never going to change. The coldest front for twenty years sat still and immovable across the eastern seaboard and if the temperature ever rose again to zero there would, no doubt, be dancing in the streets.

Across the courtyard the neon lights blazed on every floor, in every office, but the people had long since gone home. He could see their desks still littered with paper, cartons of lunch, cans of soda, all abandoned, it seemed, until the spring. At mid-morning the weather alerts had gone out and in one collective lurch the city's workforce had raised its bottom and scattered to the suburbs. Local television was screaming about blizzards. Get home any way you can, they shouted. Get home, stay warm. Stay inside.

He had caught the last flight into National airport before they closed it, and the last taxi from there. As the car limped into Washington along the deserted parkway, Florida seemed ten thousand miles away. So did Julie, and the hotel on Cocoa Beach, and the sand, and the sunsets – and all the fighting from all the years that they had compressed into a final night.

'Which part of goodbye don't you understand?' was the question he could hear her asking. And he was still thinking of the answer as she got into the rental car and pulled away towards Orlando, just another set of headlamps, past the bars and the gas stations and out into the darkness. He couldn't help feeling that the two of them had always travelled far too light. Most people were cemented to each other by the things they acquired and the friends they shared. Somehow they had never kept either for long. Photos and mementoes had always been thrown away, apartments and houses changed and exchanged, friends allowed to lose contact. He had always been travelling, always thinking about being somewhere else. And she had her work as a scientist, never discussed, and always the top priority when it became time to choose. She worked for the Government, out on the edges of the defence department. That great, grand arena of national security, which sweeps everything before it – especially marriage.

He had known the weekend would crash. Three weeks since they had last seen each other, and when he had called her from El Salvador, a single sentence said it all. 'Yes, Peter, I'll be there.'

He could hear the distant note of irritation, carried so faithfully by the fibre-optic line. What had the advert said . . . ? 'You can hear a pin drop.' Well, he could hear *her* pin dropping, but it was more like a firing pin, clicking into action on a grenade.

'You don't have to come if you don't want to.'

'I'll be there. I told you.'

That's what she'd said. But there was no 'wanting'. She'd be there like an appointment at the dentist. They'd both be there. Both endure the pain. Somehow they'd both get through it.

Only he'd got excited on the way there. Through the endless crowds at San Salvador airport, out over the jungle and a clear blue sky all the way to Miami. And then he'd hired an open-top Mustang, blazing away past the orange groves, right along the narrow straight roads, all the way to the Cape. She'd be there at the end of it, looking great with the shoulder-length blonde hair that never stopped curling and the full soft mouth that he never tired of exploring.

At the hotel he checked in and showered, tested the bed springs, remembering, imagining. Down to the bar for the first of the night – a planter's punch, just to put him into overdrive, get him in the mood.

As he sat there, he remembered how they'd met in Washington at the end of '91. It had been a busy year. The end of the Gulf War, which he'd covered with the British forces. Nearly a month in the desert. Nearly a month of diarrhoea and mosquito bites and the fear that you don't talk about because it can get infectious.

He'd hated the war but had loved the people he met. That was the dilemma. The soldiers were in *their* element with a war and he was in *his* with a story. Heady stuff – plenty of bonding and joking and rattling around in expensive machines. And yet people were getting killed: Iraqi soldiers who would stumble sleepily from their fox-holes to be cut into shreds by the helicopter gunships. Not nice for a boy from the sheltered county of Sussex, eight years out of university, with a degree in nothing very useful, and a chance on *The Times* to prove himself. Not nice at all.

Without really meaning to, he ordered another punch and watched the blood-red sun sink towards the horizon. When he'd returned from the war, *The Times* had taken him out to lunch at Langan's and told him he was on the move again.

'Christ, not another war,' he'd blurted out, and instantly regretted it.

'Not for a while,' responded the foreign editor, 'not after you screwed up the last one.' But then he had smiled and shaken his head at his own private joke. 'Washington. Three years. You earned it in the Gulf. You really did. Maybe you'll even learn how to wear a tie.'

The tie had arrived in time but he hadn't known how to fasten it. At least, not before Julie.

Peter March had gone to Washington, like most Brits, firmly believing it was London with an accent. It took nearly a month before he began to suspect that he was wrong. The neighbours on King Place had held a drinks party to get to know the young Brit who'd joined the health club. The Pearsons wanted to tell him where to get the best china, the McIlvanes advised him on curtains – 'Not the red ones, oh, dear me, no. Not red. Not in this neighbourhood.' The Fosters, well, they were so rich and important they couldn't stay long enough to talk to anyone, 'Bill's got to be in the situation room at five a.m.,' and a lady, with that uniquely Washington combination of dark suit and trainers, hurried up the steps, shook his hand and told him she was Julie Richardson – 'I don't know why I've come. I'm moving out in a couple of weeks so we probably won't ever see each other again.'

'In that case I'll have to camp outside your door,' March had said, almost without realising, taking in the white teeth and the china blue eyes. And suddenly everyone had stopped talking and started looking at them. And in the way of such things they were 'an item' even before they knew it themselves.

'Did you see the way they stared at each other?' said Mrs McIlvane, as they tripped next door.

'Like dogs on heat.' Her husband scowled at the flowerbeds. 'Never liked Brits.'

When all the others had left, Julie had gone up to March. 'We seem to have made a bit of a spectacle of ourselves.'

'I enjoyed it.'

She blushed. 'And I have to go. My car's broken down. Means an early start and catching the bus.'

'I have a car.' He looked straight into her eyes. And that seemed to decide the issue. The next morning Julie and Peter went to work together. They ate lunch together. It would be just a matter of time, said the neighbours, before they went to bed together.

He shook his head at the recollection. Four and a half years ago in the District of Columbia.

He turned round from the bar, caught sight of the blonde flash of hair, and stood up quickly, feeling a stab of expectation. Maybe it was the old Julie coming over to him . . .

But his smile wasn't answered. She touched his hand, bypassing the kiss. Half of her was somewhere else. Only the cold Julie had come to Florida. He could see that now. She had packed no basket of fun; there was just a little case of resentments, arguments and an entire collection of the undressed wounds of the last five years – spent half together, half apart.

She ordered a glass of Chardonnay before he could ask what she wanted and then sat facing the bar, turning only her eyes in his direction. 'Peter . . .'

'Darling, are you hungry?'

'No. I ate earlier.'

He could feel the evening dive into the bay. Why eat, why meet, why be there at all?

A waiter brought menus but he waved them away. He looked

down at her hand, half expecting the thin platinum band to have gone. But it was still there.

'You've been working hard.' She took a sip and pushed the glass to one side. Like a closed chapter.

'Trying.'

'I read your piece from San Salvador about the US involvement there.'

'I didn't know you got the paper down here.' He smiled. 'What is it – an air-mail copy?'

'No.'

'Someone bring it from London?'

'You could say that. They showed it to me at work.'

'And?'

'And what d'you think, Peter? I've told you this kind of thing before. I work for the Government. They don't like it when you piss on their party. Time after time. Story after story. It's almost an obsession with you.'

'I'm a journalist, Julie. You know that. You knew that when we met. Nothing's changed.'

'Yes, it has. You keep hitting the Government and pretty soon I won't have a job. It's that simple.'

'Is it?'

'I'm not going to leave my job so as to allow you to write crap about government plots and spooks and all kinds of nonsense.'

'You know it's not like that. They just don't fancy the idea of a Brit in Washington with his nose in all the wrong places.'

She turned and glanced at the other tables. 'Keep your voice down. You can be incredibly naïve when you're on your truth kick. Sometimes lives are saved when we *don't* go public, sometimes secrets have to be kept for the public good and –'

'And lies told.'

'Yes, if necessary.' She pushed away her glass. 'And lies told.'

'I can't do that, Julie.'

'Then I can't go with you. Not any further, Peter. Not any more.'

It was lunchtime when he reached the office on M street.

Christopher's was closed. C'est La Vie looked as though it had never opened. The shops were a little less active than the average graveyard and only the hamburger bars had stayed open, largely for the beggars and the police.

By afternoon the snowclouds had pulled in across the city and by nightfall the snow would come again. He let himself into the office suite on the sixth floor and picked up the mail. He was half-way down the corridor before he stopped to wonder who had delivered it. The postal service hadn't worked since Thursday, the private carriers were frozen in by the winter, and a letter with a stamp had found its way on to the office mat with his name scrawled across the front: 'Peter March, c/o The London Times, Washington Bureau. Washington DC. 20036.'

Like a glove thrown down in his path.

# Chapter two

Think yourself an animal, said the voice, and you'll be one. Get
down on all fours, shit in the woods, eat grass, sleep under a stone.
And then you'll be on your way. But you'll always have
something the animal doesn't. Orders to follow. The orders from
your commander. Orders for the good of your country and the
honour of your unit. And you'll carry them out, whatever the
cost or the danger . . .

Like fuck, thought Travis, as he sat in the hamburger bar and
replayed the voice. Special Forces had been full of voices like that.
Fully oiled, shaven-headed arse-clenchers, reciting the crap they'd
had programmed into them. Orders to shoot, orders to kill, or
kidnap. Some little piece of filth for some distant, unseen arm of
the grand federal Government. Like clearing the sidewalks.
Nothing more.

He glanced round the bar, but no one was looking at him.
Why should they? His face was a rough pathway of bruises and
cuts, leading to a dead end. And in a while some jerk, thinking
himself a notch higher on the social scale, and hired for eight
dollars an hour, would come and turf him out. Maybe this time
he'd start a fight, maybe he'd go quietly. Probably a fight was
better. Perfect camouflage for a visit to the nation's capital, where
the bums controlled the city centre and the bums in suits
controlled the Government.

And yet he knew he couldn't stay long. They wouldn't be far
behind him. Security at the plant would have been alerted first.
Then it would spread outwards, rapidly inexorably, the ripples
reaching all the way to Washington and the really nasty boys with

17

federal pay checks. The ones who do it for God and country. The disposal teams, DIA and all the other little groups controlled from little rooms in buildings the voters never get to hear about. They were the ones who'd put on their coats and gloves against the snow and go out to find him.

Careful, though. They'd have to be so careful – couldn't risk the information getting out, couldn't risk a scandal. No news conferences. No questions. Like . . . 'What's so dangerous? What have you got in that plant? What the hell are you producing?'

'You leaving?'

The man in the hamburger bar stood over him, hand on hip, tough voice of authority bestowed on him by the eight dollars an hour. 'You gotta leave if you don't buy nothin'.'

'Coffee.' Travis pulled out some coins.

'I ain't getting it for you.'

Travis put his hand down to the green holdall at his feet, checking that it was still fastened.

'What you got in that bag there?'

The man was clearly overstepping his authority.

'A fucking bomb.' Travis gave the handles a sharp tug.

The fellow stepped back quickly. 'You're crazy.'

'Wanna see it?'

The man disappeared fast into a back room. But Travis knew he'd stayed too long. This was a city where things got reported. A city that spoke and a city that listened. To everything. The conversations. The threats. The jokes. Even the wind. He'd have to get out now, get back to the hotel, sit out the weather and the night. After all, he'd completed the first of his tasks. He'd delivered the letter.

Dear Friend,

March stopped reading and sat down at the nearest desk.

Once you get over the shock of receiving my letter – do me a favor and read it. I'm not a man who writes and I'm in a hurry so there ain't no fine phrases. Another week and I'll be pumped so full of drugs, I won't know my head from my butt. So it's now or not at all.

You don't know this, because no one has told you. But all the guys who went on that trip in '91 are dead, except me and just one other. We all fiddled around with the canisters, you see, making sure the seals were still there, testing for leaks. What the fuck!

As I said, the others are all dead now. And I'm on my way.

Why am I telling you? Because the last time we met, you asked me a question and I fed you the answer. Remember? I told you it was over, that I'd had high-level assurances and bullshit like that. Well, it was a lie. I didn't know it then, but I do now. And while I've killed and maimed people more years than I care to think about, I never told a lie. Let me tell you something. Plenty of people around you have lied.

Watch yourself. This is more than you can handle.

Harden.

March put the letter down. His hand shook uncontrollably. He remembered Harden. Remembered the unaffected arrogance of the man. Remembered finding out what he did. Remembered wondering what in the name of God it would be like to be a killer. Standing in the office lobby, he wished he'd never opened the letter. For a moment, he contemplated tearing it into pieces, pretending he'd never seen it, never read it. Surely the world would be the same tomorrow as it was today.

Only then he remembered a little more about Harden, and he knew it was far too late to walk away.

Less than a hundred yards away in the blizzard, Travis searched for his bearings. All looked the same in Washington. K Street, M Street, L Street, and there on the right across the tiny patch of park was New Hampshire Avenue. Quick, man, get up there, get off the streets.

A car slides past, driver staring, questing ahead, half blind, as the storm gathers momentum.

Travis, swaying now, blown towards the hotel, hit by a counter blast, drops the bag. 'Oh, Christ. Oh, Christ, oh, Christ.' Scoops it up from the snow, moves on, face battered and punched by the wind.

*Hurry, man, so easy to find you, so easy to track you down. Only the dogs and killers on the street tonight. And the killers work for the Government. You know that. You know exactly what they were doing at the plant.*

Relief, now, because the great glass doors are there in front of him, closer than he thought. And suddenly there is warmth around him. Music, idle and cheery. The storm is left outside to go away on its own.

'Lousy night,' says the desk clerk.

'Uh-huh.'

'Guess you won't be going out on the town for dinner.'

'Guess not.'

Idiot. Punk. Stupid question when you think what I have in the bag. Travis, muttering to himself as he rounds the corner, fumbles his key–card and dives into the darkness.

It took ten minutes, maybe fifteen before his heart left him alone and the ache began to ease. He went into the bathroom, tore off his clothes and let the water run scalding into the bath. Lie here, he thought, just a few moments. Just to let me recall what I'm doing and why I'm here – and why there are people outside tonight who want to kill me.

Let's rerun the tape. Play it again. See if it makes sense.

When Travis closed his eyes he could see all the classrooms and all the teachers. That was the start. Chemistry at school, chemistry at college, and chemical weapons once he'd reached the Army. Then, of course, he'd been like a parrot with the cage covered. No talking to the outside world, not even to friends or family. 'I'm just a soldier, Dad, basic training and then some. A few jumps in the desert. Sergeant by Christmas if I make the grade. OK?'

And it was. A little frisson of secrecy. That kick from the double life. The plastic security ID in the inside zipper pocket. And it was all that a boy from Phoenix had ever wanted. Chris Travis, going places. Yessir.

Oh, they'd needed him all right for the Gulf War. Not a war. No way. A lab. That's how they'd used it. One giant testing ground in the middle of nowhere and all the goodies they hadn't been able to try out since Vietnam. All the goodies they'd want to try for the next twenty years. And, what was more, plenty of people available to die. He'd done his bit, same as the rest of them – the controlled experiments with shellfish toxin and snake venom, all the things the Agency had held back in the seventies when Nixon ordered them destroyed. The main thing had been to devise a delivery system, quiet, efficient and so deadly that even the devil would take a step back and shudder. And he'd done it, Sergeant Travis. He'd done it. And how simple it had been, after all.

Doubts? Sleepless nights? Not many. This was war. Question of national security. At least that's what he had believed until he'd seen the results. Until that one time they had taken him to the tiny Iraqi village, lost among the sand dunes. Until he had seen the dead women and children, their eyes pecked out of their faces by the desert hawks. And then it didn't matter any more who the hell's security it was supposed to be. Dying was dying, whatever passport you carried and whatever part of the planet you stood on.

When the war was over, so was Chris Travis.

And then, three months after he resigned his commission, the phone call had come, worded in the way they were so clever at wording them. He recalled the sweltering day at the house he grew up in, ten miles on the west side of the city, where the sun offered no mercy. His mom was in the kitchen, moaning about the heat, Dad outside hammering away at the air-conditioning unit, swearing for the fifth year running that they'd replace it – and the call had said come to Florida and help.

Of course, with the war over, he really needed that offer – a good job in a private company and still in his field. Only this time there'd be a difference. For once he'd be working on antidotes, not weapons. That's what they told him. Working on the very things America needed to keep it safe and give it a bright future. They really talked like that. Who could ask for more? they said. A job with a purpose.

Standing there in the kitchen with Mom looking on and Dad listening through the window, he had known it was right. And, there was nothing to tell him they were lying. Not the slightest sign or indication.

Travis lowered his hand from the bath and checked the holder on the tiles beside him.

And then he'd found out, hadn't he? Someone had talked, the way they always do. Someone hadn't been promoted, hadn't been stroked. Went out and got drunk with the boys, and when all the other boys had gone, he'd told the story to Travis, hadn't he just? Full and unexpurgated. All the pungent little details. The lies and the cover-up. And by the end it was Travis drinking, and drinking hard, while the other guy sobered up at the horror of what he was telling.

Next day Travis had called Harden because Harden had always made the decisions and Harden still knew what to do. He had gone out to Virginia to visit the man, shocked at his state of health, the loss of weight, the shaking hands, the rashes on his arms and face.

'Christ, Vic . . .'

'Christ, yourself,' Harden had said. 'You're not so fucking beautiful either.'

But then they had talked, and come up with a plan. And now he was in Washington, lying in a bath, carrying it out.

He felt calmer then, listening to the wind outside and the water around him. And then came the knocking, hard and urgent. Which wasn't part of the plan.

# Chapter three

'Hallo?'

Vince Albright recognised the super-sweet voice of Lovett's wife. The man was a putz to have shackled himself to a marshmallow like that. He took a deep breath.

'That you, Jane?'

'Why, yes. Who's –'

'It's Vince – is he in?'

He could hear her surprise. No pleasantries, no 'How's the kid?' Just business.

'May I speak with him, please?'

'I'll see if he's available.'

Do that, bitch, he thought. Do it now, because we don't have time to screw around.

'Hi, Vince.' Lovett in country-club mode. 'How the hell are you?'

'Lousy. Turn on this fucking device, will you? I don't want half of AT&T listening in.'

There were clicks at both ends as the two men switched in the scramblers, two transmitters that broke up the signal into component parts, then bounced it around in ever more complex sequences, decodable only by a twin apparatus. Vince Albright had insisted on them because he was careful and always had been.

Lovett yawned down the receiver. 'Just been playing with the kid. What's on your mind, buddy?'

Albright could visualise Lovett and his kid. Probably had a rattle in one hand and a diaper in the other. Men on second families were like that. They always had to ram their new children down everyone else's throat.

'Two little items of property have gone walkabout from the plant.'

Lovett cleared his throat. 'What kind of property?'

'Not the kind you'd serve at your dinner parties.'

'What classification?'

'Top. I'll tell you the rest.'

Albright could hear the sharp intake of breath.

'Are we talking samples?'

'What the fuck else do they make there?'

'What about paperwork?'

'I . . . Jesus, Lovett, who knows? Maybe they stole the sodas from the fucking drinks dispenser. We don't know yet, OK?'

'I have to know if I'm involved.'

Albright nearly laughed out loud. Lovett's country club had suddenly slammed shut. 'D'you want me to give you this on the phone? D'you want me to remind you how you got the authorisation for this stuff funded and approved? D'you want me to remind you of the presidential decree renouncing the production of it? D'you want to know about the profits? And you ask me if you're involved . . .'

'Shut it, Vince. Get the dogs out and shut it. Do whatever you have to.'

And Vince heard the old Lovett click in. The real Washington animal. Instantly alive to danger and risk. At the first distant sign of trouble, the brain was lighting up, all systems engaged, checking the escape routes.

Across Washington Leah Killeen stepped out of the shower and stood in front of her full-length mirror. Too many Capitol Hill receptions, she reflected, seeing the slight stomach bulge and flexing her muscles to pull it in. And yet the rest wasn't bad. Nice tits, pert, even slightly upturned – and there weren't many women her age who could say that. Look at all the saggers and droopers at the health club, all the women who'd lunched their bodies to hell and back again. She turned again and examined

24

herself over the shoulder. Nice skin, nice buns, all in working order. Nice brain, too. Not that it was a commodity much cherished in Washington. Look at it all, she told herself. Like a woman twenty years younger. So why am I always alone?

She put on a robe and went down to the kitchen. One last look at the food laid out that morning by the man from Sutton Place Gourmet, the only store that catered for working women.

'Quite a party we're having.'

She had smiled back at him. 'Quite a price we're charging.'

And now it was all wasted. The salmon, the cold meats, the caviar, the *foie gras* all grinned stupidly back at her from the table, glistening under the spotlights. Wasted. One by one the guests had phoned that evening with their pathetic excuses.

'The snow, my dear.'

'The roads.'

'Seth's back.'

'I haven't got anything to wear.'

'It's just too awful outside.'

Well, fuck them all.

Only Peter March hadn't phoned.

So was he coming? And if he did, would he come on his own? Had the little wife-thing left for good? Oh, God, she hoped so. Peter March. Her tongue played with the words like fresh caviar. She had thought about him so much in recent weeks. Thought about his eyes — grey eyes that could stroke you and bathe you and walk you away into worlds you never knew existed. Eyes that would open your thoughts and read them unashamedly in front of you. Peter March. He didn't ask questions. He made you ask them yourself and then offer him the answers. He would take you places, and you would tell him what you saw.

As she stood there she realised her hand had slid inside the robe and begun to caress her left breast. God! The lights were on and the drapes open. What if anyone had seen? She went into the front room, keeping her hand where it was, her fingers, pulling gently at her nipple, feeling it rise and stiffen.

She wished suddenly that the people from work could see her

25

like this. Some of the men had made it clear they'd like to and yet they were slow to advance, for Leah Killeen's reputation encircled her like a high wall. She would love you hard and hate you hard, and you didn't want to be in Washington when the hating began. She was the Dobermann unleashed by Capitol Hill, the congressional investigator of choice hired by the sensitive committees when the dirt began to leak and the big names ran for cover.

Killeen had no bedside manner. She was either in the bed or finding out who'd been there last. She dealt as much with missing papers as missing pants, lost reputations, bulging bank accounts. If they had toes, she stamped on them. If they had pride, she smashed it with a hammer. If they had reputations, she tossed them wholesale into the Potomac. Such was the reputation of Leah Killeen. Such were the reasons she found herself alone.

And then she had met Peter. On a fine October afternoon he had walked into her office on Capitol Hill, when the shadows were long on the ground beyond her windows and the leaves lay in piles on the damp grass. And she had looked at him and made a sudden decision. Tell him what he wants to know. This is a special man. Keep him in your life because somehow he belongs. And, after a while, as he sat across the desk, smart but untidy, sophisticated yet strangely shy, his smile seemed to warm her office, and the winter was held at bay.

They had done lunch, the way everyone 'did' lunch in Washington. Not once. But every week. Way before spring the appointment had become a ritual. The Old Ebbitt Grill, just along from the White House, the Sea Catch in Georgetown, beside the canal, and she had gone on to tell him more, realising that she needed to talk. Of course, it was understood that he would write a story. He was a British correspondent, the hack from *The Times*. Barbarian at the gate. And yet, in the course of their conversations, he never played the reporter and she never played the informant. Words passed between them. But to her it had been the looks that counted.

'You know I'm married,' he had said, one afternoon, when the lunch had stretched into evening drinks.

'You say it as though it's a disease.'

26

He smiled. 'I think I'm saying it to remind myself, not because I felt you needed to know.'

She smiled back. 'What are you saying, Peter?'

'I find your presence arresting.'

'Then arrest me.'

'But I'm married.'

'You already said that.'

He pulled his glass towards him and stared down at the wine. 'I'm sorry, Leah. I shouldn't have said anything. It was thoughtless and stupid.'

She put a finger to his lips. 'Let's agree to leave it there, my dear. We had this conversation – don't let's pretend we didn't. But leave it where it is. If there's a time in the future . . .' And she had let the words hang there, deliberately refusing to add an ending.

'Thank you.'

She raised her glass and clinked it against his. 'Thank you, too.'

It was a conversation she was to replay many times over in her mind. Like an old favourite. So many times she had wanted to talk to him, ask him if he remembered, if he felt the same, if he still found her arresting and wanted to . . .

But she hadn't.

And now, once again, she needed to talk to him. Very badly indeed.

Travis stands by the door – there but not there, bathwater dripping from his thin little body on to the carpet.

'You got a message,' says the voice from the corridor.

Receptionist. Has to be.

'What message?'

'Open the door, sir.' A plea not an order. Travis knows the difference.

'Wait.'

Jeans on, a sweater over his head. Ease the door inwards. Leave the chain where it is.

And the face outside is greasy and pale. Full of excuses and complexes. A man who's spent his life apologising for being around. Walked on by the whole world. Then stamped on.

'I need to talk to you. Let me in.'

Travis flips the chain and stands back, watches the man shuffle into the room, peering around him, quick dark eyes, like a fox.

'You're in trouble, fellah.' The fox turns round and the black teeth are open in a grin. 'Been there myself. Been inside. I can smell it.'

'Talk.' Travis has begun to work out angles. He can kill him if it all looks wrong. He's good at that. Taught in the USA. Done it for God and country.

'You need to get out of here, son. Too many cars outside, too many people on the street. Worst friggin' snowstorm of the year but suddenly it's Mardi Gras out there. Men in suits with fuckin' radios. Uh? I think. Maybe there's a guy they want to talk to. And then I look again and it doesn't seem they're in the mood for talkin'. Not this bunch.' The grin disappears. 'Then you show up.'

And Travis is picking up the few things he has with him, chucking them into the holdall. Seeing the aerosols lying there among the shirts and socks. Pulling on his coat. All one movement. Many facets.

The little figure has opened the door. 'Basement exit, leads into the underground garage, cross the street. Doors locked but I got some keys. Move it, guy. These ain't friends of yours, these mothers.'

Travis is out of the door now, and the fox is moving fast through the corridor ahead, into a doorway, down stone steps, with strip lights, power lines and pipes, under the building. Warm and dry.

They reach a door. Locked. The man fumbling with his keys. And way behind them Travis hears a door slam. Just one. No voices.

'Christ Jesus.'

Through the door now and far away he can hear the footsteps on the stone. Ten yards, twenty, counting the strip lights in the ceiling as he runs. Like counting off the years. Without warning the fox flattens himself against the wall and points ahead. 'Door at the end, fire door. You'll come out on M street, right next to a tailor's shop, forecourt of a parking lot. Don't stay too long.'

'What about you?'

The fox grins again, gasping for air. 'I got another route for me.' He taps his nose. 'Been around some . . .'

And Travis is already pushing past him, the holdall gripped tight in his hand. Ten feet to the door, wrenching at the handle, seeing the door fly open as the wind rushes in. Ice-cold. Prehistoric. Jesus. Travis sinks to his knees, his heart screaming in pain. And even as he slams the door behind him, he hears the crack, way down in the bowels of the building. Maybe a door. Yes, a door. Please, God, just the slamming of a door. But he knew better than that. Travis knew the sound of a bullet, fired unsilenced in a confined place. A high-velocity bullet from an automatic pistol. He could tell you the calibre and the make, if he put his mind to it.

As the cold wrapped itself around him he knew all too well what he'd heard.

# Chapter four

Just a few yards across the street, Peter March no longer sees or feels the cold. Harden's letter has jerked him back to another climate and another time. A dozen times he has crumpled the letter in his pocket, then removed it again and reread it. *Damn Harden. Damn him for writing. Damn him to hell for coming back.*

Of course, he could call him by phone. But Harden never used phones. And, besides, if he had something to say, you had a duty to drop the rest of your life into the nearest trash can and listen with every sense you possessed. Harden was an archive. A store of secrets. Harden was a record of things that should never have happened. And every one was dangerous.

March tried to remember the basic details of the man, but realised he knew very little. When it came down to it, Harden hadn't ever done anything normal, didn't know normal people, didn't tell normal stories. Once in a lifetime, thought March, you meet someone like that – who knows everything you want to know – and then wish you hadn't. Reality's all very well from a distance, when they lie about the nasty parts and pretend they never happen. But, seen through Harden's eyes, reality is deadly and terrifying. It's the moment when you know with absolute certainty that the world is mad; that there are wild animals beside you on the streets; that whatever nightmares you can imagine, someone's living them for real.

March was already in his car before he remembered Leah Killeen's party. Christ, on this night of all nights! He could call her on the mobile, make some excuses, say he was tired, just got into town. But you couldn't do that with Killeen. You could do that with any of the thousand other powerful women in Washington. But not with her.

She wasn't a part-time friend. A casual acquaintance. A take-it or leave-it member of the social circle. She was high maintenance, high intensity – much more than a source: she was a friend as well. But more than a friend. A lover-to-be. Did he mean that? March shook his head. All he knew was that he'd have to see her and make his excuses face to face. After that, God help him, he'd try to drive out to Virginia. He owed it to Harden.

*Can't ever leave a story, can you, Peter March?*

A question straight out of the night.

He remembered Julie saying that to him, a week after they'd met. But she'd said it then with a smile. For a brief period she'd been interested in his work, intrigued by it, watching him piece together his investigations – sanctions-busting with Iraq, a corrupt insurance syndicate, a Pentagon official taking bribes – watching him brush away the topsoil of lies and obfuscation.

News should be about new things, he'd told her. And you didn't get that by hunting in packs. You had to go off on your own, down odd alleyways, get up early, stay up late, take trains and stand on platforms for people who were afraid of what they might dare to tell you.

'It's journalism,' he would say.

'No, it's madness,' she'd reply. 'You should be doing stock-market reports, or writing a gossip column. But what do you do? You have to pick up your keyboard and try to ram it down everyone's throat. If it isn't hurting, it isn't doing any good. That's your philosophy, Peter. Face it. This is all about self-gratification. Giving yourself a kick by kicking others.'

'Not true, Julie. Not true.'

He could hear their voices, saying the same things over and over again. Endless argument, going steadily downhill.

Of course, in the days of the Cold War he had been everyone's favourite. Peter March from Warsaw. Peter March from Prague, and Moscow and Bucharest, dishing the dirt on the Commies. Very PC. Very much in vogue. They'd all liked that – even, surprisingly, the Commies themselves, who knew where they stood with him. He played his part and they played theirs. The rules had been well established.

But then when the walls came down, he'd started looking a little too hard at his own side. Hadn't pleased his own parents either. Mum and Dad always enquiring into his work with pursed lips and nervous glances. Was he sure he was doing the right thing? Was he watching his back? And then had come the little chats with the editor. An odd Lord here and there – plenty of odd ones to choose from – had started asking, *sotto voce*, if he was the right man for the job. Any job. Perhaps his stories weren't 'sound'. Perhaps *he* wasn't 'sound'. Just an idea fed into the old boys' network. A whiff of doubt. A needle of concern.

But he'd ridden out the criticism. So had the editor. So far. As long as he kept bringing home the exclusives – and getting them right.

Harden was an exclusive, had the tag written all over him.

So was Leah Killeen. An exclusive of the best and most beautiful kind.

For just a few extra minutes, Harden would have to wait.

He was half asleep when the phone call came. Or was he dreaming? Sometimes the drugs dulled his mind so much that it was hard to tell what was real from what he'd imagined. At night, when the memories flooded back, it seemed as if he was living them for the first time. All the surprise and shock, all the anger and fear hit him with a freshness and horror that he had almost forgotten.

'Vic,' said the voice.

'What is it?'

'It's Travis, Vic.'

'Right.'

'I'm in trouble, buddy. Big trouble.'

And the words seemed to clear Harden's mind, for he knew he was awake, knew where he was, eyes searching the tiny log cabin, hearing the wind outside, seeing, computing.

'What happened, Travis?'

'I had to get out of the motel. They knew I was there, for fuck's sake. How the hell could they know that, Vic?'

'I don't know. Take it easy, man. Stay cool.'

'My arse is out to dry, Vic. I'm the one with the fucking canisters. Talk to me, buddy. Where the fuck do I go now?'

'Wait.' And Harden sees it all, like words on a screen. The options. The risks. The alternatives. 'You got the list, Travis?'

'Yes. Yes, of course.'

'Remember the place we talked about? Go there. Any way you can. Get outa sight and stay there.'

'I'm trying, Vic.'

'You can do it. Remember me telling you that?'

'I remember.'

'Well, we made it before, all the other times, didn't we?'

'Yes, Vic.'

'Did I let you down?'

'No, sir.'

'Did I ever let you down?'

'No, sir.'

'Well, go do it, Travis. Go to the place we agreed. Keep your head down and I'll get to you.'

And then the line had gone. A sudden break. Could have been the storm. But Harden doesn't trust could-have-beens. He's always dealt with the facts. Always trusted the worst interpretation you could find. Planned for it. Prepared for it. Because that's how you stayed alive.

He got up from the sofa, struggling to clear his head. Arms and legs felt stiff and immovable, but they had for months. That was the disease. Progressive and unstoppable. As the months had gone by he no longer fought it. There were battles to win and battles to walk away from – and this one wasn't worth the effort. Instead, there was just a final mission. The first one he'd ever devised by himself and the most important of all. A last favour to the world, he told himself. And when they rowed him across the lake to Hades, maybe, just maybe it would buy him a better ticket.

Harden groped his way to the tiny window. The pane was ice cold and the driving snow obliterated the night outside. From the noise of the wind, the storm still had a long way to run. He turned and stared round the room. Everything was ready. The black ski-suit hanging from a peg, the boots waxed and oiled, the skis by the front door. And the backpack containing the last few things in his life worth taking with him. A change of clothes, a book, a few pictures, some names and phone numbers – and the Heckler & Koch 9mm pistol, with ammunition and silencer. The final decider.

He dressed in the light of the paraffin lamp, sweating profusely from the effort, knowing his strength was deserting him. Each button, each zip, every movement seemed to cost so much. And yet his will-power would be enough to carry him on. The disease would never take that.

Satisfied with his preparations, Harden boiled some water and poured it into a coffee cup, blowing on the surface until it had cooled and he could gulp it down.

If the gods were smiling on him, he'd make it down the mountain, get out of Virginia and find his way to Travis. It wasn't so different from any of the other impossible operations he'd handled over the years. You either did it or they killed you along the way.

Vince Albright had arrived first. A watcher by trade, he liked to be first, liked to stake out the venues ahead of the rest of the pack. It gave him a feeling of superiority. As the snow flurried across Wisconsin Avenue he lit a cigarette and sat in the four-wheel drive, with the engine running and the heater on full. Along each side of the strip there were the lights from motels and restaurants, but the main street lamps were in darkness. An electricity generator had failed in parts of northern Maryland after the storm had brought down power lines. Happened every winter. But nobody gave a fuck. That was the problem with Washington. Plenty of power talk, power meetings, power lunches and dinners. But, come the snow, there was no fucking power to light the streets.

After ten minutes he flicked on the coded transceiver on the dashboard, but the wavelengths were silent. These were the special bands reserved for government frequencies, and no surfers, hackers or amateurs played around here. The communications were invariably scrambled – indecipherable except by the person they were meant for. That, at least, was the theory. And yet as he scanned the bands Vince noted the silence and was happy with it. He'd told them all to stay off the air unless they had something to say. This wasn't a night for chatting, or sending love to Mom. This was the lousiest night of the year. This year and all the others put together.

He didn't want to be out that night, but when he thought about the alternatives, it wasn't so bad. At home the choice was to watch television or watch Laura drink her way silently through a gin bottle. It wasn't as if they ever talked. Even the rows had got lost in the rubble of their marriage. Just get to bed, get to the kitchen, and then get out again in the morning. The only goodnight kiss was the one Laura gave to the bottle in her hand. Didn't matter if he was there or not. Next day she'd stagger downstairs, promising to dry out, and for a couple of days she'd really mean it. Then by Friday, she'd be having 'just a smell' to help her through the day – and so the cycle went, and went again. Better to sit and watch the snow, and think about what he'd say to Lovett.

He could see the black Lincoln Town Car from a long way off, nosing down the street, like a boat in heavy seas. Even on a night like this Lovett had to make an entrance – but that was typical of the stupid, conspicuous bastard. His ego dominated everything he did. A real snot-nose Washington hack. A smile on his face, and a crooked deal in his pocket. Only he wouldn't be so pleased with himself once he'd heard from his little friend Vince. Vincey would make him squirm and shift on the seat then piss his pants all the way back across the Potomac to Virginia.

Vince wound down the window and gestured to Lovett to park beside him. He got out and stood by the car on the passenger side, waiting for the window to wind down. It was colder, he thought, than a pig's arse in a gale.

'Could you have driven something else tonight?'

'Get in.'

Lovett was wearing a red scarf and cap and driving in gloves. Vince thought he looked like one of those middle-aged models for Abercrombie & Fitch. The country gent, tweeds and cords, and plenty of honest money in the bank. That was a fucking laugh, all right. Honest Speaker Lovett, confidant of presidents and senators. The mentor, the arbitrator, the deal-maker – and then, when your back was turned, the silent executioner, stabbing his way to the front of every committee and every reception that mattered.

Lovett looked at his watch. 'I shouldn't even be here.'

'You better listen to this.'

'Talk.'

The Lincoln smelt of perfume and disinfectant. What the hell did Lovett use it for? Vince shook his head.

'Fellah called Travis – ex-Army, ex-Gulf, chemical specialist, passed down by someone in the same unit you served with. Remember? He came to us after the Gulf War, highly recommended, used to keeping his mouth shut. He helped design some of the biological delivery systems we used out there so we employed him for that. Good worker, no problems, until about three months ago.'

'Go on.'

'He started getting sick. Something leaked on to him. Something got out. Nobody else seemed infected. Medics took a look at him, and said he had flu and needed a break.'

'That was clever.'

Vince shrugged. 'Like, what the fuck were they supposed to say? Nobody else was down. Anyway, he came back to work after a couple of weeks, seemed better. Even went to a birthday party, which was where all the trouble started. He went off drinking with someone from the "black" programmes, you know the kind of thing.'

'I know what the fucking black programmes are.' Lovett held up his hand. 'OK?'

'Sure.' Vince sucked in his breath. 'Guy must have told Travis everything. Who knows? We took him in and questioned him, fellah called Mitchell, but by then Travis had taken the stuff and gone.'

'What stuff, Vince? *What stuff?*' Lovett's hand slammed on to the dashboard. 'For Chrissake, let's have some detail here.'

'It's experimental, hasn't even got a proper name. Just Ultra – the designation for the whole programme. Like with all the black stuff there are two sets of records. One for the oversight committee from Congress and the other for us. It doesn't appear on the oversight inventory. Nobody outside the plant has any idea that it exists.'

'What's it do?'

'Kills in a very small confined area. Normally we use biologicals for maximum spread. They kill infinitely faster and wider over large areas. This one is designed for very precise targeting. Disperses in seconds, can kill very quietly – and mostly over a long period. That means the guy who delivers can get in and out again – no suicide missions. This is point and shoot. The victim has no idea – nor does anyone else – how or even where the poison was ingested. Could take days even weeks to infect. Comes in an aerosol – looks like a hairspray. We got orders coming in from all over the world for this kind of stuff. It's a fucking revolution.'

'How much of it does Travis have?'

'Two, maybe three canisters. Mitchell didn't know.'

'Where's Mitchell now?'

'He had some bad luck.'

'Christ, Vince, what the fuck does that mean?'

'Do you really want to know?'

'I – but you can't just go round killing every –'

'Listen to me.' Vince's hand had suddenly gripped Lovett by the forearm, clamping it to the steering wheel. 'You didn't exactly object when we had that little security breach a year ago. One of our people going out with a woman from the local TV station. Remember? That was progressing nicely, until we bugged her home and discovered he was shooting his mouth off. You didn't mind about the little car accident then, did you? Two young kids dying, oh-so-tragically, in a collision with the biggest

37

truck in the state of Delaware. You didn't weep too many tears over that one, did you?'

'I wasn't Speaker of the House, then.' Lovett's voice was calm and measured.

'So suddenly you got yourself a pair of white gloves, huh?'

'There are rules, Vince, and you don't break them unless there's an unavoidable imperative.'

Vince removed his hand from Lovett's forearm. 'Or someone's ass is in the sling, huh? Well, believe me, Speaker Lovett, all our asses are hanging on this one. Get my drift?'

'Where's Travis now?'

'In the District. He was staying just off M Street. We almost got him there, but he's in the area. He won't go far on a night like this.'

'Is he alone? Did he make contact with anyone?'

'Yes.'

'What do you mean "yes"? Who, for Chrissake?'

'He called a guy named Vic Harden.'

Even in the darkness of the car, Vince could see the colour drain from Lovett's face.

# Chapter five

'Leah.'

'Peter.'

She gasped, standing in the doorway in her robe, no makeup, flushed with embarrassment.

He laughed. 'Did I get the wrong night?'

'You didn't.' She beckoned him in. 'It's all the others who cried off, the shitheads, so I cancelled.'

'You did what?'

And she was laughing too now, leading him from the hall into the kitchen where the food trays still stared from the table.

'Jesus, Leah, this is dinner and breakfast for the next six years.'

She smiled. 'Well, you're invited. Eat as much as you want. Use the place like a canteen. Otherwise it's all going to the Filipino cleaners and I'll be feeding half of Adams Morgan.'

He sat on a stool and picked up a smoked-salmon canapé.

'This OK?'

'Sure – just enjoy it.' She grinned again. 'That thing in your hand cost me about ten dollars. I'll be working till I'm ninety to pay it all off. Goddam awful night to pick for a party.'

March reached for another. 'It's a goddam awful night for a lot of things, Leah. I'm sorry, I'm going to have to go in a minute. I just didn't want to call you and make some lousy excuse, that's all.'

He could see the disappointment in her face. It was as if the petals of a flower had begun to droop.

'Is it Julie?'

He sighed. 'No, it's not Julie. Julie's another story . . .' His hand gestured into the middle distance.

'So what is it?'

'It's a letter that came for me today.'

'There weren't any deliveries today, Peter.'

He smiled. You could never play games with Leah. 'I know. That's the odd thing. Odd delivery. Odd letter. Veteran I knew during the Gulf War, said he had to talk to me. Strange guy – but he knew things, all kind of things. Trouble was you could never write any of them. It was all way too sensitive.'

'Is he in Washington?'

'No, out in the Shenandoah. Lost River. I have to get out there to see him.'

'Don't even think about it on a night like this, not with the snow. Wait till morning, Peter. You'd be crazy to go now.'

'I have to. I don't think this guy's got long to live. That was the gist of the letter. There are some things he says he wants to tell me before he dies.'

She shook her head. 'You won't make it. Not tonight. Just listen to the radio.' She was only a foot away from him, staring hard into his eyes. It was all he could do not to reach forward and pull her into his arms. She seemed to read the desire, and leaned forward to kiss him on the cheek, defusing the moment. 'I can see it's useless talking to you.' She raised her hands in a gesture of defeat. 'At least you can take some of this lousy food with you.'

He sat and drank some coffee, while she went upstairs and dressed. When she came down again he could see that a little had gone a long way. A comb through the hair, a hint of blush, jeans and a loose white T-shirt. She could have stormed Washington, he thought, and carried away anyone she wanted. She had beauty with purpose, the wildness just tamed, just out of sight, burning below the surface. You could explore her for decades and still not find the source of her power. She was raw, undiluted excitement, he reckoned, too dangerous for most people, too unattainable – like a distant mountain summit. And most people would stare in awe and never attempt the climb.

As she packed the food, he watched her and wondered for the

hundredth time about her past, her baggage. But it had long since been put away in a cupboard, and no one seemed to know where to look. Dinners with the powerful and exclusive, but who drove her home? Vacations 'with friends' – whatever that meant. Was she private or lonely? Mate or mistress? You'd never ask her – and she'd never tell.

She turned to face him, bag in hand. Her nipples were hard against the T-shirt and he pulled his eyes away, a second too slowly, for she caught the glance, considered it – and then raised an eyebrow.

'Looking's OK.' The eyes were unreadable. 'Looking's cheap. But anything else is pretty pricy, Peter. You buying?'

The question caught him off guard. 'I – I didn't mean –'

'Yes, you did. But, hey, this isn't the night to go shopping. Here's your food.' She handed him the packet and grinned. 'Don't get lost, don't drive into a ditch and come back when you've eaten it, OK?'

As he got into the car, she phoned him on the mobile. 'Try to stay out of trouble, Peter, OK?'

He laughed, looked round and saw her face at the sitting-room window.

And then she pulled the curtains, switched off the lights and there was just the voice in the receiver. 'If you need anything, Peter, I'm the best, OK?'

He was still thinking of a reply when she hung up.

Of course, she could have made him stay. Leah went into the kitchen, stood in the darkness, toying with her thoughts. He had wanted to stay. She knew that. She could almost have touched his desire. All it would have taken was a move from her. The merest hint of an invitation, a brush of her hand along his thigh, a kiss, just a second too long, the press of her body against his. And yet she had held back – and so had he.

Sweet, agonising temptation. Only one day soon she would have him. That was a promise. And when Leah made herself promises she also made them come true.

She remembered standing at the back of the class, so many

years ago, and telling the teacher and all the other six-year-olds that she would be first in the tests. 'I'm better than you guys and you know it,' said the high-pitched whine. 'And I'm better-looking too. So there.'

'Sit down, Leah. That's no way to talk in class.'

'But it's true.'

'I said, sit down, Leah.'

'They just don't like the truth, Miss Aston, and maybe nor do you.'

Voices from a summer's day, lost and then found all those years later.

Miss Aston had taken her out of class and made her stand in the corridor with her face to the wall. 'You're a bad girl, Leah. You don't say things like that. And, besides, you know darn well there are a lot of clever girls in the class. You're not the only one, you know.'

And even aged six, Leah had known that too. Which was why the other two contenders for first place suffered two most unpleasant accidents, within twenty-four hours of each other. Sally Keeps's left foot was badly stamped on during a game of softball and Lisa Manes's hand became agonisingly jammed in the door of her mother's Volvo while she and the other girls were piling in.

So as luck – and design – would have it, Leah came first in the tests.

How could I have done that? she asked herself, twenty-seven years later, leaning against the kitchen table in the darkness.

But she knew the answer. Once she'd made herself a promise, she'd keep it. She always had.

*Travis, you're dead.'* And the voice inside him keeps saying it. Only he knows it's just the fear. Harden had told him he'd make it. And Harden never lied. Harden killed, but he didn't lie.

He was warm now. First time in an hour. Off the streets, away from the snow that kept on emptying across the city.

He had stopped the taxi by falling in front of it. Only half intentionally. First taxi he'd seen since he'd run from the hotel, and it was heading south-east. And he did a deal. On driver a fifty. A rat-faced Russian – or so he sounded. dishonest voice. Lazy and ponderous. But he knew the way.

And Travis stares out at the snow-encrusted streets, not seeing, not hearing, praying the world will leave him alone. Why was he here? What the hell had brought him to Washington with a couple of aerosol sprays that could kill, maim and disfigure with just the press of a button? But even as he asked himself the question, the answer was there.

The phone call to Harden. That had clinched it. The facts about his old platoon from the Gulf. Facts. Not the regimental hand-out bullshit about God and country but the list of casualties that no one would ever reveal. He remembered holding the receiver and clutching the hall table to stop himself falling, as Harden recited the list. Franchetti, dead. Willis, dead. Utley, dead. Kozlowski, dead. Carter, dead. Tupelo, dead. The whole fucking unit that had been out there that day in the Iraqi desert, the day they'd found the canisters and killed the Czechs – all dead from contamination. Now Harden was dying, and he himself was sick – and he'd known, right from that moment, that he had to halt it. Halt the research as well as the development. Whole thing was out of control. And no one wanted to know.

Travis shook his head, trying to dispel the fear and foreboding. There was no point being afraid. Not after coming so far. He had taken the canisters and come to Washington because he had to. For the public. For Mom and Dad. Simple as that.

When the taxi pulled up, he peered out, seeing only the outlines of the street, half buried under the snow. Not a good street, this one. The houses were crooked bungalows, all different shapes, some with lighted windows, others in total darkness. In the driveways sat the cars, long, cold hulks of steel, coloured white by the storm, buried, he imagined, till the spring. Along at the end, an emergency power crew was out, working on one of the overhead electricity cables. He could see the flashing lights, and when he got out, there were bursts of voices and static from the radio controllers. Washington knew all about snow – just couldn't do anything to stop it.

taxi rolled down the street he felt a moment of panic. ouse numbers, no signs. But then he saw it. 'Hold it here. 's it, fellah.' The car slithered a few feet, brakes locked, and ravis stumbled out. 'Here.' He shoved a fifty towards the driver.

'Take it easy, guy.'

*Yeah, right. Easy. So fucking easy.*

Travis jumped the gate and trudged towards the porch. Footprints, asshole! Christ! Cursing silently, he darted back to the roadside, brushing the powdery snow with his hand, obscuring his steps as he backed towards the porch. There were no lights so he had to feel his way to the door, fumbling with the key in his pocket. The key from Harden.

Inside, he paused, leaving the door ajar, smelling the stale cold air, listening for a step or a voice. Each house had its own sounds – the things that creaked and shifted, the sound of the wind through the eaves. You had to stand a moment and sort out the normal from the dangerous. That's how they'd trained him.

Satisfied, he moved through the corridor to the back and found himself in the kitchen. And here the smell was wrong. Pungent, evil. He knew instantly, the way all soldiers know it, that something had died.

From inside his holdall, he pulled a small flashlight with a metal hood, designed to throw the light downwards. And then he saw it: a dog, lying by the back door, teeth bared, eyes wide open, locked in the rage and pain of death. Travis could see what had happened. Who couldn't? The animal was a mass of bones and fur, and there was no doubt it had died in that kitchen from starvation. As he looked round, he could see the floor covered in aged excrement, chair-legs half-eaten, scratch-marks on the wall. Why had no one heard the animal bark? Who had left it there? Why had the neighbours not been alerted?

Travis bent down by the door. All around it were tooth- and claw-marks, and blood, most likely from the dog's mouth. As its strength ran out it would have yelped and barked, then whimpered its way into the world beyond. What a lousy, lousy death.

He stepped back and turned away, trying to shut out what he'd seen. The dog's eyes had been focused right on him, cold and unmoving. Helluva house guest. Helluva welcome on a winter's night. As he looked down he could see the flashlight begin to waver and he realised his hand was shaking out of control.

The taxi driver had barely reached the end of the road before the radio call came.

'Six-oh-six, bring the fucking car back to the garage.'

He ignored it and drove on slowly. Didn't the assholes know it was snowing? If they looked outside the window, they could see it was the worst night of the year. He was damned if he was going to take the car back and then walk twenty blocks home. Bunch of chicken-shit jerks.

Five hundred yards later, the call came again.

'Pick up the mike, Dmitry, or you're fired. That taxi's coming home tonight or you can go to hell.'

'What the . . .' He slammed his hand on to the dashboard. Who the hell did they think they were? All the drivers took the cars home, if they were on the late shift. Otherwise they'd have to get a taxi home themselves. It was part of the agreement. Didn't make any sense at all.

'Do you read me, you Russian piss-head?'

He detached the mike from its housing on the dashboard. 'OK, OK. You make me sick, you people. How you think I gonna get home tonight?'

'Who gives a shit?' asked the voice. Abruptly the connection was cut.

As he drove into the garage, Dmitry could see it was deserted. Only in the inner office was a light burning, and he could hear voices. He switched off the engine and went inside. Paul was sitting at his desk, as he always did, a day's sweat glistening on his bald, Nicaraguan head, but it was the two men opposite him that worried Dmitry: they suddenly made him think of Russia, where the arrival of men in suits in a dismal, run-down, tatty garage could only mean one thing. State police. In spite of the distance and all the years, he couldn't help the jet of fear that coursed up into his mouth, forcing him to freeze with his eyes wide and his mouth open.

'Dmitry, get your ass here. These guys want to talk to you. Police. No problem. Just answer the questions.'

As they swung towards him, he could feel the same cold wind that always blew through Russia, the same malevolent intentions, the same unfettered power, the same crushing disregard for the human race.

'We need to know about any passengers you've had tonight.' It was the older one who spoke, white-haired, with a face strangely unmarked by lines. And Dmitry could tell in an instant the reason: this man never smiled or laughed. Never cracked his cheeks. Never showed a trace of emotion. This man was a killer.

'What do you want to know?'

'Like I said, the passengers.'

Dmitry thought of the fifty dollars in his pocket. Thought of what it would buy from the food store, from the liquor store, thought of the cigarettes. He wasn't going to give it up for some filth from the local police station, or the tax police, or whoever the fuck they really were.

'Lousy night. I ain't had no passengers.'

The man spread his palms wide open, slapped them on the table and stood up. 'Where you from, Dmitry? Russia?'

It took him a moment to answer. 'Yeah, Russia.'

'Grew up there?'

'Why you asking?'

'Know what this is?' And, as Dmitry stared uncomprehendingly, the man drew back his right hand and punched him with terrible speed and violence, a blow that caught his nose, crunching it, smashing the septum, ripping through bone and tissue. Dmitry's knees buckled in agony and he fell forward on to the floor. The blood is like a fountain, and he's crying and jerking in agony. But the man reaches over him, drags his head up by the hair, raising the smashed, blood-spattered face to within six inches of his own. 'I'm asking you questions, you fuck, and you're gonna answer them, OK?'

Dmitry can barely see him through the pain.

'You took a guy in the cab – yes or no?' He was going to jerk the hair out at the roots.

Dmitry's head tried to nod in response, but the wailing from his mouth barely altered.

'Where d'you pick him up? Where d'you take him? Follow me, uh?' The head jerked again, and now there was a voice from somewhere deep inside. Like no other voice you'd ever heard, born of terrible pain and fear, and defiance.

'M street to 4th Street, south-east, you fucking assholes.'

The man slammed his head forward and stood up.

In the corner Paul had shrunk to the floor, crossing himself, jerking wildly on the gold crucifix around his neck.

The man brought out a wad of bills, peeled off three or four and flung them on the desk. 'Fix him up. Get some decent drivers. Place is a fucking disgrace.'

Travis sat on the stairs and wiped his forehead with his sleeve. He'd hidden the canisters below the porch, just the way Harden had told him. 'Sit tight,' he'd said. 'I'll get to you. Leave the light on in the upstairs bathroom. And I'll see it through the skylight. That way I'll know it's OK.'

He looked at his watch. Nearly ten. He'd shut his eyes for just a moment, steady himself, let his mind switch off. Then he'd go up and turn on the light.

Sleep arrived so suddenly that he never even felt it coming.

# Chapter six

Vince Albright knew he wouldn't sleep. Some days he slept ten, fifteen hours at a stretch. Others, he could coast along with just a nap – five minutes here or there, parked in a side road or an underground parking lot. He didn't care where.

Most of his adult years had been spent that way, on the job or asleep, with tiny moments of life crammed in between.

'That's the way it is with special operations,' he'd once told his wife.

And she'd laughed back at him. 'For "special" read bullshit – all the bullshit stuff no one else will touch.' The topic had never been raised again.

He'd gone freelance after leaving the Army. Someone had put around his name and before long a few little jobs had been pushed in his direction. He was known as loyal and tenacious without being overly stupid, all qualities that could be harnessed in the interests of national security. Over the years Albright would meet a whole succession of men in dark suits in downtown Washington and they would tell him names and addresses – and he would watch them, photograph them or listen to their conversations.

They never told him who he was working for, and he never asked. Some conventions are seldom broken, but it wasn't as if he didn't know. CIA, from time to time. DIA – Defence Intelligence Agency? Almost certainly. Albright was well aware that a dozen or more intelligence outhouses in Washington took on freelances – and in the seventies and eighties the number had multiplied.

When Bill Casey had headed up the CIA, the workload had

rocketed. He never even trusted the Agency to collect his cleaning. So everything that meant anything was done out of house, with truckloads of cash for expenses. The Cold War was at its height, Congress was authorising defence overspends by the dozen, and as long as the chosen few kept their mouths shut and did the business, there was plenty of money for everyone.

Albright was grateful for those years. Of course, he had made no friends but he had formed some useful alliances, based on reciprocal favours. You received one and you paid it back instantly. There was no credit, because the business, by its nature, had a high turnover. People were always disappearing or dying or simply leaving town without forwarding addresses. So the favours were same-day affairs. You received with one hand and gave immediately with the other.

Which was why his friend from the National Security Agency said he was glad of the call. Said he could come round, even though it was nearly nine and the family was home and the kids were partying. Didn't mind at all, taking him down to the den and shutting the double soundproofed doors tight. Because he owed Albright a favour.

Harry Wilson turned on the CD player with his right hand and the computer bank with his left and gestured to Albright to sit on the sofa. He was big and bald, with the kind of stomach that had sunk to keyboard level, along with his brain. Harry was king of keyboards. King of the analysts. Didn't matter if he looked like a piece of shit in the gutter, thought Albright, his fingers could gain access to the tightest secrets in the country. It was what he did.

'You're working late, Vince.'

'It's like that in show business, Harry.' A raised eyebrow. 'You know that.'

'Want to tell me about it?' The hands began working the keys, entering the access codes, sending electronic impulses across the city.

'We had a guy called Travis. He was part of a Gulf War special team, you know the kind of thing, cleared till kingdom come and licensed to talk only to God.'

Wilson's fingers kept moving.

'Travis has gone bad. We're looking at his contacts. Frankly they worry me more than he does. We know one thing – he called his old CO, fellah called Harden – Vic Harden – and I want to know why. What's Harden been up to since the Gulf? What kind of contacts, confidants? Who's he been pouring out his soul to?'

'This could take time.' Harry punched in the parameters. Albright had a sudden vision of lights and electronic impulses and a computer tape, spinning into life in the bowels of the NSA. God only knew what they had on everyone – the files, the cross-references, the lists of contacts. And not just Americans. This was the most comprehensive intelligence archive in the world, tapping into the records of America's allies and enemies right across the globe.

As Wilson worked, Albright stared around the room. It looked like any other den, with the kids' pictures and trophies, the wife by the pool, a few certificates and badges. One happy little suburban family, you'd have thought, unless, of course, you knew.

And Albright knew. That's what the favour had been all about.

He knew Harry had just completed a messy little affair with a female clerk at the NSA, knew that he'd got cold feet and dumped her, knew that she'd been hell-bent on revenge and ruining Harry's career.

But it was never going to get that far. Not once Harry had called in his old friend Albright. And Albright had sent a few of *his* old friends to see the lady. And explained, using the barest minimum of intimidation, that she would be wise to reconsider her course of action, and incredibly stupid if she didn't. Not to say reckless with her own safety. After all, it was winter, and the streets were slippery and cars could skid and she hadn't been working for the NSA for nothing. She left town a week later, left the country, too. And wouldn't you know it? Albright had himself a favour to cash – at any hour of the day or night.

He smiled to himself. This was the good side of the job – what you found out about people, their lives, their secrets, their mistresses. Helluva kick. Better, even, than sex – if he could remember what that was like.

'Vince, this Harden fellah is some guy.' Wilson interrupted his thoughts, turning round, running a hand over his forehead. 'I'm having to go in real deep to get anything at all.'

'Is he there?'

'Oh, he's there OK. I'm just using up a ton of clearances to get at him. What I've done is put out a kind of net that's gonna scoop up any references from a whole range of sections. Least, that's the idea.'

Albright leaned back in the chair and sighed. 'How long's this going to take?'

Harry grinned. 'About three minutes.' His face glowed with professional pride.

And then, as Albright watched, the printer buzzed into life and he quite forgot where he was, kneeling down on the floor, scanning the names and files and comments that came pouring through his fingers.

The records were dazzling, extraordinary and scarcely believable. Albright forced himself to ignore the man's exploits and go for his contacts, yet he couldn't help counting the locations, whistling at the things he – and all the rest of America – had never heard about. The operations. The misinformation. The quiet, tidy assassinations. Jesus, God, you always thought . . . always knew . . . but to see it written in black and white . . .

And then something else caught his eye. A couple of newspaper articles from Britain. There was no mention in them of Harden but someone had listed the journalist's name as a contact. An intelligence report said Harden had met him several times during the Gulf War but concluded that he'd told him nothing of interest.

Albright shook his head in amazement. Even the watchers had been watched. To see surveillance reports on your own special-ops guys was extraordinary. And yet when he looked at the man's records, he could see why. Harden carried dynamite in his head – and blood on his hands. Blood authorised by the American

Government. He was therefore indispensable and deeply dangerous. No wonder they had watched him.

'Let's take a look at this journalist.' Albright tore off the
printout and handed it to Wilson. 'There's nothing else.'

Five minutes later, Vince Albright left the house in a hurry. He
got into his car and headed into the south-west of the city. Few of
the payphones there were ever monitored, in contrast to those in
the centre of Washington. And he needed some privacy. Three
calls later he knew all he wanted to know about Peter March, the
kind of journalist he was, the stories he'd broken – and the
sensitive work carried out by his wife.

And he didn't like any of it.

# Chapter seven

The three made short work of the locks on King Place. The alarm was primitive, bought some time in the seventies, probably didn't even work, but they neutralised it first. Because that's the way they were. That's why the company paid them. For all the night work, the vacations and weekends. And paid them so well.

Home of Peter and Julie March, this one. That's all they knew. Nice little street off Macarthur Boulevard, close to the Maryland state line. Nice little people. Nice little secrets. Get in there, get the papers and documents, find out what they know.

Inside it was all routine. They worked with night-vision goggles. No lamps, no flashlights and certainly no amateurs. One man for each floor.

The computer was in the den, switched on within seconds, while the hacker did his business. From the breast pocket of his fatigues he removed a CD and inserted it into the player. Designed specifically by the company it would scan the hard disc, looking for key words and phrases, searching and transferring as it went – and no sign that anyone had ever been there.

On the top floor the oldest of the team went through the bedroom. You could see at once the differences. She was tidy. He was a slob. And they didn't do a lot of sharing or loving. Everything was his or hers. Separate. Separate lives, maybe separate loves as well. Marriage is a collection of little things. Trinkets, love-notes, photos, menus, movie tickets. But they weren't there. Not in this room. He had seen it so many times before. Best not to wonder what they'd done – or what anyone would do to *them*. There was no such thing as guilty or innocent.

There was a target and you hit it, and then you found another and did it again.

Ten minutes. That was all it took to cut open the lives of the Marches, search their drawers and their hiding places, taking the essential and non-essential and flinging it into a bag.

They left by the back, through the snowy yard, out into the chill air, on a clear, starry night. Washington was doing more and more digging in dirty places. It was all damned good for business.

'Come in, Julie, sit down.' Professor Claridge manoeuvred his bulk from behind the desk and gestured to the chair opposite. 'Sorry to drag you in on your night off. This is Dr Harries from Washington – don't think you guys have met before.'

She nodded. 'Show never closes, huh?'

Harries glanced at her and smiled without warmth. He was tall and in his forties. Too smooth, too groomed for a scientist. A committee man. Born in a government corridor, and destined to stay there. She sat down, noticing that the chair was hard and uncomfortable. But, then, it wasn't a social event. There were no social events at the research station north of Orlando, not with the kind of work they did, not with the kind of people who did it. Claridge, with his giant belly and small blinking eyes, was about the most human of the personnel, but that was stretching it.

'Mrs March, I needed to talk to you about a sensitive matter.' Harries's lips were moving, but the eyes remained perfectly still.

'My name's Fairmont. I don't use my married name.'

'I see.' Harries sucked in his breath. 'But you're still married.' He looked down, brushing some dust from his striped silk tie.

She hesitated only a second but they both caught it. 'Yes, I am. Why?'

There was silence. Not just a lull in conversation, but genuine silence. The research station was empty at this level. Nine floors underground. Insulated and peaceful. She had always thought it a paradox that the most lethal weapons of mass destruction were researched in total peace. Almost as if the tranquillity of death had already settled over them. And yet you got used to it. Even

54

learned to like it. The feeling of being apart and different, and very, very special.

'Miss Fairmont, when did you last see your husband?'

She sat upright, her mouth tightening. 'Why? What's this about?'

'I need to ask you some questions.'

'And who the hell are you?'

'Someone who has the right to ask.' He turned to Claridge. 'Tell her.'

Claridge shook his head. 'Julie, this is a security matter, that's all I know. Dr Harries is from Washington. He's concerned with national security matters there. I don't know any more than that, just that his credentials have been authenticated. Please answer his questions.'

'I don't see what my husband has to do with anything, least of all my work here.'

'Do you know where he is?' Harries has leaned forward.

'What is this?' Voice rising now, cheeks reddening. 'Has something happened to him?'

'We don't know.'

'Listen, Dr Harries – Mr Harries, whoever the hell you are, you better start talking to me –'

And something in his eyes made her break off mid-sentence. No trace of warmth or sympathy: they simply studied her reactions, analysing them, storing them away.

'Your husband's enquiries haven't always been to our liking, Miss Fairmont.'

'I know that.'

'You have a very sensitive job here. I'm sure you appreciate that. And since your husband is a reporter . . .'

'I've never discussed my work with him. It's part of the reason we're . . .'

Harries raised an eyebrow. 'We're what?'

'Splitting up.' She let out her breath. There was no longer any point holding back. They had to know some time. 'We split up last night. He went back to Washington.'

'Where is he now?'

'Call him.' She threw up her hands. 'How the hell do I know? Listen, you want answers about Peter, you better tell me more than this. You bring me out here in the middle of the night, with all kinds of crap about national security. You want to know about his work? Read the newspapers. Whatever he knows, he prints.'

'Maybe not this time.'

She sat back and stared at the ceiling. 'Peter and I talked about this – I told him last night in fact. Jesus, I said, "You keep pissing on the Government and soon they'll start pissing on me."' She shrugged. 'I'm good at my job, OK? Claridge'll tell you that. I do it, I enjoy it – and I shut up about it when I'm outside.'

Harries looked at her with complete disinterest. 'You have two choices, Miss Fairmont. You can help us find your husband or . . .' The head inclined slightly. 'Let's just say that at this moment in time you only have one choice, shall we?' Harries stood up abruptly, catching both Julie and Claridge by surprise. 'Does the name Vic Harden mean anything to you?'

He hadn't ski'd that way for years, down a mountain in darkness, through the trees, feeling the wind grasping at his face. He fell once. Twice. Badly the second time, twisting his right ankle, feeling the pain stab into him when the binding failed to release. Lousy equipment, Vic Harden. Should have prepared it, checked it, made sure it functioned. That was the always the drill, you asshole.

Propped against a fir tree, he pulled himself to his feet, feeling the sweat pouring inside the ski-suit, his heart like a runaway train. And yet the exhilaration was still there. The mind was living it, even if the body couldn't. The thrill of an operation. Twenty years of darkness and madness had given him his edge. Go back five years, he thought, and there was no one to touch Vic Harden. He went into things that no sane person dared imagine. He came out of things where only corpses escaped. And now his body was giving up, driven only by purpose and will, and when that disappeared, it would shut up shop and go home. Wherever that was.

Brushing down his suit, he pushed off once again into the

night, hearing the metal skis slush their way through the fine damp snow. He still knew the moves, could still make the turns – such an elegant athlete. A pile of boulders came up and he executed a perfect spun Christie, throwing up a shower of snow, pressing on down into the valley. Pleasing for an old guy to give out one more performance, one swan song, alone on a mountain in the heart of Virginia.

And yet he wasn't alone. Even as he ski'd, he caught the clatter of the helicopter, far away behind him. Even on a night like this, they were flying – probably a Huey, much beloved by the ex-Special Forces, the kind they'd have hired to hunt him. The kind of dogs that were cheap to feed and cheap to buy.

But the noise spurred him on, as he knew it would. There was always more energy in the bank than you thought. For the body kept its own reserves out of sight, never telling the mind, in case the mind fucked with them and wasted it all. The body was a wise old thing and always kept something back.

Three miles to go, he thought, and he'd need everything he could muster.

Had she done the right thing? As they drove her back to the condo, Julie stared out of the white Lincoln Town Car and thought back to her conversation with Peter. If they'd spent more time together, loved a little more . . . if the relationship had contained some passion . . . then maybe she wouldn't have done it. But she'd warned him less than twenty-four hours ago – and that hadn't been the first time. She was a government scientist with an important job to do. She'd trained for it, spent six years at university and research institutes, studied in Germany on government grants. For Chrissake, she owed them her loyalty, didn't she?

Maybe it had never been right with Peter. Relationships were about more than timing, weren't they? And when they'd met, they'd both been lonely: he in a new country, she obsessed with her work and the opportunities they were holding out. In time, they'd said, she could go to Washington, meet the top brass on the National Security Council, eat all the right dinners and breakfasts, and carry the standard for the scientific community. After all, she was bright, articulate and damned attractive. And in these times of shrinking budgets they would use her – and she would use them.

Peter hadn't fitted into any of that. Peter was off on his own pursuits, digging here, digging there and upsetting all the people she needed to influence. It couldn't have continued. She knew that now.

Ahead of her, in the front seat, she could see the bald head of Dr Harries – but there was no way he was a doctor. This was a fixer, a persuader. In everything he had said there had been the implication of threat, of power unlimited and unaccountable. All governments possessed them. Such people wouldn't be bothered by laws. They were simply employed to get things done.

Was this the kind of government she wanted to work for?

'I believe this is your house, Miss Fairmont.' Harries didn't bother to turn his head.

She was silent. A sudden, unexpected shard of regret hit her and, with it, an old snapshot memory – Peter's laughing face and one of the few glorious, trouble-free vacations they had spent together. She could see it quite clearly. The beach-house on stilts and the blinding white sun along the Outer Banks of North Carolina. Her parents had come for the first weekend, father dour and immovable, insisting on wearing a sweater on the beach, mother ditzy and nervous, always running to the lavatory, oh-so-anxious never to offend.

'How did they end up with a daughter like you?' Peter had asked, when they were out of earshot.

'I woke up one night and stole the family brain cell.'

He had laughed. 'Keep running with it, 'cos if they ever steal it back I'm out of here!'

And she had punched him playfully and run off around the stilts, allowing him to catch her, and pull her on to the sand, his hand snaking into her bikini.

'No, Peter, they'll see.'

'They might learn something.'

'You're terrible . . .' But she didn't stop him, lying back, lifting her buttocks, letting the hand move on down, the fingers straying and probing . . .

Voices and sounds and crystals of sunlight on the surface of the ocean. A summer long gone.

They had driven her parents to the airport at Charlotte, and she'd insisted on waving the plane goodbye, crying as she always did at farewells, feeling the tears flow uncontrollably down her cheeks. He had turned towards her and put his hand on her cheek. 'What is it, Julie? Why are you crying?'

And she had taken a moment to think about it, perhaps for the first time in her life. 'Because they take a little of my certainty with them whenever they go.'

'Why do you say that?'

'They belong to the past, Peter. That's pretty certain, isn't it? Everything else is in doubt. It has to be.'

'And us? Are we in doubt?'

She could see his face darken, as if covered by a cloud. 'I don't know, Peter. I just don't know.'

Wisely he had left the subject and they had driven back to the house on stilts and he had made her laugh, and somehow the evening was rescued.

Much later they had taken a bottle of champagne and two glasses and strolled the beach at sunset, huddling together on the sand as the wind came up and the great orange ball went down. And then, because no one had been around, she had lain on top of him and they had made love, pulling aside their costumes, screaming with the joy of it all, the contrast of the warmth within them, and the cold outside . . .

'I said, I believe this is your house, Miss Fairmont.' The great head turned this time, an eyebrow of annoyance cocked in her direction.

'Yes,' she said simply. She closed her eyes briefly, but by then the memory of old times had snapped shut and the decision to forget about Peter was made.

# Chapter eight

Travis heard the glass shatter even as he forced himself from the depths of sleep. The cold air hit him first, and with it the sensation of a crowd punching into the corridor, heading for the stairs where he tried in vain to stand. Faces and dark uniforms stampeding in the darkness. Too fast to take in.

When they reached him the pain seemed to come from all sides, a massive onslaught that made him cry out to the depths of his soul. Something had paralysed him for, in that instant, there was no movement in his arms or legs, no focus. No centre.

They must have carried him into the living room before tying him into the chair and switching on the lights. And he couldn't work out if he'd been transported to another world as the shock took away the pain, locking out the fearful certainty of what they would do to him. Everything seemed to come from a distance, the light, the noise, and the blood he could see running down his shirt in a tiny stream, collecting beside his trouser zip.

'Travis, where are the canisters?'

There's an echo on the voice, and an immediate surge in pain, but he can't work out where it's coming from. All he wants to do is shout out, 'I'm in America, five miles from the White House, in the District of Columbia, the nation's capital. This can't be happening, can't be true. You don't have the right . . .'

He couldn't have said the right thing, for the pain began again, stabbing him from behind, surging like a blast of volts around his body. Someone was screaming. Was it his own voice? He couldn't be sure. There's only so much the mind will take before it stands up and runs away.

One thing he knew, if they went on much longer they'd lose him. He didn't have the will to stay there. He wanted peace and a breeze. A little bit of sunshine and someone to tell him it would all be OK in the end. Someone like Vic. A name wrapped in sadness. Because he'd never see Vic again. Vic, his mentor. Vic, his instructor and leader. Vic, the invincible, who'd promised he'd be fine.

They must have stopped hitting him, for the relief was almost tangible. And he looked around at the masked faces, even offering them a smile, thinking it was all right and maybe they could work something out. But the faces were a long way off, the hands and bodies moving in slow motion. And no one approached him, no one held out a hand.

For a moment Travis lost his concentration, or maybe the dull ache of pain robbed him of it. He never saw the hypodermic needle, never felt it as it jabbed his upper arm, administered from behind. But suddenly he could see his mother, standing in the kitchen, swore she was cooking omelettes and hash browns for the family, the way she always did on Sundays, swore his father was giving him that same sceptical look, just the way he always had, as if to say, 'You don't know what you're doing, son, but go for it, see if you can . . .'

He could see the face so close – Dad's face. The lines and the moles, the left eye always moist, the right one squinting – never had good eyes, poor dad, couldn't see close, couldn't see far away . . . He'd go out on to the porch, even on the coldest of nights, and stare into the sky, trying to make out the stars, seeing nothing, straining that teary left eye, hoping he'd see the light. Until Mom led him back inside.

'Bye, Dad, says Travis, 'bye, Dingo – the mutt with half an ear and a sawn-off tail, best mutt in the whole damn state.

'Bye, Vic, my friend.

And just as he was wondering why it all took so long, the hand appeared in front of him, floating, disconnected, with a piece of steel bolted to the end.

'The canisters, Travis, where are they?'

And he began laughing, because now was easy. Goodbyes were

said, regrets were sent . . . and fuck 'em if they couldn't take a joke.

A thought to take with him, as Vince Albright pulled the trigger on the Heckler & Koch 9mm pistol and blew the back of Travis's head on to the wall behind.

# Part two

# Chapter nine

Leah Killeen removed the doctor's letter from her bedside table and held it under the light. You're never ill, she thought, until the doctor tells you. You go into the consulting rooms, happy and healthy, with a whole future to play for, and then comes a letter some ten days later and you're a basket case. Only takes a few seconds to slit open the envelope, read the contents, and feel the first of the tears rolling down your cheek.

But the tears had gone now. She had never spent long on them. Tears didn't get anything done. They won you smiles and sympathy but you couldn't cash them in. That was one of life's great myths. Besides, in her experience, it was more often than not the men who did the crying. Especially the high-ups, the princes of politics or business or the arts. The higher they went, the more whining and weeping they did. And she had no wish to join them.

Alone in her bedroom, she could read the letter quite coldly. Dr Friedman had wanted her to come in for another consultation 'to explain it all', but she'd insisted he write what he had to say. She'd rather face it alone. 'Besides,' she told him, 'you charge me a hundred and fifty bucks every time I sit in your lousy waiting room and read last summer's magazines. Why should I pay to see your sorry face when I don't have to?' Friedman had known better than to argue.

So what did it all mean? She got up, went into the bathroom, and ran the shower as hot as she could stand it. Better get into practice for hell, she thought, if that's where I'm going.

As she dried herself, she looked at the options. Multiple blood disorders, chronic fatigue and a general down-turn in the immune system. She could live with all that – for a while. But there would come a growing inability to tolerate light and smells. This would be progressive, and deeply unpleasant. She recalled visiting a serviceman who had taken part in some of the nastiest chemical experiments conducted by the defence department in the name of progress. A sergeant, Jack Tree. Tall man, proud man. At least he had been once. Now racked by pain and sickness, he was forced to spend his life crouching in the shadows.

Go to see him in bright colours and he'd throw up at the sight of you. Wear make-up or perfume or any pungent smell and he'd shrink away into the dark. Multiple chemical sensitivity, they called it, brought on by poisoning from any number of top-secret warfare agents that had never been acknowledged and should have been banned from the face of the earth for all time. That was the scenario that awaited her – with no cure in sight.

She knew all too well how it had happened – and she knew where to direct her rising anger. Running downstairs, she headed for the antique desk in the living room and began to tear out drawers. Souvenirs from half a life tumbled on to the Turkish rugs. Photos, letters and passes, a scrap of cardboard with a phone number, and then the dog tag she had worn, on a journey she should never have made – to the Gulf War.

With a man she should never, ever have loved.

It was October 1990 when she met Dick Lovett at a party for the Senate Judiciary Committee – one of those absurdly overdone Washington galas where the grandees huddled and plotted in the corners and the wives and mistresses flaunted what nature had given them, and silicone had enhanced. She remembered thinking that the only things that hadn't been lifted, tightened or pushed out were the canapés. And that went for the men too. But Leah enjoyed these showcases: as a lawyer in her late twenties she had already handled three major investigations for the Senate, and had access to some of the capital's most sensitive gossip so it was fun to see who approached – and who shied away. Fun to see the raised eyebrows and the nervous tics. Mingling and chatting that night, she could sense both admiration and fear – and an undercurrent of danger. It was never far from the surface of the capital. Too many powerful and ruthless people in one place. Too many deals, too many promises, too many riches. You never knew where one crazy operation began and another ended. Who was running it? Where did it lead? How many secret agencies existed in parts of the city where no one even thought to look? Unless you were careful, Washington was a journey into darkness. Don't turn your back, she thought, or look away or close your eyes. Otherwise the dogs will have you . . .

At around nine thirty she had glanced at her watch and decided she'd had enough. Wives were being hurried out into taxis, the powerful were mumbling about having to be in the 'situation room' at dawn, the party was fraying around the edges. And then she had felt an arm snake through hers and had turned in surprise and delight to find her old law professor, Jack Richardson, grinning from ear to ear, trying hard not to cough his guts into his glass.

'Jesus, Leah . . .'

'Jack, I don't believe it . . .' She patted him on the back until the coughing fit died down. 'Thought you were going to stop smoking years ago.'

He shook his head. 'Stopped everything else. Just couldn't give up the goddam weed.'

'You're crazy.'

'I know, but I had to be to think I could teach you law. By the second year you were teaching me, for Chrissake. Remember?' He took a step back. 'Look at you . . . You've done fantastic things, Leah. Been following your career, you know. We're all very proud of what you've done.'

'You're very kind.'

'Nonsense.' He took her hand and guided her towards the window. 'Want you to meet an interesting friend of mine.'

And, of course, as the friend's handsome grey head had turned towards her, she took in the medals and the uniform and the victory smile, and had no trouble at all in recognising General Dick Lovett, one of the principal commanders of US forces, then on their way to the Gulf. She had stared at the face, counting the lines, wondering if each represented a military campaign, unable to prevent herself being impressed. Everything about him said power, action, the ability to make rapid, life-changing decisions. Richardson did the introductions and there were handshakes and the bonhomie flowed like treacle – and every time she looked up, his eyes were targeting hers. It wasn't aggressive, but it wasn't uninterested either.

Of course, it was too late to talk. The party was almost over. Richardson had been coughing again in a corner and the drinks had dried up and the waiters were clearing the glasses. However glittering, Washington parties were always sudden-death affairs.

'Do you have transport, Miss Killeen?' Lovett had raised an eyebrow. So had the other guests, aware that they were not included in the invitation.

The thought amused her. 'I do, General, but when you've got so many men and machines to take out to the Gulf, you're going to need all the transport you've got.'

He laughed. 'We're getting there, Miss Killeen. Thank you for being so thoughtful.' He held out his hand and she took it, barely noticing the scrap of card that he left in her palm.

When she let herself into the ladies' room, she could see the phone number quite clearly. A downtown Washington exchange, probably a hotel or military guest-house. And she made a decision then and there not to call it. After all, it was such a typical Washington gesture. Soldier away from home sees pretty woman, wants a fuck after a long day. Scraps of paper like that were a dime a dozen in the capital. Pathetic! And doubly pathetic that it came from a man with such a high-octane reputation and a family tree growing right out of the *Mayflower* itself. But, then, wasn't it always the way?

In fact, as she drove home, Leah became increasingly angry about Lovett's advance. It was high-handed and disrespectful. Worse, it made her seem like a cheap hooker, who didn't even have the price of a ride home.

Damn Lovett, and damn all the Washington men who thought they could get any skirt they wanted by dint of wearing a uniform and a few ribbons. They never, ever grew up.

For more than an hour, she lay in bed unable to sleep. It wasn't the first time she had been propositioned. Far from it. But this time it had unsettled her and she didn't know why. In the end she sat up and switched on the bedside light. Only one thing was going to help her sleep. She needed to call Lovett and tell him what a skunk he really was. Then she could forget about him and get some rest.

It was a mistake she was to regret many times over.

Of course, Lovett had apologised profusely. He'd had no wish, no inkling, not the slightest desire to cause offence. He was desolated and sincerely sorry for causing hurt. He was, it went without saying, deeply ashamed that he had done such a thing.

And suddenly, for reasons she couldn't begin to explain, she had begun laughing down the phone line, unable to stop herself, tears cascading down her face, until he, too, had done the same. And for a few moments neither had been able to talk coherently. When they'd collected themselves, it seemed obvious that he would invite her to lunch. 'I'm just here for a couple days, then out again to the Gulf, so if you had some time . . .'

So very hard to refuse. Just like the flowers he brought to the lunch table, and the old-fashioned New England manners, helping her to her chair, making sure she was served and pampered, that doors were opened, that waiters fawned. She didn't know it but it was part of his game, and by the time the second Bloody Mary came along, they were talking about their childhood, their schools, their parents, as if they had known one another for years.

Three weeks later, he was back in Washington, and they did it again for dinner. He had booked at an Italian restaurant, just a few yards from the White House – a noisy, crowded place, where the lights were turned low and you could lose yourself in the gossipy intrigues of the city. Snippets of conversation were as tantalising as the food – and Lovett had plenty of his own. He was wonderfully indiscreet about the Pentagon, about George Bush and Colin Powell. He told of the tantrums and scenes with the allies, who didn't want to get involved. The bribes and sweeteners handed over to some of the Arab ambassadors, the cowardice of the ruling élites. And, of course, she'd been hooked. Who wouldn't have been? This was, after all, the lifeblood of Washington. This was why she'd gone to the city. This was what got her up in the morning and made her lie awake at night. And she was enthralled by the man, who had just returned from the Gulf, and who, by all accounts, would fight a war there in a few months' time.

Leah didn't reply when Lovett suggested a stroll to his hotel. She simply allowed her hand to be taken, her body to be steered, out of the restaurant and down the hundred yards of 18th Street to the Willard – the most luxurious and grandest billet in town.

It was the best of evenings in Washington, the end of a long, hot fall, the sky a deep turquoise, blotched by dark blue clouds, pulling east across Virginia. 'You should see the desert skies,' he told her, planting a dream. 'That's when you realise we're part of something truly magnificent, and that anything is possible.'

And she had allowed him the conceit, stifling a natural urge to tell him it was still all bullshit – and a pretty sky didn't make a damned bit of difference to anything. But, as she later told herself, she had suspended normal critical faculties. Didn't happen often. Shouldn't have happened at all.

He had started to undress her even before she was fully inside the room – and that had excited her even more. His hands cupping her breasts, then reaching behind, pulling the silk blouse from her skirt, his mouth exploring hers with an urgency she had not expected. The bra had disappeared in a second and her breasts fell into his hands, the nipples taut and aching as his tongue stroked over them. There were sounds in her throat that she had forgotten she could make, and she could feel her climax building from a long way away, powerful and unstoppable as his hands moved down her belly.

Dick Lovett, the power and the glory . . .

He had been fit and hard, as she expected, precision entry, practised movement, no stranger to the ways of womankind, she thought. But there was something clinical about the way he handed her a Kleenex when it was all over, about the mint candy that he sucked and offered to her from a packet beside the bed, and the way in which his hair was newly combed and coiffed once he returned from the bathroom.

Sex had taken place between them. Not love.

But maybe, she imagined, the one would lead to the other. And even if it didn't, Lovett had something else about him that was hard to resist: he was a ruthless sonofabitch. And so, in her own way, was she.

Together, they might go far.

Sometimes, in the weeks that followed, they would stay at her house and she would kid herself that their lives were merging. But it didn't happen. He never left behind any clothes or mementoes, no notes or trinkets. He simply visited her life and her bed and then he went away again. And the less he gave her, the more she had to imagine.

By this time, of course, the coalition war machine was building into shape. There was plenty for him to think about. And he had less and less time to return to the US. Once there was a call from London, and another from Geneva, and he promised a little bit of excitement 'if it can be arranged'. But she thought no more about it. The war was probably only a few days away and he would surely get no extra leave until the conflict was over.

And then she had arrived back home on a Friday night, to see the blue staff car parked outside her drive, with a signals officer inside and a sealed cable in an envelope marked with her name.

As she read it, her mouth fell open as if it was no longer connected to her face, and her heart started beating loudly enough to wake the neighbourhood. The note told her simply that she had the chance to board a transport plane, leaving at midnight from Andrews air force base outside Washington, and be flown direct to Saudi Arabia where Lovett would meet her. All she had to do was say yes to the messenger and the arrangements would be put in hand. She could be back home in Washington by Tuesday.

Leah stared at the officer, who stared back without expression.

Such things, of course, didn't happen. She chuckled at the stupidity of it. It was a good joke, and she'd almost been fooled.

71

And yet the longer she stood there, the more she began to shake her head. The soldier was waiting for an answer.

She looked again at the cable and knocked on the car window. 'What would you do if I said a simple yes to you?'

'I'd ask you to bring a bag with your personal items and I would immediately make arrangements for your journey.'

Jesus, God, Dick Lovett. What have you done?

'I'm sorry,' she told the officer, 'there's been some mistake. I can't possibly do something like this.'

'I understand, ma'am.'

'Goodbye, then. Thank you.'

And she had walked inside the house and the phone had rung and Lovett had worked some of his old, and now familiar, magic over the line from Saudi. There were, as he put it, people and places to see. The trip would be exciting and important – and who knew what the future might bring? And what the two of them would do when the conflict was over?

It was the throw to the future that clinched it. Leah Killeen broke a long-held promise to herself, about being taken in by men, and packed her bag.

By mid-afternoon the next day she was in Saudi and Lovett's fellow officers were going round the mess telling everyone he'd won the first battle of the war.

As she sat on the rug, Leah could still see that winter's day in the desert six years earlier. She had flown into an air-force base near Riyadh, amazed at the biblical chaos unfolding in the middle of the desert. Everywhere she looked there was noise and dust, as tens of thousands of soldiers were massing in tents and the first of the tanks took up positions, pointing north towards Iraq. From the skies came the ceaseless droning waves of supply planes and the frightening array of fighters as the American war machine kicked into top gear. She couldn't help the twin jabs of fear and excitement, couldn't help realising that, although it was terrible and sinister, war was an aphrodisiac. War was a hard-on.

Lovett's colleagues had been bursting with it – frothing at the mouth to start shooting and killing. Fingers were itching to hit the firing buttons, to test the toys, to send out the rockets and the laser-guided bombs and prove once again that they could kick ass whenever they wanted. All so young, she thought, and all so ready to kill.

It was a shock to watch them over dinner, where she could sense the resentment. She was the General's woman, flown out courtesy of the USAF, the little miss bimbo from Washington, overdressed, under-informed, come to suck the old man's dick before the battle began. They wanted to talk strategy and throw-weights, guidance systems and battlefield shells. And you couldn't do that with a skirt.

'I shouldn't have come,' she told him later, as they made their way to the hotel commissioned by the US military.

'They're keyed up. Don't take any notice.'

'I want to pay for my plane ticket.'

'Don't worry. I'll take care of it.'

'I'm serious, Dick.'

'And I said I'll take care of it. I'm a fucking general, for Chrissake —' He stopped, knowing he had gone too far.

She removed her hand from his and turned to face him in the back of the jeep.

'Let's just get one thing straight, OK? I don't take orders from you or anyone else — least of all from you. If you don't understand that, you don't understand anything. And if I say I'm going to pay my way I pay it, OK? Now, stop the car.'

'Leah, it's the middle of the desert.'

She leaned forward to the soldier in the front seat. 'Stop the car, please.'

The man looked nervously back towards the General.

Lovett nodded. 'Do as she says.'

She got out and stood by the side of the road, breathing deeply. A thousand stars stared back from the clear night sky. What an idiot she'd been to come here. The entire world was waiting for war. He was on edge, she was on edge and the whole thing was a disaster.

Lovett touched her arm. 'I'm sorry, Leah, I was out of line.'

'Yes, you were.'

'Will you get back in the car now? We shouldn't be standing around like this — it's not safe.'

She climbed back in and ten minutes later they were at the hotel. But the row was like a fence between them and she knew that neither of them would attempt to climb it that night. She undressed in the bathroom and, as they lay in the darkness, they could still hear the planes droning in on final approach to the airfield. Headlights flickered on the wall behind them. 'I shouldn't have come,' she whispered, but Lovett didn't answer. Turning to the wall, she wondered if she shouldn't simply get dressed, return to the air base and wait for a plane out. But she was asleep long before she'd decided one way or the other.

It was around three a.m. that the sound of urgent knocking forced her awake. When she opened her eyes Lovett was already at the door and she could hear furious whispering in the corridor.

'Jesus fucking Christ . . .' Lovett shut the door and switched on the light.

Leah raised herself on to her elbows. 'What the hell's happening?'

'Some kind of alert — don't know for sure.' Lovett was sitting on the bed, pulling on his battle fatigues. 'Go back to sleep. I won't be long. Probably nothing to worry about, but I should go and check.'

'What kind of alert?'

'I'll tell you later. Nothing to concern you.'

And then the light was out and he had gone.

Leah lay for a while, trying to sleep, but then she began to cough and sleep became impossible. She got up and it seemed her throat was on fire and her chest swollen beyond belief. As the panic set in she ran straight out of the room, her breathing now in short jerks, her temperature rocketing.

And there, in the foyer of the hotel she saw something she would never forget. It was like a scene from another world. She stood in shock before the screams escaped from her throat.

In the half-light from the fluorescent strips she could see a dozen or so figures with masks and chemical suits and an array of testing equipment laid out on tables. For a brief, wild moment, she imagined they were aliens – but it was suddenly clear what it meant and that was the moment at which she cried out.

Two rushed towards her, up the stairs, catching her as she fell to her knees. The last thing she remembered was falling forward on her face, choking and trying to throw up at the same time before the blackness overcame her and the lights in her mind went out.

When she came to, she was inside a breathing tent. Two nurses were checking instruments and a medical orderly was writing notes on a pad. There was the low hum of electronics and the steady swish of a fan. Leah tried to sit up, but a wave of nausea hit her. She called for water, feeling the burning in her throat – which brought back the memory of what had happened.

As she sank back on the pillow, one of the nurses zipped open the tent and took her hand.

'Water . . .'

'I'll get you some. How do you feel?'

'Lousy.' She was whispering. 'Where am I? What happened?'

'You're in a US Army medical centre near Riyadh. You were brought here after a gas leak at your hotel.'

Leah shook her head. 'No gas leak . . . chemicals . . . men in chemical suits . . .'

'Wait.' The nurse slipped outside the tent and murmured to the orderly. She came back with a plastic cup of water.

'Here, drink this. We've told General Lovett you're awake. He wanted to be informed as soon as you came round.'

Leah took the cup and drained it while her mind raced back over the events she had witnessed. A gas leak? This had been no gas leak. You don't get soldiers climbing into chemical suits because of a gas leak. She closed her eyes, seeing the figures rushing towards her, recalling again the terrible burning in her throat.

And then Lovett was beside her bed, holding her hand, telling her how devastated he was, and all the things he would do to make up for what had happened . . .

'What did happen?' She looked him straight in the eye.

'Didn't they tell you? It was a gas leak. Jesus, we were lucky the whole hotel didn't blow up. The place is a death trap. I've moved all our things out.' He smiled. 'The medics tell me you're fine and they'll let you out later in the day. Then we're heading into Riyadh and the most modern hotel they have. Somewhere quiet and peaceful where you can rest up.'

'Tell me the truth, Dick.'

His eyes opened wide. 'What do you mean? I just told you.'

'The hell you did. When I clawed my way out of that bedroom last night I saw soldiers in chemical suits and I was coughing my guts up. That was no gas leak, that was a full-scale chemical warfare attack and I had no protective suit.'

'Leah, you have to have been dreaming. I swear to you, I've heard nothing of soldiers in chemical suits. Far as I know they haven't even been issued yet. And there was no chemical leak. I can show you the reports. This was gas – nothing more, nothing less.'

'Don't lie to me, Dick.'

He opened his palms in a gesture of full disclosure. 'I wouldn't lie, honey, I swear to you.'

'Then what was that alert you got called out for?'

'An accident on the base. Two of my men got killed when their jeep veered off the road. They were drunk – you can see the reports if you want.'

'Dick, I know what I saw.'

'You were delirious, believe me. The medics said you were brought in coughing and muttering and making no sense. The gas can do that to you, specially the foul stinking kinda stuff they have here.'

'Dick . . .'

'Just close your eyes and rest. I'll come and get you in a couple hours, and we'll drive into Riyadh. It'll be OK, I swear.'

She lay back on the pillow and nodded, convinced that Lovett had lied to her.

By the time he returned she was dressed and in no mood to go anywhere except home.

'Take me back to the air base, Dick. I'm leaving.'

'Leah, what the hell's going on?'

'I don't know – you tell me, for Chrissake. There's some kinda cover-up going on here and you're not telling me about it. So, unless you have any more convincing explanations of what happened to me, I'm leaving.'

'What the hell can I tell you?'

'The truth would be a start. You can tell me about the chemical attack on this godforsaken fucking place. You can tell me why there was no protective suit for me when everyone else had one. You can tell me all kinds of things that wouldn't insult my intelligence – and until you do, I don't want to speak to you again. Is that clear enough?'

She glanced behind him towards the dispensary where the nurses and orderlies were trying hard to listen to their conversation while appearing not to. Lovett followed her eyes.

'Let's talk outside.'

'Let's not talk at all.' She stood up and walked towards the door. 'This is getting nowhere. You seem to think you can treat me like some kind of imbecile, full of strange imaginings and no longer able to believe her own eyes.'

'I'm sorry you feel that way. Nothing could be further from the truth.'

'You don't know what the truth is, Dick. And if you do know, you're not going to tell me.'

Leah walked out into the sun, momentarily blinded by the brightness. A warm wind was blowing in from the desert. To the west lay the city of Riyadh, to the north the air base where planes were landing incessantly – the vast transporters in their sandy camouflage, bringing America's men and machines to the war.

Odd that there was no element of surprise. The largest army in the world was heading off in the full glare of the world's television cameras, bringing in its tanks and planes and soldiers. And when it had assembled enough of them the killing game could begin. No secret manoeuvring, no subtlety. The enemy would just sit where it was and wait to be annihilated. What, in God's name, was going on?

And then there was last night. She had spent the last few hours believing that the hotel had come under attack from the Iraqis.

What if that wasn't true? What if, by some terrible chance, it had been American germ-warfare agents, released by accident? Wasn't that the emergency that had sent Lovett scurrying away in the middle of the night? One thing was certain: he wasn't going to tell her.

Lovett drove her in silence back to the air base, didn't kiss her, didn't say goodbye. When she looked into his eyes, she could see it was over. Whatever had passed for affection was lost in a range of emotions that she couldn't fathom. Annoyance, frustration. Fear?

'There's a C-130 leaving for Andrews in a couple of hours. I'll make the arrangements.' He turned on his heel, then stopped and walked back. 'Nothing happened here, Leah. Believe me, nothing at all. You should know that.'

'You're a liar, Dick Lovett.'

'If that's the way you want it . . .'

'I'm going to find out what did happen. Count on it.'

'Just go home and leave it.' And there was something in his tone that she hadn't heard before, something a million miles from the Dick Lovett who'd seduced her in Washington and barged his way into her dreams.

'Are you threatening me?'

He was silent as a plane roared in over their heads. Then he said 'Do I need to?'

As she sat there on the rug, the memories seemed to come at her through a thick mist. Only now they were clear. Now all the pieces fitted together. There was a pattern and a sequence – and a chapter of lies that was still being written years after the book had been closed. To this day Leah had no doubts about what she'd seen – or the extent of the cover-up that had followed. Throughout the Gulf War, there had been repeated detections of germ-warfare agents. All had been denied. Even after the conflict, they were still denying the existence of nerve gas in areas that had been under Iraqi control. But the first denial of all had come directly from Lovett.

That night in Riyadh the whole ghastly chemical scenario had begun – and a new generation of weapons was released for test.

Neither side had ever admitted it because neither would accept responsibility for a new phase of lethal conflict from which there could be no retreat.

Washington had locked all the doors of the citadel and let no one in. They could never take the chance. One room would have led assuredly to another, and another after that, and still more rooms, containing still more disastrous secrets, until the whole appalling picture had come to light.

Two years earlier, Leah Killeen had bought the piece of information she needed, the key which unlocked that citadel. She had come across proof that a high-level Pentagon official had been having a homosexual affair – and she had confronted him with it, threatened to go public.

The man was facing ruin and offered to do anything to save his career, his family and reputation.

Over lunch at a restaurant in Glen Echo, just outside Washington, Leah Killeen had told him what he had to do. She wanted the Gulf War story, pure and unadorned. She wanted documents and papers, names and conversations. And he was to deliver them to her within a week.

Exactly seven days later he met her at the same restaurant and gave her what she had demanded: proof positive that both sides in the war had released chemical weapons, that US and other coalition troops had been exposed to lethal nerve agents and that most of the substances had been refined and produced in top-secret American laboratories. For that reason alone, the cover-up could never be lifted.

Leah had looked at the papers, placed them back on the table and excused herself. In the bathroom, suddenly overtaken by a fit of shaking, she had run the water as cold as she could. Her breathing became rapidly arrhythmic and sweat broke out on her forehead. As she stared at the mirror, she could see one of her eyelids fluttering involuntarily. There was no way to stop it. She waited ten minutes before the searing flush had cooled and she could step calmly back to the table.

Of course, the man had gone – and so had his documents. Somehow, she had known what would happen.

Next day the *Washington Post* carried a story on page four about a senior Pentagon official, whose car had careered over the edge of a scenic overlook close to the Capital Beltway. The vehicle had exploded and the driver and all contents had been burned beyond recognition.

Leah had tried to feel pity, but by then she was beyond it. The anger and the sickness were growing inside her.

For a while it was hard to recognise the symptoms. Niggling pains, excessive fatigue, eye strain – didn't everyone suffer from that in Washington?

And then the different infections, the colds and the attacks of flu. A whole succession of viral onslaughts as her immune system developed holes and gradually lowered its guard.

So now there was the proof from Dr Friedman. And Leah Killeen knew exactly what she would do.

The first opportunity that came her way, she would kill Dick Lovett.

# Chapter ten

Winston found Travis's body, sprayed against the wall of the sitting room. He stared at the sight for more than minute before his mind could absorb it. Then he went out and threw up in the hall.

'Jesus, man . . . oh, Jesus Christ.' For a few minutes he crouched by the stairs, eyes shut, giving little grunts of pain. He was only a thief, he told himself, a petty thief at that, fucked about by the world at large, only come into the house because they'd told him this was the one. Check it, they'd said. See who's around, see if it's cool. But he hadn't asked why. And they hadn't said anything about a goddam corpse − or half a corpse, blown away in the night. He stood up, feeling the dizziness in his head, mouth dry and acid, eyes running. 'I gotta get outa here . . . Oh, Jesus, man, how the fuck did I get here?'

Winston was fast. A man of perpetual motion. He was fast even when he was cruising. As he came out of the house, he crossed the street, checking the sidewalks, computing the distance to home, the short-cuts and the blind alleys, just in case he was followed. The nausea was still in his throat so he spat as he ran. The world, he told himself, was a skunk-pit, and he was a voyeur, and nothing good would ever come of his life, however hard he tried.

Past the church now, and he should have been there on Sunday, should have listened to the fucking sermon, filled his time with God and good works − and maybe then he'd have got himself a life. But that was a long time past. He'd tried it for a while, met the big, bald Reverend Harrington MacFarlane, with his big name and big ideas and big speeches about the world to come.

But it was the here and now that Winston needed. Someone to listen and understand. Someone to help him wrap up the past and put it away, and never make him look at it ever again. And that was when he'd found the family and they'd found him. Yes, a family – a real one. Joined by blood – but not their own. Joined by the blood of people they'd killed in the service of their country and wished they never had. People who were against the armies they'd served in and the state terrorism they'd committed and would do everything in their power to destroy them. Such were the people who had welcomed Winston in.

One day a week he'd go on the streets for them, do the errands, steal a car, deliver a letter, pay off a friend. Once he'd even had to beat a guy – just to give him a warning. But he'd told them all he didn't do violence no more. Not since his time in the US Army. So they'd never asked him to do that again. They were good like that – the family – the people he hung out with. The people who made him feel he belonged.

Christ, they'd go crazy when he told them about the corpse.

Past a garage now. Shut. Shops, a restaurant, all shut. Life had been like that before the family. Shut right down. And maybe it was his own fault. Couldn't get the war out of his mind. The Gulf War of '91. The one the Army never talked about any more.

Of course, he'd only stayed in the service for a couple of months after coming home. And why was that? Too many corpses. That was the simple answer. Too many people cut down in the biggest duck shoot since ducks were discovered. He'd seen it happen, flying navigator in a helicopter gunship. He'd seen the Iraqis stumble sleepy and petrified from their foxholes, heard the order to slice them down where they stood, gazing up into the lights of the machine that hovered and clattered, like some prehistoric monster, just above the ground. And then the high-velocity cannons had stitched patterns right across their chests and they were dead before they hit the sand, some cut in two in mid-air. Something you should never, ever witness, never hear about, never tell . . .

And now he'd seen it again.

As he ran, his mind began retrieving the details. He didn't know Travis's name but he could see what they'd done to him. He could picture the scene. The last moments of a man's life. The mounting terror. The shocking, brutal act and the darkness that follows.

Sometimes, he recalled, there is peace among the dead. Those who have departed naturally lie still and quiet, with hushed voices around them. There is a cool solemnity in the air. But not when the death is violent. Then the face is contorted, the hands and legs splayed at terrible angles to the body. The violence can be felt, almost touched, and just when you think it's left you it returns to sit at the end of your bed, caught and captured by your mind and never released.

Winston knew how it would go, knew that he was in big trouble.

'What happened to you?'

He was back at the big house in south-east Washington, five miles from the Capitol, four from the river and right inside hell's backyard. Those were the first directions they'd ever given him. And he'd found it OK. Found it again this time, Christ knew how.

It was a broken-down, rambling neighbourhood, just like the people who lived there. Oddballs, vets, the retired and the frightened. Crime was like the wind. Always there. Sometimes it died down, then it flared up again. Never went away for long. He felt cold looking round the house. They'd knocked all the downstairs rooms into a large meeting area, with a kitchen tacked on and a courtyard for the motorcycles. And as he stared up at the first-floor landing, one or two of the family emerged from the dormitories, leaning over the rail to hear what he had to say. Of course, he hadn't said anything yet but they could see from his face and his clothes and the straining eyes that something had gone wrong. People who've lived through wars have an extra sense, not given to others. They know when an emergency has walked through the door and is standing in front of them. They don't need flashing lights or sirens. They just know.

'Winston, talk to me . . .' Angelo was standing in front of him, sad-faced, sick, but still in charge, still knowing what to do.

'He was dead, man, just dead, OK?'

'It's not OK. How did he die?'

'Every which way, man. They'd tied him to a chair, then beaten him about the head. You could see that, then shot him in the face. Jesus, man – blood all over the wall . . . I never saw nothing . . .'

And then he stopped because, of course, he'd seen too many things like it far too many times . . . Until the horror had set in and he'd walked away.

'Did you see anyone in the area?'

Winston shook his head.

'Think man, think . . .'

He shut his eyes tight. Ice-covered cars and snowy front yards and barking dogs crowded into his mind. And, as the tape rewound, he could see the car that was different from all the others.

'Jesus, man.'

A squat, grey Chevy, a Caprice, the one they called the Mob's staff car, about a hundred yards up the street. Different. Why? Because the windows were misted from the inside. Which meant there had to be someone sitting there out of sight. Maybe two or three people. And what in the name of the sacred Virgin was someone waiting out there for on the coldest, lousiest night of the year, when the rest of the city was cowering at home to keep warm?

As he told what he'd seen Angelo's face turned another shade of pale. 'Fuck, man, did you lead those guys here?'

Winston shrank back in horror. 'No – for Chrissake!'

'Steve.' Angelo snapped his fingers and a younger clone appeared at his side. Beard, T-shirt and combat pants, ten or fifteen years lighter on his feet, a sweatband around his forehead. 'You check the front. Take two of the boys and cover both ends of the street.' He put out a hand, stopping Steve in his tracks.

'Break out some firepower. Nothing showy, OK? Take the Magnums and a couple of grenades, case you need 'em. Back in twenty – now move it.'

And when he heard the orders, Winston was back in the field, shielding his eyes against the desert sun, knowing that the war was imminent. Angelo had been out there as a young lieutenant with all the prospects in the world: word in the battalion was that he could go all the way, Pentagon, joint chiefs – and right along the road to a plot at Arlington if he ran out of luck. Meantime, he was dressy enough for the parties in Washington and cruel enough for the killing fields of Iraq. He'd been launched on his way to the future – and now, just six years on, he was trying to escape the past.

As Winston looked around, he could see them all receiving their orders – all the bums and stiffs who'd once stood straight to attention and been proud to salute the flag. But they were still a mean bunch. Still a force. And no one in the city would dream of coming near them.

He went over to Angelo, who had drawn a pistol from his waistband and was checking the ammunition in the clip.

'What d'you want me to do?'

'We're outa here, man. We're compromised and if we stick around we're dead. We gotta head for an alternative location.' He looked around the main hall. 'What we're gonna do now is split up and move out separately across the city. It's the only way. If a guy's followed, he's gotta lose 'em or go somewhere else on his own. We can't risk screwing up the mission.'

Winston's eyes bulged. 'What mission, man? I didn't think there was any more missions. Ain't that the reason we got out?'

But he was already being pushed aside. One by one the family was lining up to receive an address, scrawled on a piece of paper, to be read and memorised, then chewed and swallowed. On their backs were small rucksacks that held their only possessions. In their pockets a gun and some ammunition. They were to meet, said Angelo, in three hours at the new location. If they made it, they made it, if they didn't he'd understand.

'You guys, take care,' he told them. 'There's a bunch of crazies out there who ain't fussy about punchin' holes in you. But you're better than they are. They've never had to do what you did. So think of that. You know the procedure. We went through it enough times in the old days. And keep the faith.'

Winston watched them leave, six guys he had known well, eaten with, cried with, and reminisced with about better times and places. 'Hey, guys, take it easy,' he whispered as they passed, but they didn't respond.

He went up to Angelo, who had begun burning papers in a trash can. 'Think they'll make it?'

'I guess. They know how to lose themselves in a city – that's what they were trained for. That was the speciality, urban warfare, in case we ever had to go into some fucked-up European city and get the Commies out. These guys blend in with the buildings and the cars and the beggars.'

And then he stopped because there didn't seem any point going on. To him Winston was a decent guy who'd drawn a fuckin' short straw. It was just another lousy mission, and it was always the good ones that went down. Winston caught his glance, and the expression he couldn't hide.

'Hey, man, you gonna give me this address everyone's going to?'

'You know I can't do that, Winston. That's the rule, son. You've been seen. We gotta assume they know who you are.'

Winston stood frozen to the ground. 'What – what am I gonna do, man?'

'You run, fellah. Go to ground. Give it a week, maybe ten days. Then we'll find you, OK? Once this has died down we'll put out the word and bring you in.'

'I – just –' Winston could feel the tears beginning to well out of his eyes. 'But I did what you wanted, man. I went to the fucking place. Not my fault the guy'd been wasted.'

Angelo put a hand on his shoulder. 'Hey, we're not shutting the door, OK? We gotta get out of here. That's it. For the guy's sake and for yours too. It'll be fine, you'll see. Ten days, and we'll pull you in.' He dug in his pocket. 'I ain't got too much money, but take this.' He pushed a wad of notes into Winston's hand. Winston shook his head.

'Don't need money.' Winston wiped his eyes, and a toothy, seriously crooked grin lit up the dismal hallway. 'If I can't steal it, man, then nobody in this city gonna be able to. I'll do just fine.' He shook Angelo's hand. 'Take care, fellah. I'll see you soon.'

Without looking back, Winston walked out of the house, crossed the road and moved fast towards the main street. He clocked Steve and another lookout but they didn't acknowledge each other, eyes didn't move. It was getting lighter now and the first of the buses were trying to plough their way through the snow, churning it into dirty slush.

He had eyes for the darkness and eyes for the light – and maybe he was too upset to do the checks in the window, the stops and starts, and the double-backing that he should have done.

At any rate they picked him up three blocks closer to the White House, two cars and a biker, and he never spotted any of them as he wove his way into the early-morning traffic.

# Chapter eleven

'Hi, honey.' She was waiting for Lovett in the hallway, pink and polished like a boiled sweet, her hair swept back into a ponytail and that same stupid smile he'd seen on all her family photos, going back to when she was a kid. Not a smile of love or affection, or even amusement. Just a vacant, mouth-open grimace that she'd probably carry with her to the grave.

'Coming to bed, honey?'

Oh, God, he thought. Not that. Not another hour of her little whimpers and giggles and baby-talk. She was like a poodle playing with a bone, rather than an adult trying to get it on. But, then, she wasn't an adult – never would be. Christ only knew how she'd ever given birth to a kid. When he thought back, he couldn't remember even coming inside her, let alone in the same room. Most of the sessions had ended with him feigning orgasm and then sloping off to the bathroom to handle it himself. Some · fucking marriage he'd got himself. But it was her dad he'd married. The old straight-up-and-down Washington fixer, part crook, part benefactor, habitual liar, cheat and charmer all in one. Yeah, he'd married Dad for all his money and influence – and the promise that he'd get him on the Republican ladder and keep him there. And that was a marriage in anyone's book.

'Is something the matter, hon?' She stood under one of the spotlights on the stairs, her cheeks glistening with moisturiser.

'Nothing. I'll just get a drink from the kitchen.'

'I'll get it for you.'

He headed down the corridor, turning on lights as he went.

'You go to bed. You know how tired you've been last coupla days. I'll be up soon.'

Her grin widened. 'I won't be asleep.'

Lovett shut the kitchen door behind him and reached into the fridge for a soda. He flicked it open and drained it in two gulps. As he sat down at the table, he could feel his pulse like a runaway horse.

Slow down, fellah, keep steady. Look at all the options. Rewind and review.

Old precepts plucked from the past.

After all, things had been bad before. Washington was forever on the brink. You set things up and someone tried to knock 'em down. Always the way. But, Jesus, this was a bad one.

A guy in the plant with a conscience. That was all they needed. Look at all the millions of dollars spent vetting these people to make sure they didn't have one. Conscience, for Chrissake. These were people who had fought dirty wars and done things they shouldn't have done. How the hell were you to know that one of these dumb fuckers had found Christ on the bus home – and decided to shoot his mouth off?

This had to be cleared up fast. If the whispers got out, they'd have every fucking watchdog in Washington sitting up and howling, calling committees, rummaging around in all the cupboards where they'd no business to be, mouthing off to the press about freedom and rights. What the hell did these people think *ensured* them their grand rights and their fancy homes and cars and all the fuck-witted little brats at private schools. Jesus . . .

Hold it, Dick, get a grip, don't go wandering off.

The mind checking itself.

He threw the soda can into the trash and poured himself a whisky.

And then he saw it.

The kids' calendar stuck to the door of the fridge, with all kinds of scrawlings and drawings and brightly coloured letters attached with magnets. Thursday had been circled in red: some kind of party had been scheduled. But he knew what Thursday was. The Gulf War anniversary at the Pentagon, six years on from the whole ghastly débâcle, and just three days away. Three days before the President and all the chiefs of staff got together with the seniors from the Gulf, to shake hands and to meet the widows and families. The whole thing was for the cameras, with all the networks and newspapers invited . . . Jesus.

That's what this was about. That's where the canisters were going.

He picked up the receiver and called Albright's mobile phone.

'Yeah?'

'It's me.'

'What?'

Lovett lowered his voice. 'I know what this is about. You know the reception at the Pentagon on Thursday?'

There was a moment of silence, but he knew Albright would get it. 'You mean that annual thing for the Gulf vets? Jesus . . .'

'They'll be going for that. I'm certain. Going to disrupt it and probably kill –'

'That fits.'

'This is why Harden's involved. Has to be.'

'We're onto him. Don't worry.'

'Find him, Vince, and kill him. Harden's about as dangerous as they come. You won't get a second chance.'

Upstairs, Jane replaced the receiver and stared at it. She had been listening to Dick's calls for some time, thinking he was probably having an affair. After all, he didn't want sex. He hated coming home. And he couldn't have cared two buttocks in a snowstorm if she was alive or dead.

But what she had heard now was far more upsetting than adultery. Vic was up to his eyes in bullshit, she knew that. Serious bullshit that could ruin lives and careers, and went way outside anything she could ever understand. She knew she couldn't stop it, but she also knew that she couldn't just turn away and let it happen.

Sometimes when she looked at herself in the mirror, she would speak sternly and admit quite frankly that he didn't love her any more and probably never had. But even that wasn't the worst of it. Somehow, for the first time, she had the impression that he was probably an evil sonofabitch and she really didn't want that kind of father for her child.

She reached over to the bedside light and turned it off, lying there in darkness, staring towards the ceiling. Of course, her father had been the same type of man. Washington bred them, drew them in, made them and corrupted them – she had seen it all and heard it all, way back into the early days of her childhood. The conversations, the plots, the whispered, hurried phone calls. And no one had paid her any attention because she would simply stand there, with the stupid smile, looking as though she had left her mind in the subway and someone else had taken it home. And yet she understood well enough what it was about – and somewhere along the line there were limits. There had to be. What would she tell the baby if there weren't?

Jane rolled over on her side and faced the wall. If Lovett had been able to see her, he'd have noticed that the habitual smile, which he always took such pleasure in mocking, had gone.

As he drove away from Leah Killeen's house Peter March could see the police lights. But they barely registered. Washington was never short of emergencies: whatever the weather, the dying was constant. Week after week relentless gang battles were fought out in the south-east and north-east suburbs, same areas, same body count. People were killing other people where before they'd have thrown a punch. On some streets, life itself was a luxury.

It wasn't even as if Washington was the worst. Other east-coast cities had more shootings, but their trauma units were quicker and better so more of the victims were saved. In Washington they sometimes died where they fell, waiting for the ambulances, bleeding under the noses of the nation's politicians – with other things on their minds.

March had done his share of the violent stories but finally the paper had had enough. Besides, with the presidential elections just a year away, it was the political assassinations that interested them. That and the other things Washington did best – sleaze and intrigue. Sex and power. On that level the US capital never disappointed.

March headed the Jeep up 23rd Street towards Dupont Circle, skidding a little as he accelerated into the traffic. The top snow was soft and flaky but there was a hard layer of ice beneath it. The worst night of the year. The night Harden had chosen to make contact.

He shivered, but it wasn't from the cold. Harden did that to you – just the memory of the man, the things he'd done, worse, the things he believed in. Harden and all the other paid-up lunatics, schooled and modelled in special institutions for special missions in which special people always ended up dead.

March had met him first when they were both on leave in Dhahran – the front-line base in Saudi, launch point for some of the low penetration strikes into Iraq. They had talked for twenty minutes about other places in the world they hated, and then Harden's tone had altered abruptly. He was tired and bored, and wanted nothing more than to lord it over a Brit in the al-Bustain hotel bar. Besides, Saudi was dry. Saudi was the last stop before the end of the world.

'Ever heard of the Jedi knights?' He'd pointed a finger at March, then jabbed it into his arm.

March had laughed.

'I'm serious, mother-fucker . . .'

And it was suddenly clear that he was. More than serious. Harden was on a kick, driven, and very focused.

'It's *Star Wars*.' March had shaken his head. 'Characters from the movie.'

Harden laughed. 'Top of the class, Brit. You've won a drink. Give him a lemonade. Give him the fucking barrel, for Chrissake.' The barman put a bottle on the counter and Harden picked it up, gesturing for March to follow him to a table.

'So what about the Jedi knights?'

Harden took a long drink and set his glass on the table. 'They're here, fellah. All around us. They're called Jedis because they design wars for the future. They got a base out in the Midwest – Kansas – and they map out the battles for the next century. Who we're going to fight, what kind of weapons, the chemicals, and biologicals, how many are going to survive ...'

'So what are they doing here?'

Harden shook his head. 'You don't get it, do you? To those people a war is like a giant lab. You use it to test your systems and weapons, your soldiers. In this case they're using stuff that hasn't been taken out of its box since Vietnam. Then there's all the new things they want to test into the next century. That's what the Gulf is about. Testing. Making sure the whole kit works. Sending a few signals to some other potential enemies around the world, who may be watching.'

'And you're part of this?'

Harden finished his drink and replaced the glass on the table. 'I gotta go. Here endeth the first lesson.'

'Can we talk again?'

'Who the fuck knows?'

March shrugged, stood up to shake Harden's hand, but the hand wasn't on offer.

'You believe in this stuff, don't you?'

'What stuff's that, Brit?'

'All these wars of the future. The can-do spirit. If it moves we'll find a way to kill it. If we invent it, we use it.'

'Don't be so glib, my friend.' Harden's fist had described a long circle that ended about an inch from March's nose. 'You may not like what the USA does, but look at the rest of the shit-can world we live in. States so drugged up that their governments couldn't even lie straight in bed. Organised crime running whole nations, secret police ramming cattle prods up the dissidents' assholes. Tens of millions diseased and dying in poverty and ignorance. Like I said, you may not feel too happy about America but go out there and pick a side you prefer. Go ahead. Fucking do it. But I guarantee you'll come running back to Dixie.'

As he drove March could still hear Harden's voice, still see the wiry, dark New Yorker, still recall the man's razor-sharp commitment. Of course, he'd met soldiers before, but this one was different. He wasn't designed for open conflict on the fields of battle. Harden wouldn't take prisoners or follow the rules of war. Here was a licensed killer, who'd made his choice, torn up his doubts and scruples, and given away his soul to the cause.

He had met Harden another half-dozen times before they parted for good. Harden had wanted to talk, March had wanted to listen, knowing full well he could never write the stories. They weren't the kind you could slip into the paper on the back page, or bury in the weekend section. They were international headline scoops, which he couldn't attribute and couldn't confirm. And if he had ever printed a word, Harden would have shot him down on any street corner in the world without the slightest compunction. That much was certain.

He felt for the letter in his pocket and shivered again. Harden was lousy news at the best of times.

# Chapter twelve

Winston flattened himself against the shop window as the wind lashed the street, blowing away the fresh top-snow in powerful gusts. He had fastened the hood of his parka, but the cold seeped in all the same. And as the fear hit him he began to dribble, shivering helplessly, his trousers flapping wildly in the gale.

He had seen the car and the biker – how had he missed them? No one hangs around on street corners in downtown Washington on the day of a cold-weather alert. Businesses would be closed, transport would be minimal, government offices and schools empty. So they weren't exactly clever, sitting there watching him till his nerve began to fray at the edges and then snapped completely.

*Winston, baby, you ain't gonna make it to Paradise, but you sure as hell are going on a journey.*

He tried to quieten the voice inside him, and the drumming of his heart, but they wouldn't quit. He wondered what Angelo would say if he were there. 'Create a diversion, man, run into the open, make 'em break cover. And if the worst scenario happens you got yourself a gun and you take 'em with you.'

Didn't sound so convincing when you're on the corner of a street at five a.m., and they're moving in on you.

As he stood still, he couldn't prevent the anger rising from his gut. Anger that they had begun another mission and hadn't told him. That they'd put him in danger when they'd told him just to check a building. That they would sacrifice his well-being and his new-found security – and do it so cheaply. The family had deserted him. All the confidences, the late-night discussions, the new sense of belonging signified nothing. When it came down to the wire, the people he trusted had thrown him, on a winter's night, into the shithouse.

*Run, guy. Run, Winston. You ain't a human sacrifice. Don't let 'em take you without a fight.*

And, like a machine, his legs begin to move, the muscles responding, as the great engine in his chest begins to pump. Winston is on the move, straight out across the road, dodging a car, then a second and down a side alley.

Even as he runs, he hears the biker engaging his gears, the metallic clatter as it comes to life, and the swerving skidding sound of the car behind it.

*Don't turn round, man. Never turn round.*

And running is Winston's thing. Zero to thirty, they used to tell him, and the only thing faster was a Corvette. Been doing it since he was a kid, since he robbed the first candy store, then a 7-Eleven, and then the liquor store – but only when he was sixteen and his dad let him do it. Even then there were principles.

You know the business. Don't enter a building. Buildings are cages. Never shut the door behind you. Only the stupid do that. Keep it fast, man. Fast and smooth. Keep the rhythm, keep the pace.

It was good to know that the legs still performed. Winston was so proud of his speed and his style.

Out of the alley now, and the road surface is bad. Patches of black ice beneath the light, flaky snow.

*Watch it, guy.*

Behind him the buzz of the motorcycle. Fifty yards. Maybe seventy-five. Too close, man. But the biker can't speed in the snow. He's got to slow up. Got to watch the traffic. And then there's the car. Where the fuck's the car?

*Keep dancing, man. Weaving and dancing.*

Winston is into his stride now. Second side-street. And this is good. People on the move. Digging the snow. Community at work. Clearing a path. Clearing their cars.

*These are my witnesses. No one can harm me. No one can touch me.*

But they're not giving up. Not letting him go.

He's heading now for the bus station, forcing the pace, forcing the issue. If they let him inside they'll lose him. He'll stay close to the bums and the winos and the rest of the hopeless and homeless who've sheltered there from the freezing night. So they'll block him if they can.

All this he knows as his legs power him forward.

Winston, man, you're an athlete. Run for your town. Run for your state. Run for the USA. He'd had the dream, but that's where it had stayed. Winston had run for his life, not for medals. Run to steal, not for glory. Just a small change along the way and it could have gone well. Smiles instead of tears. Fame instead of jail.

He can see the signs now, at the end of the street. The bus station. Lights on. Someone at home, in the dismal tatty hall behind the grimy windows. But it's still five hundred yards away. Might as well be the moon.

Where are the people? Where's the traffic? Suddenly it's quiet when it should be damn noisy.

As he ran Winston couldn't help seeing Travis's face. The death mask of a man who hadn't gone quietly. Travis had departed in a scene of bestial, primitive violence, his body torn apart, his mind blown away in fragments. And suddenly the memory made him tired. Tired of seeing the dead. Tired of the culling.

Four hundred yards to the bus station. Only his legs had begun to slow and the fatigue was spreading fast.

When he'd got home from the war, the memories had come back. Moments that he could see and relive a thousand times, especially when he didn't want to. He would be sitting in an armchair and he could see an Iraqi soldier at the end of his rifle sight. There, in terrible colour, was the moment when he pulled the high-velocity trigger and saw the man's right arm wrenched from his shoulder by the bullet – literally blown off the torso. And he had begun to cry, wishing for all he was worth that he hadn't done it. But he knew he had.

Standard après-war, they called it. And yet it wasn't standard at all. It was a deep furrow of mental damage, ploughed, scarred, never to recover.

Three hundred now and the silence is strange. No longer can he hear the buzzing of the motorbike, or the skidding car. Even as his mind hopes for release, Winston knows the reason.

Somewhere high above the street, a sniper is positioned – and someone else will fire the single bullet to tear off his arm or his leg, and do so without a care in the world.

Two hundred yards.

So why are they waiting? Winston has slowed his pace because the great legs couldn't go on. When you lose the will, you lose the energy, each pace an effort, each yard a mile . . .

And he never hears the shots, just a blinding sledgehammer through the back of his knees one after the other, cutting his strings like a puppet, tearing through the bone and the tissue, sending him face down into the snow.

And then nothing. Even in his agony, Winston knows it's not over. Two shots from a silenced hi-power rifle and he could have been dead twice over. But it was just the legs. And now they'll come to get him. The orders were clearly to leave him alive.

Even as the thought comes to him, he can hear the noise of an engine approaching from behind. Turning, screaming with the pain, he can see a single bus lumbering down the street, faster than it should have done on the slippery surface.

*They'll use the bus as cover. That's what I'd do in their place.*

And as he stares into the snow his legs have gone numb. There's no feeling below the thigh. Maybe they were shot away, severed from the rest of him. Leastways, he would never run again, never set the pace.

Only now he has an idea. Close to the kerb, lying face down, he can see the snow flurries, gusting along the street, blowing the newspapers and candy wrappers. And the idea takes shape. Even as the wind flattens him, carrying away everything in its path, he knows what he has to do.

Maybe it was the sermon he'd heard, all those Sundays ago. Maybe it was just the way he felt about the guys in the family.

Sure, they'd done him wrong – but you had to forgive. That's

what the preacher had said. Life was pain and life was giving . . .
and now Winston had been chosen for both.

As he looks over his shoulder he can see the blood, lying in
pools in the snow. A deep, dark red – the serious kind. Either
awfully simple or simply awful, as the medics used to put it. And
this was the awful type.

*Concentrate, man. Keep the focus.*

The bus is coming closer, and it still makes no sign of slowing.
Winston can see the green and white livery. A snub-nose coach,
grinding along with a ton of attitude. The driver is looking only
to the station ahead, peering straight into the snow and wind,
trying to make out the road. Doesn't see Winston. Doesn't know.

*Just a moment away, and I gotta find the strength. Gotta win.*

To the east the cloud base has lightened. Dark blue to grey.
And the only promise is snow. A pale, unhappy day, with the cold
draped low across the city like a shroud.

Winston has little strength, but he has kept some back for his
final act.

Twenty seconds, fifteen, ten – and the bus is almost upon him.

Like a wild animal, he seems to curl into a ball, launching
himself across the ground, curling over and over again, trailing his
shattered, bloody legs as he heads into the vehicle's path.

And someone must have seen him. Maybe a passer-by. A friend
or an enemy. Someone who shouts out a warning. Someone who
knows what is to happen. But it makes no difference.

On a dawn winter's street in Washington, the bus has no eyes
and no reactions.

When it happens, it catches Winston with the giant chrome
fender, just as his head comes up to meet it. A steel punch that
sends him right out of this world and delivers him damaged and
forlorn to the next. So he doesn't know how the giant tyres grind
over him. Doesn't feel the splintering of a hundred bones or the
pressure squeezed from his chest as his life escapes.

Oblivious, the bus charges on towards the station.

But behind it, a motorcycle and a sedan pull up beside
Winston's body. One man in a beige coat gets out of the car and
examines the remains. It's no more than a couple of seconds

before he climbs back inside and the vehicle speeds away in the direction from which it came.

The passengers reckoned Winston had had a lousy death, but they agreed he had done himself a favour. Had they caught him themselves, he would have died in far greater pain.

# Chapter thirteen

As Julie watched, they searched their way through the condo, aggressively unapologetic, ripping the cushions from the sofa, rummaging through kitchen cupboards, lifting, sorting, patting her clothes. She shut her eyes, hearing doors open and close, zips undone and refastened, the slow methodical invasion of her secrets.

'I'm sorry, Mrs March. You know the rules.'

As she watched, Harries seemed like a robot, shifting from room to room with practised obscenity. The kind of man who wouldn't know what to do with a life of his own. His hands always in other people's drawers or clothes or cases. His eyes roaming over their papers and books. Mr Voyeur – all in the service of the country, all in the name of national security.

It was like being in hospital. You lost your inhibitions and your dignity. Yes, they would find your tampons or the cap or the letters from Mom and Dad, a few from Peter. The photos of an old lover she had never been able throw away. But so what? They were strangers, never seen before, never to be seen again. It wasn't much worse than the initial vetting – the endless interviews, and the piles of personal documents she'd been obliged to show them. And then had come the little telltale signs of surveillance: the mail that arrived late, because they were intercepting it, the phone calls with the hollow, dull sound, because they were listening. All this, so that she could function as a US scientist with the highest of security classifications and the brightest of prospects in the unit. She knew the price for that. And so did they. For inside her head she could recite the state of readiness of the entire strategic nuclear forces under US command. She knew the areas of research, the successes and the setbacks. She was government property – had been since the day she had signed the national-security directive that appointed her. And despite the crest and the eagle, and the numbered clauses, with all the protocols and sub-sections, that tied this piece of paper to the law of the land, they would crush her without mercy if she ever stepped out of line. This she had always known. But now they were giving her a sharp reminder, the only way they knew how. So there could be no misunderstandings.

Forty-five minutes later they stood in front of her.

Harries put his hands behind his back. 'You don't seem to have much from your husband. None of his mail – faxes, phone bills. Anything at all that might give us a clue where he is. Does he have family or friends?'

'Of course he does, he's British. His family's in London, friends in London. He works for *The Times* newspaper, for Chrissake.' She stood up, flushed and angry. 'You still haven't given me a single clue why you want him. And until you do I'm not saying any more – and you can recite fucking national security till it comes out of your ass.'

'You're not being helpful, Mrs March.' Harries took out a handkerchief and wiped sweat from his forehead. 'This is a very serious matter, and we require . . .' he paused for a second '. . . we require your co-operation.'

She stared straight through his thick, horn-rimmed spectacles, through the colourless eyes, right to the back of his head, but said nothing.

'Listen to me, Mrs March, it's possible your husband is in serious danger. Not possible. Let me be completely open with you on this. It's our assessment that his life could be at risk.' The eyes didn't leave hers. 'You know the kind of work he does?'

'So he's discovered something you don't like. That's what this is about, isn't it?'

'Of course not. This is a democracy, Mrs March. We may not like some of the things your husband has done in the past but he has his constitutional rights –'

'Bullshit.'

'If I can finish what I was saying . . .'

Harries's expression hadn't altered since the conversation began. She stared at him, seeing the same flat, dull eyes that he had brought into the world, and would take with him when he left. Indifferent. Programmed. Unmoved by doubt or argument.

'If I can finish, we believe he may have contacted one of the right-wing militia groups that are seeking to overthrow the Government of this country. We believe he went into this looking for information and may have become an instrument in one of these group's activities. In short, Mrs March, he may be used and then killed – if we don't find him first.'

'You don't seriously expect me to believe this?'

Harries walked to within three feet of her, and she could see that his attitude had changed. The apologetic government servant, simply carrying out his unenviable duty, had turned once again into the Government's thug.

'At this point it's of no interest to me if you believe it or not. We can talk this through now and you can be helpful and co-operative – or we can continue at the plant, through the night, into the morning, past lunch, past dinner, into another night and all through the days to come till you tell us what we want to hear,' the voice rising now to a crescendo, just as she had known it would, 'do I make myself fucking clear?'

If it hadn't been about Peter, if they hadn't broken up just the day before, she might have laughed at Harries as he stood there. The ridiculous, staged antics, the brutish ape performing in her front room, the little band of jackals who go round searching through women's knickers because their own lives are so pathetically unfulfilling . . . She could have laughed at them under other circumstances. But not today.

Harries took a piece of paper from his inside pocket and handed it to her. 'This is a bill for your husband's mobile phone. Call him. Ask him where he is. Do it now.'

Over Washington's Key Bridge and out on to Route 66, and the Jeep was doing its best. As he passed the snowploughs and the highway police, the night seemed to close in around him, and the flurries of snow slammed straight at the windscreen. Ten miles out of Washington and he had slowed to a crawl, with only the occasional light visible and the hulks of abandoned cars by the roadside. On the radio, it seemed, they were talking just to him. 'You fellahs out there, you need some serious psychotherapy. This is the storm to end all storms. And you have to get out of it, get home and get treatment for being stupid enough to come out in the first place.'

March reckoned it was pretty good advice. But it wasn't what he needed. He had done plenty of stupid things in the past – hadn't all reporters? – only this was something different. Most people would go through life without ever meeting a Vic Harden – a man from the other side, the dark side of your safe and civilised society. You could walk away and pretend it had never happened, but you'd always wonder. And then, in a year or two, something would happen, a death, a bomb, a little war, and you'd see just a tiny paragraph – and you'd know, yes, *know*, that Harden had made it happen. Somewhere far away, in distance and time, but it would carry the Harden stamp.

After an hour and a half March pulled over to the side of the road and got out. His eyes ached badly and the cold gnawed at his jacket. There'd been no time to go home and pack, get warm clothes, a parka, the Russian hat. And yet, when he thought about it, something had told him not to return to the little house in the Palisades. Just a feeling, just a tiny flickering sensation at the edge of his consciousness. A little gust of warning.

Despite the noise of the engine turning over, he could feel the vast night sky and the dark snowclouds pushing down on him. Get on, he told himself. You have to get through. Have to make it. Nothing will ever be the same in your life after this night. But it's too late to turn back.

When he climbed back into the driver's seat, he noticed that the mobile phone was flashing. It had registered a single call, but it didn't store the number. And he hadn't heard it ring.

Instinctively he called Leah Killeen's house. It went on ringing until the answering machine picked up, so she must have gone to bed.

Which meant that his instinct must have been wrong.

# Chapter fourteen

Angelo stared out of the window and into the street below, trying to imagine how Winston had died. A few isolated cars crawled like insects towards the Interstate but there was no one on the sidewalks. And he wondered for the twentieth time what Winston had thought as the bus bore down on him on a street much like this one, shrouded in snow, less than three miles across the city.

Of course Winston had died for a reason. He'd been recognised and identified. There was no way he could have got to the safe house. He'd have blown the operation and they would all have died in excruciating pain. Angelo had no doubt about the methods of the interrogators. He'd used them plenty of times himself.

'You thinking what I'm thinking?' Steve had entered the room soundlessly from the hall but Angelo showed no surprise or concern.

'Yeah, just thinking about Win and the piece of crap he died for. He didn't have to die, you know?'

'Wrong.' Steve came round in front of Angelo and pointed a finger at him. 'It was Winston or us. You know that, man. No choices. He did a brave thing back there. Ellis followed him all the way. Saw exactly what happened. Winston was a real hero, but it was him or us. He knew that. So should you.'

Angelo turned back to the window. Soldiers were always wonderful at explaining things away. If they'd shot Jesus Christ on his way to the second coming, someone would have said, 'There was no choice, had to be done. The guy was asking for it.'

He breathed on to the icy pane, watching it cloud over instantly. 'Waiting's the lousiest thing. Bad enough wondering when Harden's gonna get here, but with our guys out there looking for this stuff at Travis's house . . .' He let out his breath. 'What a nightmare.'

Steve came and stood beside him. 'I ain't too happy about having this place full of biological crap. You may have been toying with it, but it's kinda out of my league.'

Angelo stiffened. 'I never used the stuff and you know it.'

'No, but you were part of the group that shipped it into the Gulf, right? Wasn't that what your little band was all about – the SSG, huh? Remember, my friend? The Special Situation Group, set up by Ollie North – the one everyone said had been closed down after the Iran-Contra scandal? Well, it wasn't, was it? Just kept on rolling along ever since, taking on one lousy, shitty and extremely deniable assignment after after another.'

Angelo shot him an unpleasant look. 'You got a fucking way with words, man. You really have. You know that?'

The team had gone into the house with minimum planning but maximum skill. They knew the road and the surrounding area, but there was little time to survey the ground in advance – and they had calculated the risks. To tell the truth, each was enjoying it: the chance to take on a mission, carry a gun, and feel the pulse begin thumping the old rhythms for the first time since they'd shed the uniform. They'd sworn never to do it again for the tarnished eagle and a corrupt, double-dealing government – but this one was personal. This was for the family. This was for Winston. For Travis.

The three had formed part of a US Navy 'seal' team, the brightest and best of the covert-operations teams. They had been picked because they were single and largely unable to form lasting attachments. That was the profile required by the unit. They had to go places and not mind about coming back.

Dressed in shabby civilian clothes and boots, there was a confidence among the group that was evident by their silence and the economy of movement. They took two cars, and two high-frequency Morse transmitters on wrist-watches. But there would be no voice communication: a tiny series of bleeps would signal what was to be done and when.

To them, of course, it was textbook, but they'd expected better opposition. One guy at the back of the house, two at the front. Both in Oldsmobiles. This was low rent, low budget, and smelt of hurried, desperate measures. The men were probably Mob – gunmen with a free hour or two, and in search of some extra money. Most likely from out of town. They were often used when an internal operation went wrong because high-level officials liked the 'flexibility' that came with them: if they died or disappeared, no one shed tears. And once they'd performed their tasks, you simply started rumours that they'd gone bad – and the Mob would execute them for you. Wasn't that a tidy little number?

At the back of the house, the youngest of the seals approached the Oldsmobile and, at a distance of fifteen feet, dropped to one knee, drew a pistol from his jacket and fired two silenced bullets through the windscreen. They landed side by side, drilling identical holes in the driver's head. The so-called double tap, speciality of the British SAS. The move was carried out with nonchalance and calm. The seal was no more or less involved than a worker in an abattoir. Animals were served up to him for slaughter. He simply dispatched them and went about his business. After seven years without a kill he was surprised at how little he felt. And yet it was just as he remembered. Nothing to think about, once it was over.

The seals at the front of the house picked up the twin beeps signalling a hit and decided not to wait around. They approached from different ends and different sides of the street. One was limping, the other appeared drunk, calling out names and incoherent drivel, shouting at the moon. The men in the car examined them both with binoculars and concluded they were dropouts. This was the area for them – full of bums and stiffs.

And then comes the lethal dance, so finely choreographed, so casually performed. The drunk starts banging on the trunk of the car. After three seconds the driver gets out, yelling at him to fuck off. But even as he points a finger, he can see the flash of a matt black sliver of steel racing towards his throat, flinging him backwards on to the icy road. As he falls, though, he leaves a clear line of fire for the man with the limp, who has drawn level on the other side of the road. The rhythm is perfect. The timing exquisite. The dance has reached its climax. With a silenced Heckler & Koch in his hand, the bum releases his high-velocity bullet to smash itself into the passenger's forehead, tearing through bone and tissue, burying itself in the right-hand hemisphere of the brain. The dance is over.

Years ago, in Florida, when they'd done their training, their best time for the manoeuvre had been 9.4 seconds. This time it was eight – dead. As the instructors used to tell them, there's nothing like doing it for real.

The drunk reaches into the car and disconnects the radio. They all know they have less than three minutes to do the business. If only Travis has followed the rules. If only the canisters are buried where they should be.

Into the front yard now, through the house and out to the back. Recite the formula. Recite the code. Six steps forward on to grass, four left, four right – all turns are right angles. Soft ground. Softer now.

Oh, Jesus Christ Almighty.

One prayer released into the night.

And it's only then that they start to worry. Not the killing in the street. Not the sight of Travis, spattered against the sitting-room wall. But the fear of a colourless, odourless substance in a couple of aerosols, buried in the ground, that emerges as they brush away the snow and mud with their hands. A package. A consignment. Nothing to tell you that these were weapons from a doomstay still to come.

One of the seals shivers and holds out the NBC container, a folded black bag with a special military lining. For the first time in his life, his hand is shaking with fear.

# Chapter fifteen

Vic Harden had memorised the route down the mountain, held it in his head like a keepsake, left it there for the day he'd need it.

He'd never told them about the house in the Virginian mountains or the set-up behind it. The rent was paid monthly by a shell company, incorporated in Delaware and linked to a trust in the Cayman Islands. His name appeared on no documents. All the signatures were made by a lawyer. It was safe and secure and that was the way he'd wanted it. A haven among all the dust and killing. He always went there alone because only in silence was there honesty. No need to tell lies to a friend or a wife. No need to make excuses for the trips away and the lost weekends and the cuts and wounds you picked up along the way. In the isolation of the mountains, he could talk to himself, cry to himself and then go back and do it all again.

Hadn't always been that way, though.

June 1985, and Vic Harden had possessed the finest, cleanest record in the 82nd Airborne division, the saddest face in all the photos and a future in civilian life. A friend, Harry Dinkins, was setting up a security agency in Miami – where, God knew, you needed all the security you could get – and he had offered Vic a partnership. 'For now, we'll do the work ourselves,' he'd said. 'Some protection, some bugging, some matrimonial stuff, but in five years' time we'll be breaking open the fat cigars, ticklin' the typists' fancy and someone else'll be out on the streets, working for us. You betcha sweet life, man, that's the way it's gonna be.'

Vic Harden had left the Army a happy man. Happier still when he met Dinkins's sister at a birthday party, a shy twenty-seven-year-old blonde in white socks called Margie, with white all-American teeth and a smile that he told his mum could light up Times Square by itself on a winter's night. It was three months before he dared summon up the courage to kiss her, three months and one day till he asked her to marry him. She told him afterwards it had never occurred to her to say no.

Three days before the wedding, Margie went out late to a 7-Eleven because the family had run out of bottled water and she didn't want to drink from the tap. The sky was an angry clash of reds and blacks and the wind hurtled in from the Atlantic, whipping the waters of the bay, heralding the storm.

She got into the car and shivered. Something was wrong. She didn't know what but she knew that the world had somehow been jerked from its orbit and was badly out of kilter.

And then she froze in terror as the voice from the back seat told her what he wanted.

'Give me the keys, lady, nice and easy and no one gets hurt, OK?'

Only she was too frightened to move.

'I – I –'

'I said, give me the fuckin' keys, like now, you hear me?'

And still Margie hadn't moved, her eyes fixed straight ahead in terror, her body paralysed, as never before.

'Gonna ask you one more time, lady, and if you ain't said nothin', I'm gonna fuckin' loosen that throat for you, you got it?'

Only then did she scream, a loud, shrill cry, full of primeval horror. Just one scream, cold and clear into the night. And then a grotesque choking, followed by silence.

There was no witness to what had happened but ten minutes later, when the ambulance was called, the orderlies found more than fifteen stab wounds in the back of Margie's neck and a torrent of blood that had spilt out of the car and on to the road below. They told Harden later that she had died instantly – but that wasn't true. They had found her semi-conscious and in terrible agony and she had died on the way to hospital. The culprit was never found.

That was why Harden no longer cared.

Six months later he was back in uniform and had volunteered for Special Forces. Inside he was half a man. On the outside he became exactly what they wanted. A killer without ties or distractions, cold and indifferent to his personal safety.

It was the only marriage he was destined to enjoy.

At the edge of the woods he slipped the bindings on the skis and buried them. In a half-hour, he reckoned, the traces would be covered along with his footprints. Besides, the darkness would work in his favour since he alone knew the route down into the valley.

Ten, maybe fifteen minutes earlier he had heard the single helicopter, clattering low over the trees, heading north. Just as he'd planned. He had carried out the standard diversion tactics. A sheaf of papers left none too tidily on a bookshelf, a bill of sale for a car and a garage rental in a town called Stark, forty miles north-east, which he had never even visited. All clues for them to find. And now they had.

Odd to think of them going through his things, tearing apart his little haven, violating the very private life of Vic Harden. But what the hell? It was all over, bar the ending. And he was doing it the way he'd always said he would – with a gun in his hand, and a target in the sights.

The town was deserted when he entered it: small clapboard houses frozen in snow, icicles on the mailboxes, leaning telegraph poles with their cables criss-crossing the skyline, connecting little America to big America. Harden walked fast but didn't hurry. If anyone looked out of the windows they'd see nothing more than a figure in the cold, no sense of urgency, nothing to remark on. Not until he was ready.

At the southern edge of the town he could see the coach and truck park, about five acres surrounded by wire fencing and watched over by a guard. This was where he wanted to be remembered.

The windows of the little hut were frosted over but Harden could just make out the fellow inside. A grey head, at least two days of beard, a tired, old guy on six bucks an hour, if he could stay warm enough and live long enough to collect it. Harden knocked on the window, watched as the face registered first surprise and then boredom.

'Come for my car,' he shouted.

'Uh?' The old man rose stiffly and pushed open the door. 'What d'you say?'

'Said I've come for my car.'

'You'll have to dig it out – look around you.' The hand described an arc stretching out into the middle distance. A heap of trucks and other hulks lay half buried beneath grey snow.

'Can you help?'

'No way, kiddo. Asthma. There's a shovel along the fence somewhere . . . young fellah like you . . .'

'I'm in a hurry, that's all.'

'Me too.' The man grinned. 'Where you headed?'

'Upstate New York – Albany.'

'That's aways from here, fellah.'

'No kidding.' Harden shook his head. 'You got a map I could look at?'

The answer was automatic. 'Nope.' And then, a second later, 'Yeah wait. Used to be one in here someplace.' He climbed back into the shack and rummaged around on the table. 'Where d'you say you were heading?'

Harden removed a square of paper from his pocket and screwed up his eyes. 'Albany. Upstate New York.' He could see the man relaxing, dropping his guard. 'Visiting my sister. She's just had a son – her third, I should say. Lives in a suburb there called Peabody – yeah, that's it.' He looked at the paper again. Keep going Vic, he thought. Nice and chatty. 'Gloster Drive, Peabody.' He returned the paper to his pocket. 'Well, I better go dig out that car o' mine.'

The watchman smiled. 'I'll have that map for you when you get back – and a cup of coffee!'

Harden clapped him on the shoulder. 'It's a deal.'

Twenty minutes later he was outside the hut again, but this time with a plain black Mustang coupé, swept clean of snow, its exhausts thumping out like a bass drum across the parking lot. It was nothing special to look at. Five years old, tatty and rusty. No flashes or spoilers. Harden had even removed the decals, showing the size of the engine for it was there that the car excelled: five litres of rock-hard American muscle, rebored and tuned and capable of burning holes on any Interstate in the country.

Harden left the beast running, climbed inside the hut and drank his coffee from a filth-encrusted mug. And when it was time to go, the piece of paper from his pocket had miraculously found its way back on to the table – where he had intended it should stay. Hide in the open, they'd always said. Leave traces, start a fight, drop your papers in a crowd, goose the woman in front of you – but get noticed. Let everyone know what you're doing and where you're going – and then go somewhere else and do something different.

Of course, the old man didn't notice the paper until Harden was driving out of the lot, heading towards the mountains. And by then it was too late to call him back. 'New York, New York,' he muttered to himself, and closed his eyes to think about it.

Twenty miles away, on the other side of the Shenandoah, the wind had dropped and the storm was heading out towards the coast. Even the radio forecasts were reluctantly admitting that the worst was over. March could hear the disappointment in their voices. Wasn't often the weather boys got the lead story – normally they had to make do with the closing spot after basketball – so they were milking it for all they were worth.

Five miles before the Interstate turn-off he could see the rows of flashing red and white lights and knew there'd been an accident. A big one, by the look of it. Police cars and trucks were blocking the oncoming traffic, filtering it between the cones, waving it slowly forward. And yet as he approached, March could see no sign of any pile-up. No wrecked cars or ambulances. This was something else – more like a roadblock, with state troopers in wide-brimmed hats and capes, rifles in hand, checking each of the cars, heading back the way he'd come – into Washington. He wound down the window and the cold night air struck him in the face like a punch. One of the troopers waved him to the side.

A face appeared at the window. 'Road's pretty much impass-able from here on in, sir. Better turn back.'

'I've got to get to Lost River.'

The face was raw and earnest, important, full of the mission. 'Unless your journey's urgent, I have to ask you to turn back and wait till morning.'

'Wait where?'

'There's a motel about a mile off junction seventeen. Go two miles west of that – it's a Days Inn. They got rooms.'

'Journey's urgent.'

'I can't stop you, sir, but if you run into problems there's no guarantee we'll be able to help.'

March nodded and depressed his right foot, feeling the Jeep slither forward, leaving the trooper staring after him. Something about the man wasn't right. In fact, the whole set-up was odd. Why were they checking cars coming out of the mountains? Why the rifles? And then he realised there'd been no markings on the trucks. He'd simply assumed they were police but there was nothing to confirm it. On the contrary, he'd been in Washington long enough to know that unmarked trucks with flashing lights had nothing to do with the police. They were either Secret Service or CIA, or any of the half-dozen other security agencies no one ever talked about. Christ! What was going on?

He drove on, more unsettled than he'd first realised. The road lay covered in light snow but underneath there were ridges of solid black ice. A careless touch on the accelerator and the wheels skidded wildly.

*Christ, Harden, you'd better be worth this, with all your hang-ups and prejudices and wild, unprovable tales. I'm not driving out for a bedtime story. This time I want the goods, Major. Facts and dates, times and bodies.*

Always bodies around Harden.

For a moment his heart seemed to miss a beat as he entered the valley and caught sight of the first road-sign to Lost River. On each side of him the woods had thickened out, caked in sugar-white snow. As far as he could see, the landscape stretched unbroken into the darkness. And then the gradient increased sharply and the Jeep slithered and clawed its way along the narrow road, its headlights picking out mounds and bends and shadows. In the snow everything seemed one-dimensional, shaped and reshaped by the winter.

Then, a hundred yards ahead of him, he could see a fork in the road. March pulled up and, for the first time since leaving Washington, drew Harden's letter from his pocket. The directions had been crafted with military precision: left at the fork, 120 yards, then left again, follow the curve of the side road into the trees, and it was the first cabin you came to. 'Watch yourself,' said the letter. 'This is more than you can handle.'

*More than I can handle.*

March shivered involuntarily.

*Get away from here, Peter. Turn back. Head fast to Washington and knock on that beautiful, warm and friendly door called Leah Killeen. A place to crouch low and wait for the storm to pass. A place with a future. Because suddenly this doesn't seem to have one . . .*

And yet the Jeep was already moving through the gates of the park, already climbing towards the trees.

March stops at the first bend, pulls the car over to the side, switches off the engine. No lights. Just the sound of the forest, the drifting snow and wind. He moves forward on foot, crouching involuntarily, half walk, half run, keeping to the trees, the cold biting deep inside his coat.

What had the letter said? Jesus, you just read it. Five hundred yards, first cabin you come to, but which side?

And then he hears it – the burst of static from a radio. Clear, unmistakable. No more than a second and a half, but he knows what it is. Might as well be a foghorn or a factory siren. His first thought is Harden.

So call out his name. Would be just like him to wait outside. Only Harden has no radio. No friends. Harden is alone in a log cabin.

The radio is someone else.

Thoughts scream at him as he stands there, fearing to step forward or back.

Harden is two miles down the road when it hits him – the letter he wrote and the way he knew March would respond. Why had he written it in the first place? Maybe he thought there was more time. Maybe he thought March deserved to find out what it was all about.

He had a clear memory of the tall English reporter. Tougher than most, better informed than most. A good reporter, too. Someone who listened and took it in. Didn't ask damn-fool questions. On another planet, in another age, they might have had some beers together and talked about the truth, whatever that was.

But now? March would get to the log cabin and find a very different reception from the kind he'd expected. Tough. They'd give him some heavy questioning then send him home to Washington. After all, he didn't know anything so couldn't embarrass them, couldn't start talking to the wrong people.

Harden pulled over to the side and sat still, listening to the thump of the engine.

Damn the letter and damn March with it.

In his heart of hearts he knew they'd never let the Brit go. Not on this one. Not when so much was at stake. They'd kill him there and then – make it look like an accident. Perfect weather for it. Simply knock him out and drive the car over the ridge. Another couple of days and it would be in the papers. Ten lines and the end of Peter March. How sad. What a shame.

Christ Jesus, Almighty.

Harden turned the car around and headed back fast the way he'd come.

# Chapter sixteen

March forces open his eyes. In the snow there is no such thing as darkness, just a range of hues and shadows, too subtle for a human to distinguish. And yet he knows he's not alone.

A hundred yards from him sits the log cabin. Two lights are burning in the windows, one on the porch. Smoke rises in cotton tufts from the chimney. Harden is home, it says. There's a welcome at the inn. Food on the stove. Walk to the door. Come in from the cold.

But it's too cosy for Harden. Not a man to leave lights on for guests. Hated lights, hated guests. Left to his own devices, he'd have crouched in the forest and waylaid any visitors as they came close. Stalked them, frightened them, made them confess to things they had never done and never even imagined. Harden had been trained for that.

And now he has slipped away like a soul departing and others have taken his place.

Even as he realises it, March can see the way forward. The moment of panic has passed. Ice-cold calm takes its place.

As he cronches low among the trees, the advantage is with him. There is no pressure of time, no action to co-ordinate. He is free to move alone.

Wait and watch. Let him come to you, whoever he is. Let him break cover first. If he's heard you, seen you, he'll make his move.

And, for a moment, March is back ten years in the streets of Warsaw, as the tanks came in, and the union leaders were bundled into military wagons, carted away for internment. They had put the snatch teams into the crowd, searching for trouble-makers, weeding them out, beating them senseless in the side-streets, or later, and more scientifically, at the makeshift detention centres outside the capital.

Even as he watched in the narrow alleys of the Old Town, March had felt the arms grip him from behind, and the first of the truncheon blows landing on his shoulders and spine. Rubber truncheons, they were, with steel rods running down the middle, bitter and vicious. He fought back, but they were dragging him hard now, as the tear gas fell in canisters and the crowd went mad.

Over his shoulder he could see the figures in gas masks and blue combat fatigues, as they forced him further into the alley. And he couldn't escape the feeling then – as now – that they would kill him if they could. While the crowd ran for cover, his body would be lying in the gutter with the life beaten out of it. And no witnesses would ever come forward.

He recalled the anger building inside him, recalled the strength that surged in his arms. A big man, Peter March, fit and trained for sport. A boxer in his day and a calm, cool figure that you should never provoke, never cross.

Reaching behind him that day, he had torn the mask from one of the riot police, slamming his fist into a jaw, feeling the whole skull jolt, and the surge of power in his fists. He seized the man's truncheon and brought it down hard on the head of the second officer, watched him fall away, saw the light go out in his eyes as he lay immovable in the gutter. For a moment March had leaned against the wall, gulping air, trying to think in straight lines – and then he had run. But even as he tore through the streets there was exhilaration at what he had done. The knowledge that he was a fighter and a survivor, the realisation that never again would he crouch in fear when threatened.

A memory to cherish as he stood motionless at the edge of the forest.

After Warsaw, of course, he had fought many times in his own defence. In Russia, in Beirut, in the north-west frontier of Pakistan. There had been times when he'd needed his fists far more than his brain. People who had sought to rob him, or scare him, had quickly discovered that Peter March was the wrong target. They had imagined a gentle giant, friendly and open – an easy touch.

No one made that mistake twice.

March had gone on to refine his fighting, martial arts, boxing – he had spent his twenties visiting summer schools in Japan, Hong Kong and America. Never a fanatic, he had had little time for the clubby circuit but he had found himself among a group of highly unexpected people: not the sadists, bouncers, or assorted gangland crooks he'd expected, instead, a group of profoundly ordinary people, from shopkeepers to postmen, who had tired of the abuses of daily life and simply wanted them to go away. Beyond that he had found little in common with them – but he had known that the effort would pay off. One day someone would try as hard as they could to kill him. And he would be ready.

Maybe that day had arrived.

As he stared into the gloom, he was grateful for the cold – kept him sharp, awake, every sense tuned.

Without it, he might never have heard the shuffle behind him, never have sensed the figure who had moved so silently towards him.

Swinging round towards the darkness of the forest, he realised, in that single stiletto second, that there was nowhere to hide.

Harden cursed as he reached the outer edge of the state park. He was still a mile from the cabin but now he would have to make it on foot – and his strength was failing fast. The mountain route had tired him more than he had anticipated. Time was when he could ski for hours at a stretch, rest for thirty minutes and do it again. Now each step was a project, each thought took double time.

Before leaving the car, he removed the false bottom from the boot, extracted the hardware. The Heckler & Koch pistol was ice-cold, wrapped in oily sacking, but it still fitted into his palm, the grip custom-made by a weapons factory in Florida. Eight clips of ammunition went with it, together with the silencer and an AK47 Russian assault rifle that he had 'found' during the Gulf War. The previous owner had obligingly died to make the find possible. Harden, of course, had dispatched him with the minimum of ceremony.

As he clipped the rifle to his parka, he sincerely hoped he wouldn't have to use it. Anything that noisy was simply a weapon of last resort. So were the two grenades he plucked from their foam-rubber casing. But you should never go light. That was the rule. Never depart the world wishing you'd taken just another rifle or an extra clip because it only gives them something to laugh about when you get to the other side.

Harden let the thought go. There were plenty of others to concentrate on. As he set off, he didn't know if he was angrier with himself or March.


'Just raise your hands, it's all you got to do.'

The voice behind him was low and steady. March assumed that the gun now pointing at him was also steady. Automatically, his mind began to compute range and options but right now the man was too far away. Even if he dived at him he'd die twice before he got there. This was a professional. No stupid mistakes.

March raised his hands, still unable to see the man's face. 'I'm trying to find one of the cabins –'

'You found it.'

The accent was hard to place. Central America? Miami?

'I'm visiting a friend.'

'Turn around and step towards the clearing. Keep the hands up.'

March swivels his head and shuffles in the direction of the road. There's very little time left to make a move. Just a few paces and they'll be out in the open. And then the others will appear. He stops in his tracks. 'I'm sorry.'

'Do that again and I'll kill you.' The voice hasn't changed tone. 'Keep walking.' And now March has no more doubts about the man behind him. This is a freelance operator, confident and practised. Hired to turn the living into the dead. And, unless something is done to alter the odds, he'll be the only one going home.

March stands perfectly still. 'I want to know where I'm going.'

Then, without warning, he senses the jolt even before he hears it. And with it the sudden, terrifying shock that a bullet has passed within a hair's width of him and that what he has felt is the slipstream – the massive, unstoppable power of a shell, the act of cool, matter-of-fact violence directed at him.

As his hand probes he can feel the warm blood on his temple, the sting, the merest fraction of a graze. He turns again towards the man: fear is pumping faster than he's ever known it, the heart crying out for oxygen. Had he meant to kill him?

For the first time now he can see the outline of a face and body. Medium-height, chest like a castle rampart. A human dispatcher. Built by mankind, programmed as a robot. A step back into evil.

Even in the freezing early-morning air, the man is wearing a half-smile. The confidence of a gunslinger, built on one simple yet complex operation. The speed of impulse between brain, eye and finger, and the practised ability to co-ordinate the three. When you face it, nothing is more deadly.

'You gonna walk now?'

For the first time in his life, March can't see a way out.

When you've been around, thought Harden, you know when a gun has been fired. You don't have to see it or hear it. The mere displacement of air and the sudden heat in your vicinity puts you on guard. Call it soldier's instinct or sixth sense, but he knew that March was in big trouble.

Without thinking, he could calculate the risk, assess the requirement. The bullet was silenced. That meant a freelance government killer. Exactly what he'd expected. How many? One was unlikely. Two on the ground, with a radio-control point somewhere out of sight. That was the best option. And yet they'd be keeping this one as tidy as possible. No extraneous personnel. Two, if he was lucky.

He could feel the tiredness as he ran. More than tiredness. A sense of the body closing down. A taste of finality. And yet you can't give in to it, can't let it take you over. There's the pride to consider.

Harden doesn't want to be taken out by a bum from the streets of Detroit or Portland or San Diego, doesn't want to give it away. Not after the training and the operations, and the manuals he wrote about how you do it.

In the old days this would have been playtime. Not even a challenge. He'd have gone to the candy store first and sorted them out on the way back. But this one was different. This would be scrappy and difficult and it wouldn't win prizes in the regimental scorebook. Be like pulling out weeds from the ground.

Messy.

Harden slithers forward, as he has a thousand times before. But his feet seem heavy and lifeless.

Move it, man. A life is on the line. You put it there.

He's a hundred and fifty yards from the house, stopping now because his eyes are no longer what they were.

Everything looks the same. Trees. People. How the hell can he make out the difference?

And, even in the ice-cold night, there's the sweat of fear, breaking out from deep inside. Been a long time since he'd felt it. Old Father Fear. Long time since he'd been scared and shaking, stuck out somewhere on his own, not knowing if he could hack it. In the past the boys were always with you. They'd get you out or they'd take your body home. Never leave it to the wolves. Soldiers care about their bodies.

Quite suddenly the mist in his eyes seems to clear. Through the trees two figures emerge silhouetted against the snow in the clearing. And now it's business. Nothing more or less. Same old routine, done it a thousand times before, the autopilot kicking in. Body and mind going for it.

The MP5 is in his hand now. Thirty yards distance. Just a bit too far. But there's good separation in the figures. March at least six inches taller than the other guy. If he had to shoot now he could probably do it. But better to get in close. Better to wait a while and see who else shows up.

He was being taken to the cabin. That much was clear. Peter March, herded up the hill, presumably to be questioned and shot.

He knew enough to realise that such things went on. Over the years he had even written about them. Extra-judicial killing, they called it. Denied at the highest of levels – but the sources were just too good. When it happened the scenario was always the same. The US had become over-exposed in some kind of horse-shit operation dreamed up by freaks in the Pentagon and farmed out to idiots who didn't know any better or were desperate for the cash. Then it would start to unravel. Someone would talk and suddenly the light would get in through the cracks – and you'd start to see a chain of command. People with too many pips on their uniform began reaching for the Prozac, phoning politicians, meeting late at night in roadside cafés, and then would come the reaction. Magically, as if of their own accord, people would die all over the place. Cars would start going out of control or rolling down hills with their drivers asleep. Instead of getting on trains, people took to walking in front of them. Others would mysteriously take fifty sleeping pills before getting up. And so it went, on and on, until the fortress got boarded up again and the daylight no longer shone through the cracks and the madness was over. For a while. Of course, the government leaders would never order assassinations. They simply appointed people who knew what had to be done. Like the man four paces behind him.

'Get in there.'

March has no choice.

Up the steps and in through the porch. Harden's domain. Lights still blazing.

The gunman has an unmarked almost baby face. He's a meticulous, fastidious man. Clothes clean, shoes shiny. He's proud of himself, the half-smile still playing across the cheeks, gun stretching out parallel to the floor. Small calibre with silencer. Minimum force to do the job – and there's a sign of confidence.

And as March gets through into the cabin he can see what they've done. Instead of holding out that winter's night welcome, they have comprehensively trashed the place. Chairs are broken, covers ripped, shelves and cupboards splintered in an orgy of destruction. They hadn't just done a job – they'd enjoyed it. And over by the kitchen there's a second figure turning towards him that he likes even less than the first.

'Thanks for coming, sir.'

Military type, this one. But something is wrong. There's the Marine haircut, the stance and the bearing. But the eyes are out of control. So is the sweat on the temples.

'Against the wall, sir. Keep the hands up.'

They're both facing him. Seven feet away. Only the short figure has the gun.

'We can do this nice and easy, sir.'

And the sir is a taunt, sir is an insult. Somewhere along the line this one was thrown out of the Army.

'It's your call, sir, just tell us what you were doing out here.'

'Who are you?' March is pleased with his voice. Steadier than he thought — or felt.

'Government, sir. That's all you need to know. We're employees of the federal government,' and they're both grinning now, 'authorised to ask what you're doing.'

'Why the guns?'

'Sensitive area, sir. We're investigating a possible crime.' He wipes away some of the sweat with his sleeve. 'We're in a hurry, sir. Need some answers pretty quick now.' Tone is rising, the eyes are losing it.

'I'll call my lawyer if you don't mind.'

And then the teeth bare, and March can see the avalanche building, a great wave of violence, fighting to break loose. Wouldn't be long.

'Fuck you, sir.' And the grin has gone. 'Fucking give us the answers or we'll blow that great fucking head of yours into the woods.'

'And if I do tell you?'

He turns now to the shorter figure. 'Sir's jerking us off, Bill, because Sir's a fucking idiot. Sir's gonna have to be punished for this.' He takes a polished metal pistol from his pocket. March can see a clock on the wall. Just seconds of life left.

'Sir's going to answer the fucking questions — now.'

As the gun comes up, and the voice becomes a scream, Peter

125

March braces against the wall, ready to launch himself towards the man's throat.

Six feet from the porch Harden hears the scream and knows it's over. No time for stealth. Running now with a soldier's prayer in his throat – to anyone who can hear it – to deliver him safe from evil. And even as he reaches the window, he glimpses a figure in the air and fires beneath it. The back of a head, grey and curly, flashes into frame and the MP5 is pumping death, the way it always did. A dozen snap decisions in the pull of a trigger. And it's the gun that makes them. You point it and it fires, reading your mind, reading your fears.

One down. How many more? Through the window now, shattering frame and glass and he's on the floor, eyes scanning and the heart shouting pain from every valve.

It was March who'd jumped – had to be – there's a figure half buried beneath him, and he fires again, watching the flesh jerk. Again to be sure. Dull, silenced thuds, puncturing light and life as they go . . . Pulling March away from the figure. Eyes scanning. Revolve, revolve, 180 degrees, keep moving, turning. Two down. How many left? The old routine kicking back in, recite it as you go, practised over thousands of days in dozens of countries . . .

March sitting up.

Thank Christ he's alive. Passing him a gun.

Harden checks the two bodies. Now the window. This is only part one. Getting in – always easier than getting out. Half your strength already gone.

March isn't talking. Just shaking his head from side to side.

Harden slaps his face hard.

'Christ, Harden.'

'You or them. That's all you need to know.'

Crouching on the floor, he turns away, focus blurring, the tiredness coming again, washing over him. Lie down, Harden. Rest, Harden. Just for a moment, shut your eyes . . .

But he knows he can't.

Outside, beyond the cabin, there's no light or movement. Just the two of them. Two alive and two dead.

He takes a look around the cabin, and there's a flash of pain at the chaos and destruction. His haven. His life alone. And even though you've said goodbye, part of you has been torn to pieces with it. He picks up an old picture and . . . the world suddenly takes a dive into darkness. Inches behind him he hears the movement and braces himself for the shot that he knows is coming. Hand outstretched against the bullet – and you're dead, Harden. Lost it. Took your mind off the job and now they've finally . . .

But as he turns it's March who's fired the gun. And the man on the ground has a fresh hole in his forehead as he's blown back against the wall by the bullet's impact.

There's a gun in his hand that you missed, Harden.

Basic fatal error. Would have cost you your life. And now you're so far gone you've become a danger to anyone who's with you.

March drops the gun and his gaze freezes.

Harden can read the signs. When a man has killed for the first time, he's crossed into a world for which nothing can prepare him. The complex arrangement of rituals and standards by which he has lived has gone for good. Nothing he does tomorrow will be the same as the things he did yesterday. He's cast away from his former life – and can never return.

Worse, he's both hunter and hunted and there isn't a sanctuary in the world that will take him.

That much he could read on the face of Peter March.

# Chapter seventeen

'We gotta move.' Harden looks over to March, but he's slumped against the wall. Eyes open, mind on the run.

March has aged twenty or thirty years since he last saw him – and the last half-hour hadn't helped. Slap him again, get him moving. Never stay at the scene. Check the dead and get the fuck out. Simple rules, written for survival. And Harden still wants to survive; still has the mission; still a few days before he can walk to the terminal and catch the last plane out.

He reaches over and slaps March – harder, this time. Right across both cheeks. And March's fists come up clenched, teeth bared like an animal, and suddenly the lights are on again, the anger flowing.

'What the hell have you got me into, Harden?' He pulls himself painfully to his feet. Can't look at the bodies. Can't accept what he's done.

'I came back for you, sonofabitch. Came back when I saw what they'd do to you.' Harden shrugged. 'You wanted stories, man. I got you one. Biggest story of your life.'

March's eyes showed a flash of anger. 'This isn't a story, it's a death trap. It's your world, Harden. Got nothing to do with reality and nothing to do with me. I don't want to live on your planet, don't want to share your daylight, 'cos every time you move, someone around you seems to die.' He ran a hand over his eyes. 'Now, talk. Who wants me dead? How far does this go? I don't want a story – I want to get out of this with my life.'

'I'll tell you, but right now we gotta move it.'

'We need help, for Chrissake.'

Harden raised his hand like a stop sign. 'You don't understand, do you? There *is* no help. No one. Everywhere you go they're waiting for you, watching you. This is too big, man.'

'Words, Harden. Just words. What's it all mean?'

'Means government. Authorities. Secret agencies. All the geeks and piss-heads controlled by Washington who sit dreaming and planning for war – and believe they're protecting our country. They're the ones producing all this chemical filth that we used in the Gulf and went on producing it. Even when they said it was over the project kept running. It was unstoppable. Nobody could halt it, 'cos nobody had the power. Jesus, man, this crap was made in US labs, tested in the grand USA, 'cos we have to kill better than anyone else.'

'You're talking bullshit. Where's the proof?'

Harden laughed without humour, and when the laughing was over, the coughing began, deep in his belly, rising to his chest, racking it with pain.

'Rest, Harden, you're sick. Rest a moment.'

'Listen, man, I'm dying. Didn't you read the letter I wrote? Dying. *Comprende*? I got too close to the little bag of tricks they took out to the Gulf. Just at the time they were using the whole place as a giant lab. Tested everything they hadn't tested since Vietnam – everything they wanted for the next century.' He wiped his mouth on his sleeve and his breathing had quickened. 'No one talks about it. No one admits it. But all the others are dead and I'm next.' His right hand shot out and gripped March's arm above the elbow. 'Well, now it's out. We found the new stuff and we're gonna show the great US public what's been done with their tax dollars. Kinda State-of-the-Union address.'

'Harden . . .' and March is pulling him down on to the floor, flattening him fast against the boards. Suddenly there are headlights on the wall behind them.

'Christ, Jesus.' Harden on his back now, with the MP5 in his hand, checking the magazine, slamming it back into the grip. So practised. Not even the illness can take it from him.

Outside they can hear the voices, the slamming of doors. One car, two doors. Three of them at most. Harden's mind is computing fast. He gestures to the rear door and March is on his front slithering and crawling, past the kitchen, around the bodies and the debris. And for Harden, the tiredness has slipped away. He's back where he always was, under threat, with far too many of the odds against him. The way they always lived in Special Forces.

Lived and died.

He pulls at March's leg, slides round him, reaches the door and eases it open. Seconds, he tells himself. That's all you've got. The footsteps were twenty seconds away, maybe twenty-five. And now there's the sound of a boot on the wooden porch, and they're faster than you think. Faster and more confident. Because the door's open and there's no one posted at the back.

Pulling now at March, dragging him through the door, down the three steps, close behind him, as the first of the footsteps enters the cabin.

Cut it fine, Harden. Oh, so fine.

Into the snow, with the sudden shock of the cold. Keep low, keep fast. March, you fucker, run.

Both of them on their feet now, heads down, sprinting and slipping across the clearing towards the trees.

A foot ahead, Harden throws himself into the thicket, counting the seconds, always counting, because that's how you keep alert and alive. Somewhere, right in front of you, the next deadline is running out.

From an inside pocket in the parka, he takes a small transmitter – no more than a three-inch square – and raises the aeriel.

'What the hell are you doing?' March beside him, peering through the darkness.

Harden on his back again, switching on the device, watching the lights come on. 'Blowing up my house – what do you think?'

'I think they're going to die. You can't keep doing this.' Whispers in the night, but they're not reaching Harden. On the keypad, he's punching in the security code, activating the system.

'You're crazy, Harden.'

'Been that way all my life.'

'These are people.' And then he stops without warning, seeing a face in the rear window.

Harden's caught it too. And he's seen a thousand faces like this one. A thousand animals in suits or uniforms, tools of the state, brainless and programmed. And you can't even call them evil because they're the same as you are. It's just that, in your case, the programme wore off, you saw the light, chased it and were never the same again. Couldn't sing the college song any more. Couldn't play the college game.

That's why they need to kill you.

Another second and the face at the door will see the footmarks. Two sets leading off into the snow. It's like a racetrack. Harden shakes his head. How can he miss it?

And then the man points and shouts, and suddenly there's another, bigger, face and a torso in fatigues. As he watches, the Uzi sub-machine gun comes up, held high, in a gloved hand.

Count me down, says Harden to himself. *Count me out.*

And even as the two seem to launch themselves through the door, he presses the button on the transmitter.

It's a moment he's always loved, when technology, planning and stealth all come together. Whatever the place, whatever the country, this is a defining moment. The time when you take out the targets and send them off to hell in little pieces where they've always belonged. Christ, it was good.

After a while, he thought, you know what to look for and you can see all the lightning stages – the initial crack, like a tree hacked in two, then the roar from deep inside and the fireball launched as a rocket, forging upwards through the superstructure, out through the roof, shattering and blasting everything as it goes. An act of supreme, primeval destruction, a massive eruption in the middle of a forest, in the middle of a winter's night. An assault on the natural world, and everything within it.

'You're mad, Harden.' March leans against a tree as the fire takes hold and the chunks of wood and debris burn in the snow, just yards away.

'You wanted to be killed? Listen, fellah, you get down to some pretty stark choices here. No frills. No extras.'

'But this was your house, your own house, you've destroyed.'

Harden snapped the transmitter aeriel back into its housing and returned it to an inside pocket. He looked at March without expression. 'I didn't need it any more, did I?'

They're out of the forest now, heading down the slope, and there's almost nothing left to burn. Only as he looks back does Harden glimpse a tree on fire but he puts it out of his mind. That's another thing they'd given him: the discipline to order the mind. Tell it what to think, and what to erase so that when you go for it, there are only the essentials in front of you. The mission, the target and − if you get it right − the way home.

On the edge of the path is the Jeep the men had come in. And Harden is into the driver's seat, searching for the key, cheering inside that he's found it, still inserted in the ignition. Jesus, they were amateurs. They'd sent amateurs to get him. He even laughed as he let in the clutch and the car skidded down the hill.

Out of the state park now, and there's still no one in sight. The biggest explosion in the state of Virginia since the Civil War and no one's even come to look at it.

'Which way, Harden?' March has strapped himself in, breathing steady, the blood seeping back into the system.

Harden flicks on the heating. 'There's a flying club about fifteen miles from here . . . little place, run by redneck veterans.' He grinned. 'Like me.'

'Don't be stupid, you can't fly in this kind of weather.'

'Helicopters, boy. Take 'em up and put 'em down again. Been flying 'em for twenty years.'

'And you don't think they'll have covered all the places like that?'

'These guys? Hell, no. Fuckin' amateurs, man. This is definitely the vacation team. If I'd had any of them in my team they'd have been out on their asses, first mission we got. Either that or dead.'

March didn't answer. Even with the heating his hands were solid blocks of ice.

Harden leaned down and rummaged on the shelf beneath the steering wheel. 'Gloves,' he announced. 'Put 'em on.'

'I don't wear dead men's clothes.'

'So that's it, huh?'

'That's what?'

'You're pissing yourself because you popped one of the gorillas back there, and your conscience is screaming at you and you wanna run off and tell your mom – that it?'

'Listen to me, Harden. I don't know how many people you've killed in your life, and the worst thing is, you probably don't even remember yourself. But if you're asking if I like shooting people, the answer's no. It really doesn't feel that great. So forgive me if I don't share in a fucking great celebration of death, the way you and your comrades seem to like doing. I told you, this isn't my world and, frankly, if you'd left me in peace, I could have gone on happily – without half of Washington trying to shoot me.'

Harden swerved the Jeep round a corner, turned sharply to the right and the car screamed up a country track, slicing through bushes and branches that seemed to reach out to try to claw it back. As he glanced out of the side window he could see the first streaks of light appearing in the east, pushing back the darkness.

'Jesus, we gotta hurry this one along.' His right foot hit the floor and the Jeep lurched and thumped over the track. He shot a quick look at March. 'This isn't the time for in-depth discussion. But in this business if you leave it too long you kinda miss the chance. So I'll tell you what I want to tell you and you can make up your own mind.'

The gradient was suddenly much sharper and Harden had to fight to keep the Jeep pointing straight.

'Tell you the truth. I ain't too happy about the killing thing myself. Maybe that's 'cos I'm about to go down that same road where I sent all the others. Guess there's a chance they might be waiting for me, and not exactly with flowers in their hands . . .' He grinned again. 'But there's another reason. I ended up working for a bunch of assholes who didn't deserve me.'

March turned and stared at him. 'What happened to all that Truth, Right and the American Way that you used to give me out in the Gulf?'

'I grew up. Our own side turned out to be just as lousy as the other one. Different, OK, but full of sick bastards who just want to kill for the sake of it.' He swung the steering wheel, but one of the front wheels must have hit a boulder because there was a terrible jolt and March had to grip the seat to stay upright. 'Me? I needed a target. I needed to know they were a threat, a danger.' He stopped. 'Except for one time out there in the Gulf, and now I'm dying for it. And you know something?' He lifted a hand from the steering wheel and gripped March by the elbow. 'That's justice too. I deserve it for what I did. Yes, I was ordered to do it. Yes, the operation was sanctioned. But it was wrong, March. You understand? Wrong all the way down the fucking line.'

'So you wanted to do something about it.'

'And then some. I wanted this thing stopped. Now. Dead in the water. Didn't matter for me any more, I was on the way out. But I kinda wanted to put something back for all the things I'd taken out.' He coughed painfully, holding his chest as if to contain the agony.

They were reaching the summit of the mountain. March wound down the window and the cold, clear air flooded in. Beneath the moaning of the engine, you could hear the tyres biting deep into the fresh, crisp snow.

Harden gestured ahead. 'There's a plateau up there and the airfield's slap in the middle of it.'

March shook his head. 'You mean guys are living up there?'

'I told you – coupla old rednecks like me, vets. Like father and son. Came back from some fucking battle that was never supposed to have happened and guess they only had each other. Landed up in Virginia where a lot of the geeks went. Either their brains were shot up or they came back with odd numbers of arms and legs. Buncha crazies, most of 'em. But these guys are OK.'

'How d'you know they're still alive?'

'I don't.' Harden peered through the windscreen, trying to make out the track. 'This is kind of a night for surprises.'

'Yeah, well, before we get any more, why don't you finish telling me how I came to be involved in this?'

'You want to know? OK, this is what happened. Ten days – no, two weeks back I get a call from Travis. Travis and me, we'd

worked together in the Gulf and a bunch of places. He got out of
the service and began working for one of these chemical plants –
Christ knows why, they're the places that are developing all this
chemical shit. Anyway, I don't hear squat from Travis for a coupla
years, then he rings me up in a panic and says he has to meet me. I
say, fine. So he comes out here, looking pale as a rat's ass on a
winter's night, and tells me his story. And it ain't nice.'

Through the windscreen Harden glimpses the final approach to
the airfield, a tiny sign that says simply, 'Keep Out'.

He chuckles to himself. 'Friendliest people in the world, these
guys. Nothing they wouldn't do for you – including knife you in
the back. Anyway, where the hell did we get to? Yeah, Travis.
Well, when he came to me, it was clear this company wasn't just
producing this junk for the security of Uncle Sam. There were
commercial reasons that had gotten far more important. They had
started selling the stuff world-wide. And selling it where? To all
the tin-pot repressive regimes around the world that could cough
up the money for it. Dictators in Africa, Burma, the Far East,
Central America – we even had it going through front companies
in Eastern Europe and ending up back in Iraq, for Chrissake. If
that ain't the sickest thing I'd ever heard . . .'

'Did Travis tell you all this?'

'Some of it. But some I knew already. When General Lovett –
now, of course, Mr Important Dick Lovett, Speaker of the
goddam House of Representatives and number three in the line
of succession to the President – when he told me after the Gulf
that it was over, I knew he was lying. This is a guy who couldn't
even lay straight in bed if he tried.'

March smiled for the first time.

'So I had to stop him, and Travis gave me a way to do it. He
stole a couple of canisters from the plant, a new, experimental
substance that he says can kill fast or slow, depending on the
dosages. It's carried in an aerosol and just a few puffs does the job.'

'Jesus Christ Almighty . . .' March let out his breath. 'No
wonder they want you dead.'

'Us,' said Harden. 'They want *us* dead.'

He stopped the Jeep beside a fence. March could see nothing

except a vast expanse of snow, and a sky that was turning light all too fast.

As he wound down his window, the barrel of an AK47 came through the window, forcing him hard against the back of his seat.

'Welcome, boys,' said the voice from a blackened face. 'Can't you read the fuckin' sign?'

# Chapter eighteen

As he looked at the canisters Angelo didn't say a word. None of them had spoken, not since the team had returned and they had removed the protective cover, setting the package in the middle of the wood-block floor under a bright single light-bulb. There was no celebrating, no triumph and no words of congratulation.

For several minutes they stared at the objects as if unable to turn away from them. Two plain metal canisters, cylindrical and about six inches long, sat looking back, both containing vials of colourless liquid, visible through tiny Perspex windows. One of them also held a row of paper sachets, like tea-bags.

Then they knew exactly what they were dealing with. Tear open the paper and a lethal substance would be released immediately across a small area. It was biological warfare, complete with its own delivery system and already in production. It was not a moment for pride.

Eventually, Angelo let out his breath, and stared at the semi-circle of faces. 'Christ Jesus, guys. The only thing that's missing is the Made in America label. What the fuck are we doing manufacturing this junk?'

'We ain't just manufacturing it, you know that.' It was the youngest of the seals. He had killed first outside Travis's house. 'We're selling the goddam stuff as well. C'mon, guys, exports, balance-of-payments, happy, smiling shareholders, that's what matters these days. For Chrissake, even when we were in the military we carried around chemicals and biologicals and never gave it a thought. Like it was the weekend food shop at Safeway.'

'We had to, man.' Angelo held out his hands as if they were tied together. 'We didn't exactly have much choice.'

'Yeah, well, now we do.'

'What's that supposed to mean?'

The younger man shifted his weight from one foot to another. 'I say we get rid of the stuff. Lose it, bury it – and get the hell away from here. Who knows if they can't track this shit with some kind of scanner or something?'

Angelo snorted with contempt. 'You gotta be kidding. That's the attraction of this stuff to everybody. No one can trace it. Period. Not in airport security, not through Customs. No one. They just don't have the technology.'

'All the more reason why we get rid of it. The way I see it, the package should never have come here. We have no idea what the risks are just being close to it.' The seal looked round at his colleagues, counting the ones who were nodding, working out the odds in his favour. Three out of four had moved over, almost imperceptibly, to his side of the room.

Angelo could feel the temperature rising, feel his cheeks redden. The younger man had picked up the protective bag and was unzipping the secure compartment.

Slowly, pointedly, Angelo positioned himself between the seal and the canisters. 'Put the fucking bag down, man.'

'To hell with you.'

'I said put the bag down,' and then Angelo was aware that his time had run out. There could be no more mixed signals, no hesitation, no question of who was in charge. These were men who had lived with guns. They would have to be given a clear and unequivocal message. Already they were closing in around the seal, forming a security cordon, building towards a show-down.

Angelo removed his pistol from a holster inside his waistband and, without taking aim, shot the seal in the thigh. The act was so sudden that the group stood open-mouthed in shock as the young soldier screamed in pain and terror, catapulted against the wall behind him by the force of the blast. Only when he lay on the floor, yelping in short, agonised bursts, did they realise what had happened. Angelo reached down and knocked him out with a swift, sharp blow to the chin. He turned to the others. 'Stevens, Mazer, Woike, patch him up, give him morphine when he's awake.'

'Jesus, man, what the fuck are you doing?' Mazer stood stock still in the middle of the room.

'Just do as I say. Now! This weapon carries another eight shots. I can spare you one each – and more for the obstinate. So make a decision what the fuck you want to do. And do it now. You all knew the plan, you all went along with it.'

There was a moment of hesitation as the men glanced at each other, weighing up the odds. Each was well aware that Angelo had been an Army marksman. Long range or short, he didn't miss.

'This stuff is fucking lethal, man.' Mazer had frozen where he stood. 'None of us knew we'd have to live with it, sleep with it. For Chrissake, why do we have to risk our lives for it?'

Angelo stood up. 'Because we've been chosen to do something. You understand that, Mazer? You understand what it's like for the first time in your shitbag life to be chosen to do something important? Uh? You never had that before? Uh? All your life you obey orders from one asshole or another on some goddam mission that means nothing to you in a place you couldn't even find on a map. And you go do it, right?' He looked at all of them in turn. 'And then you get a call from a guy you really respect, an officer with balls, for Chrissake. Not one of the West Point fuckheads that doesn't want to get his shoes dirty, but a guy who's come up through the ranks. A guy who wants to get things done. Vic Harden, who never let down a fellow soldier in his life. Man, I –'

'So where the fuck is he?' Mazer shook his head.

'He's on his way. I told you. Why don't you fucking listen?'

''Cos he ain't coming, man.' Mazer snorted in disbelief. 'Harden ain't coming. He got cold feet or died or something, I dunno, but he ain't coming.'

'He'll be here.'

'He better be, man, or I ain't staying around.'

Angelo spread out his hands and made a calming gesture, like a priest. 'Harden doesn't quit. Trust me. I know the guy. OK?'

Nobody said a word.

# Chapter nineteen

Lovett is up at five, an hour earlier than usual. There's an alarm mechanism, built in long ago, that can wake him at any time in any country. It's familiar and predictable but seldom offers any comfort. It's called fear.

As he dresses, he can feel its drumbeat, feel the left eyelid fluttering out of control. Odd that he'd never felt nerves on the battlefield. Only in Washington, where the deaths were sudden and silent and the assassins came at you from behind. Beware the Ides of March, April, May and all the other months, he thought. Ancient Rome was alive and well within the Beltway.

But the public never saw that. All they were given access to was the smiling and gladhanding, not the treachery that travelled hand in hand. Lovett stared into the mirror and fastened his Dunhill tie. And yet the priority was to protect your position. He had responsibility, influence, a central role in the event of a crisis. A confidant of the President. His own position was even more important than he was. He would do anything – everything – necessary to protect it.

When he slipped out of the dressing room Jane was still sleeping. He hated her inactivity, her ignorant serenity – and that stupid smile. Hated the baby thing as well, only he would never admit that. After all, the baby was the ultimate political prop, brought out and dusted at every opportunity, held up to the crowds, even coming equipped with his own makeup for the photographs.

And there was Jane's father. Red-faced Tartar, hovering around the eighty mark, doting on the child as if he'd never seen one, then turning round and shafting his associates in the back. If you knew what was good for you, you watched out for old man Piedmont – from one of the best-known New England families, a man who could trace his devious and duplicitous ancestors all the way back to the Founding Fathers. Whatever the administration, he remained one of the chosen few with instant access to the White House. He didn't wait to be invited, simply told the chief of staff he was on his way and didn't want to 'dawdle' at the gate. He was a permanent member. More importantly, he possessed the money to make up the rules. Nobody turned Piedmont away without a very good reason. You courted him, flattered him, massaged the monster ego, and hoped your name would trip off his tongue at the right reception or power dinner. And yet for every favour he did, he would take one away. Even Lovett, who had never shied from treachery, had been astounded at the gratuitous cruelty of the man: his enjoyment at destroying careers and reputations, his penchant for mockery, his unique ability to identify the weakest point in a person's character and use it against them. He was known in Washington as a consummate sonofabitch, to be feared and treated with maximum care. Piedmont may have been old but the volcano was still active.

Lovett shivered as he stepped out into the cold morning. Fifteen miles outside Washington, it felt more like fifty. The house was in a dip so you couldn't see the road or the other buildings nearby. And as he looked east towards the sunrise, the land was draped in white, the countryside locked in the cold stillness of dawn. Inside the garage he climbed into the Lincoln Town Car, turned the ignition and heard the distant purr of the engine. As he headed on to the Beltway, he could tell that the snowploughs had been busy: three lanes were clear in each direction. Another hour, he thought, they'd all be clogged, and the skidding and swearing would start as the Washington commuters battled their way into the city. Half the day's business ended up getting done on the carphone. Most people, he reckoned, only came in for the coffee. And the kill.

Driving into Georgetown he could feel the wheels skidding a little so he didn't attempt the hill off Wisconsin Avenue. He parked the car and began to walk the half-mile to Piedmont's house. People had come out the day before and cleared the sidewalks in front of their houses, piling the snow high on the side of the road, so at least there was a way through. In any case he was glad of the walk. Piedmont was the one person in Washington he dreaded seeing. The one person whose power and influence he couldn't begin to fathom. He needed some cool deep-breathing before he saw him.

Of course, Lovett hadn't called the house in advance because he knew he didn't need to. Piedmont slept only three or four hours a night, rising at four, opening the windows, whatever the temperature, and letting the cool air circulate through the house. Since his wife had died three years ago he lived, according to legend, on venom alone. And on the news they brought him daily from his empire. For Piedmont's low profile disguised nothing less than one of the major arms-dealing operations of the century. And scarcely anybody, outside the centres of power, had ever heard his name.

Once, and just once, in the early fifties, *Life* magazine had devoted a cover to the man, naming him as one of the international wheeler-dealers of post-war Europe. But the cover had since disappeared from the newspaper's offices and, along with it, all traces of the edition in which it had appeared. Many years before computerisation, there had been a fire in the archives and all relevant records had been destroyed. Lovett had checked exhaustively and had grudgingly given Piedmont his due. He was thorough and he got the job done. It was as if the article had never existed. Since then, the old man had never once been interviewed and no reporter had ever called at his door.

Lovett stood in front of the distinctive yellow house and marvelled at the deception. Even as he watched he could see the tiny camera above the main door swivel and point straight at him. Another on the roof would get the broader picture. There were probably several others in the trees along the street. In the basement, a twenty-four-hour team of two private security guards were watching the monitors, with instructions to notify Piedmont immediately if they saw anything suspicious. Within a minute,

Lovett knew that the door would open and the man would be there with a welcome about as warm as that of a snake. No need even to ring the bell. Everything would happen by itself.

Even as Lovett's count reached fifty seconds, he could hear the lock turn in the main door. Piedmont stood there in dressing gown and slippers, wearing an expression not of annoyance or even concern but similar to that of a tiger, whose breakfast had unexpectedly come calling.

'What happened to you, Dick? You look lousy.' The thought clearly amused him for a smile spread across the craggy, freshly shaved face.

'Mind if I come in?'

'Mind? Why should I? I've long grown accustomed to your mannerless unscheduled visits. Is my daughter fit?'

'Absolutely.'

'Because if she wasn't I'd kick your ass all the way to Cincinnati.'

'I said she's fine.'

Piedmont stood aside and let Lovett pass. The temperature inside the hall was little different from outside but the old man was in pungent good health. A little slower over the years, a little watery around the eyes – but they could still pierce a tank at fifty paces.

'You want coffee?' Piedmont gestured to the kitchen. A large espresso pot sat fizzing on the hob.

'Sure.'

Lovett took a cup and sat at a table by the long French windows. The early-morning wind was blowing the snow off the tops of the trees and it looked as though more was on the way.

'So what have you fucked up now?' The smile still sat there at the edges of Piedmont's face as he eased himself into a chair opposite Lovett.

'There's a problem.'

'I figured you hadn't come here to lick my ass.' The old man chuckled. 'Though I guess you have, figuratively speaking.'

'You know the chemical plant that Albright runs –'

'Why wouldn't I?'

'One of the experimental substances has gone missing.'

'Don't lie to me, Dick.'

'I don't understand.'

'One of the experimental substances – bullshit! You seriously imagine I don't know what's been going on at the plant? This wasn't a substance, it was a biological warfare agent, made in the USA with finance from abroad, which I set up through my own associates. And it hasn't gone missing. A lousy fucking employee, who your people had vetted up to his gonads, stole two canisters and is threatening to turn us all into mutants and pot plants for the next ten years.' Piedmont pointed a finger at Lovett. 'Listen to me, Dick, and get this straight, or I'll ram it so far up your asshole you'll need a spade to dig it out. Don't come here at six in the morning and try to sell me crap. Don't come any time at all.' The face was reddening fast, but the eyes were ablaze. 'I know what happened. I know what you've done. And I know how you and Albright are fucking up the entire operation.'

'Albright isn't the man for this.' Lovett's eyes narrowed. 'He's not getting results. And I'm not certain how committed he is to it. He could be trying to shift blame.'

'He's too dumb for that. But he can always talk.' Piedmont sniffed with distaste and stared out of the window at the snow-filled garden. 'I'm not going to let this run indefinitely.'

'What does that mean?'

'It means I'll bring my own people in and get the job done properly. For the last fifty years I've managed quietly and efficiently below the surface. That is, until my daughter began associating with a putz like you. Since then I'm running round Washington like a fucking nursemaid, clearing up your mess. Jesus!' He turned away and began to cough into a handkerchief. 'If you people had to run a commercial enterprise you'd be fired in your first half day. You couldn't even cock your leg on a tree without mechanical assistance.'

Lovett pushed away his coffee cup and stood up. There was a limit to what he could take from Piedmont, never mind his stupid, whining daughter. Jesus, he'd paid a high price to get the old man's political support and now even that was in doubt.

145

Piedmont stayed where he was. 'If you've lost confidence in Albright, then get rid of him. Personally I never had any. But you were always a lousy judge of character.'

Lovett turned away, and moved towards the front door.

'And one more thing, Dick . . .' The smile was back, writ large across the pale, cold cheeks. 'You got twenty-four hours to end this circus. No more.'

Piedmont sat at the kitchen table and stared out at the garden. Then he slid his hand below the surface and pressed a small button.

Thirty seconds later a man in a blue pullover came up the side stairs from the basement, let himself into the hall and knocked on the kitchen door.

Piedmont looked up as his head of security, Charlie Richards, ushered first his stomach then the rest of his bulk into the room. With Charlie there, the place seemed suddenly much smaller.

'Did you get it?'

Richards nodded. The question was rhetorical. If he hadn't got 'it', he'd be fired on the spot and out of the house within minutes. After more than ten years with Piedmont, he knew exactly where he stood. If you delivered, you were fine. There were treats and extras, holiday money, gifts for the family at Christmas. If you didn't, you'd better get out and move town. The old man was a vindictive bastard.

Richards slipped a video-cassette into the player on the sideboard and switched on the television. As the picture stabilised you could see Lovett talking into the middle distance, but the rest of the room was out of shot. There was no sign of any interlocutor. Both sound and vision were crystal clear.

Richards ejected the tape. 'We'll edit out your questions and replace them with another voice. There won't be any trace of you.'

Piedmont grunted with delight. 'So we can move any time we feel like it.'

'Want me to get some of the team together?'

'Find out where they are. See if they're in town and have 'em stand by. I want to move last on this one, not first. We'll wait and see what everyone else does, then we clean up. Top to bottom.'

He stood up and patted Charlie's shoulder. 'Sure you don't want some coffee?'

Richards shook his head. The less he ate and drank in that house the better. Especially knowing what he knew about Piedmont and his activities over the last ten years.

It was late in the afternoon when he went out. The sun, which had appeared, pale and cheerless, for a half-hour, had hurried back behind the clouds and the day stood on the brink of darkness.

For an eighty-year-old, Piedmont walks with amazing ease, swinging a stick for show, luxuriating in his fitness and sense of well-being. Of course, he's looked after himself. Nothing but the best, when it come to food, or holidays or exercise. And his clothes, although muted in colour, are nevertheless of the finest quality.

But he had never been seen in a store. Not Mr Piedmont. There were designers who came to the house with their materials and their tape measures, their sighing and muttering, and their cases full of Italian silk ties, from which he chose only the dullest. Greys, blacks and pin-dots by Cerrutti and Armani. Always just the tiniest bit understated and self-effacing. 'Let the quality speak for itself,' he used to tell his wife. 'Not the colours. It's the cut that matters.'

So it was in the brutality that had characterised his life.

Louis Piedmont hailed a taxi on M Street and told the driver to take him to the Washington Hilton. He walked into the lobby, looked around for less than twenty seconds then strode out again, shaking off the attentions of a porter, who wondered, in broken English, if he could possibly help.

Another taxi took him to the L'Enfant Plaza close to the Air and Space Museum, where he made a call from a payphone in the lobby, admired some of the jewellery and watches in the glass showcases, then walked back on to the street, stopping ten minutes later at the corner of Constitution and 18th. Even as he stood there, a black sedan moved alongside and the passenger door swung open. Piedmont inserted himself deftly into the space offered and landed comfortably on the leather back seat. He was the only passenger, separated from the driver by a smoky-grey screen. The temperature had been set at around seventy degrees, roughly forty degrees higher than the world outside, and the streets of Washington looked distant and unreal through the tinted windows.

Four blocks later, the car disappeared into an underground garage, in a row of brownstone houses and came to rest in an unmarked parking space, against a concrete wall. Piedmont's door was snatched open smartly. He got out to find a man in a suit, somewhere in his thirties, anonymous, and with a face that was instantly forgettable. No introductions were made.

'If you'll follow me, Mr Piedmont, sir . . .'

Piedmont said nothing.

The man led him to a passenger lift, turned a key and pressed the call button.

Piedmont entered but the man stayed outside.

'It's automatic, sir. It only goes to one floor.'

The lift doors slid shut behind him.

When they opened again, Piedmont stepped into a room that could have been anywhere but Washington.

Half of it was in darkness but the light, filtered through shutters on the window, cast all manner of shapes and shadows on to the wooden floor. As his eyes grew accustomed, he could make out a long table at one end, a door to another room and, close to where he now stood, a sofa and two armchairs.

'Louis, is that you?'

A voice boomed out from the other room. A voice so familiar that he might have been listening to it on television.

Four words that would identify their speaker instantly and to almost anyone in the country.

Piedmont stood where he was. To him it didn't matter who the man was. They were all the same, men like this. They had their strong points, their weaknesses, their money and their insecurity. What mattered was their power. And this man had plenty of it – although a lot less than he thought.

'Louis,' said the voice again. 'Don't just stand there, man, talk to me. Come in here. Make yourself at home.'

Piedmont smiled to himself. 'I'm right here, Mr President,' he said quietly. 'Just catching my breath.'

# Chapter twenty

Under Albright's instructions Julie March was flown in an unmarked twelve-seater jet to a private airfield in Maryland for transfer to Washington.

Harries had spoken to her only once during the flight, 'Some things are more important than one's personal feelings. As one of its most trusted employees I need hardly tell you about your duty to the Government,' and she had sat back in her seat, closed her eyes and wondered for the thousandth time where her duty really lay.

Peter had stumbled into something serious, and they needed to find him. Fast. For his own good – or theirs. When you thought about it, that wasn't so unreasonable. Except for the approach and the search, and Harries himself. And yet she had met the breed before. Harries was security, a particularly brutish, rude and aggressive incarnation, but she had always known of *their* interest in her work. Besides, when you got paid by the Government you never knew which part of it you were serving. The whole grand edifice was just a series of committees, some more secret than others, but always fighting each other for funding or turf – or the latest advances that the scientists were making. So where did your loyalty lie? Which committee? Which boss? Was it the man with the highest security clearance? Or the gun under his armpit?

Like the other scientists she had enjoyed her status on the cutting edge. Enjoyed the pampering and the privileges, the *knowing* of things that others would never know. The feeling that, by her brain and efforts, she could in some small way advance the future of the United States and the causes it espoused around the world. It was all very right and very proper because it was in the name of her country.

And people like Peter tried to come along and upset the whole thing, for the sake of a few misplaced scruples. She couldn't suppress the anger, only it wasn't for herself or for the Government. She was angry because he was wrecking his own life, and spoiling his own chances. He wasn't a bad man. Far from it. He was kind and gentle and caring, and he was about to learn a lesson she wished he'd learned many years before: that the meek don't inherit the earth, after all, and that Uncle Sam was a cold, ruthless bastard when you crossed him.

Whatever he had done, she wouldn't be able to save him. She knew that now, staring out of the aircraft's window as the snow-covered Maryland countryside came up to meet them.

Harries left his seat and stood over her. 'We're going to be co-ordinating this whole operation in Washington. It's a safe house over in Adams Morgan – multi-ethnic place, lot of activity all hours of the day and night, so we won't be attracting any special attention.'

'How are we going to find Peter?'

Harries didn't answer until they had left the plane and climbed inside the car that had drawn up beside it. 'We're checking into some of his friends and associates.' A smirk appeared on his face. 'There could be quite a few of them, people of all kinds you know nothing about. But we may need your help in approaching them all the same.'

She knew all too well what that smirk meant.

Harry Wilson replaced the receiver and put his head in his hands. One call from Vince Albright was bad enough, but two was abusing the privilege. Hadn't he already penetrated the inner recesses of the NSA's computers on some damn-fool request? Christ! He'd put his own security clearance on the line for Albright's sake. Now the guy had called wanting more. Damn him.

Harry went to the sideboard and poured himself the fourth bourbon of the night. From the den, he could hear the mayhem upstairs. Now that the kids were home the whole house echoed to the sound of pop music, clumping feet and shrieks of laughter. He needed a late-night visit like a bullet through the foot.

When he arrived, Albright led the way down to the den, as if he owned the house, hardly registering the presence of Claudia Wilson, who leaned out of the kitchen to see who had arrived. He was in a ragged, lousy mood, Harry could see it: the face was unshaven, one of his shirt-tails had drifted out of the waistband, he was too tired, too overweight and too worried for a man in his fifties.

'This thing's pissing me off,' he stood in the middle of the den, hands in his coat pockets, 'and I need help.'

Wilson shrugged. 'I gave you what I could last time, Vince. Every time I go digging it leaves a trace. There ain't no silent paths. I can't get in and cover my tracks once I've been there. Each day I go in expecting someone to ask me what the fuck I'm doing . . . So what the fuck am I doing, Vince? You tell *me*.'

'I can't. It's national security, Harry.'

'Then go to the fucking NSA yourself. Why have I got to try to sneak in under their noses when it's their business all along?'

'Sit down, Harry.'

'Don't tell me to sit down in my own house.'

Albright parked himself in the rocking chair and lit a cigarette. Harry could see his hand was shaking. 'I'll forget you said that.' The voice was quiet, controlled. 'I'll forget everything you've said tonight, Harry, which has been unhelpful and uncooperative. And I won't go upstairs to that nice little wife in the kitchen and tell her about the piece of skirt you were fucking at the Pentagon, at the same time as she was having her cancer treatments at Sibley Hospital. I won't go and tell her that, Harry, because maybe she might be a little upset, maybe she'd start crying and screaming and waking up the neighbourhood. And then the kids might come down and ask why their mom's so upset, and she might tell them and it could all get so very nasty, very quickly. But I won't do that, Harry, because I don't want to fuck up your family life. But you have to do something for me instead.'

'You're a shithead, Vince, d'you know that?' Harry sat down in front of his computer.

'If there was another way I'd take it.'

'Would you really, Vince?' Harry looked back over his shoulder and stared straight at Albright. 'I wonder if you really would. Maybe you like doing this to people in the name of national security.' The voice was sneering. 'I think maybe Vince Albright gets himself a hard–on by threatening to fuck up people's lives because this country wants it. Right, Vince? Beats going to the ballgame, uh? Beats screwing the wife, I bet, uh?'

'You don't know shit, Harry.' Albright stubbed out the cigarette on the arm of the rocking chair and flicked it on to the carpet. 'And you're better off not knowing. Get into the damn database. I haven't got all night on this one.' He lit another cigarette, but the hand had steadied. 'Guy's name is March – Peter March. Brit journalist working in Washington. I need to know if they got his friends and associates. They should have done. He was under low-level DIA surveillance for at least three months. Seems the guy was nosy.'

It took Harry more than an hour to access the files he needed. When you don't know the individual filing systems, they make you work for it. There are no road maps or short–cuts. You have to do it all by yourself. And Harry had done it all by himself.

He printed out the results, tore off the paper and handed it to his visitor.

Albright held it up to the light. 'You look pretty pleased with yourself. And, frankly, I can see why. It's a pretty thorough job.'

'The last one, Vince. That's it. No more.'

Albright chuckled. 'Hey, buddy, old friend. Don't get serious on me all of a sudden. The debt's repaid, OK? It's cool. This is the way it should be, friends doing favours for each other, helping out –'

'Just get the hell out of here, Vince. I'm gonna have a helluva lot of explaining if any of this comes out.'

'It won't.' Albright got up, yawned and ran a hand through his hair. 'Trust me. Nobody's even gonna come looking. I guarantee it.'

'I wish you hadn't said that.' Harry stared straight in front of him and logged out of the database. One name stuck in his mind and he didn't know why it wouldn't go away. Maybe he'd seen it or heard it somewhere before. Certainly not a Washington name – although it'd be bound to make something of a stir with the lady herself.

Leah Killeen.

He rolled the sound around his tongue and liked the way it tasted.

# Chapter twenty-one

March glanced through the front windscreen, taking in the bleak dawn landscape, the contours of an airfield, with the stiff-cold airsock, frozen immovable beside the control tower. Under other circumstances, the gun barrel held against his nose by a man with a blackened face and army fatigues would have pushed him into blind panic but after the events of the last three hours he considered it with a certain equanimity. Especially since Harden was sitting beside him with an expression of some amusement, which turned rapidly to laughter.

'Jesus Christ, Sergeant Henry Jaworski,' his finger pointed towards the blackened features, 'you look almost human. First time in your military career, son.'

Jaworski's mouth opened in shock.

'You're getting rusty, fellah. Safety catch is on. We could have blown your balls out from under you by now and you'd still be trying to pull that trigger. Didn't I teach you anything, all them years ago?'

'Fuck you, Major – sir!' The face grinned and the gun barrel was lowered. 'What you doing here on a day like this, for Chrissakes?'

'Need a ride.'

'Hell you do . . .'

'Where's Billy?' Harden pushed open the passenger door and came round to face Jaworski.

'Billy's not good, Major. He's in the control tower.' He jerked his hand in the direction of March. 'Who's your boyfriend?'

'You don't even want to know.'

Jaworski grinned again. 'Right. If he's anything to do with you, the less I know about him the better I'm gonna like it.'

March got out of the Jeep. He could feel the sense of urgency slipping away. This wasn't the time for banter and old camaraderie. 'I think we ought to get moving.'

Jaworski turned his head a moment, then his eyes refocused on Harden. 'Your boyfriend's nervous.'

'We're all nervous, Sergeant. Remember? That's how we used to stay alive.'

The control tower was little more than a two-storey shack, but March could feel the warmth as they went inside. He was struck at once by the tidiness and sense of order. The wooden floors had been freshly polished. He could smell detergent and disinfectant, and it wasn't until they made their way to a room at the back that he could see the reason for it.

Jaworski knocked on the door, but didn't wait for an answer. Inside, the light was intentionally dim. Two lamps in the ceiling cast only narrow beams on to the floor and had been shrouded to reduce glare. Billy was half propped up in a bed by the window, coughing out his heart, but the curtains were drawn and he was wearing shaded glasses. For a second it seemed to March as though he was watching some grotesque comedy. But then he took in the oxygen cylinder and the mask beside the bed and realised there was nothing funny about Billy.

On the contrary, Billy was most likely dying and suffering horrendously in the process.

'Billy, there's a couple guys here to see you.' Jaworski leaned down towards the face.

'Have you offered them refreshment?' The voice was surprisingly strong. Educated. Confident.

'You don't know who they are yet.' Jaworski grinned. 'Major Harden's here, for Chrissake.'

'Harden?'

'It's me, Billy. Good to see you again after all this time.'

A half-smile appeared on Billy's face as if by magic. 'You're still a liar, Harden. I'm not good to be seen any more. What about you? Rumour a while back that you weren't too fit yourself?'

'Not long to go, Billy. Reckon I picked up the same cocktail as you, but I haven't suffered the way you have.'

'That's too bad.' Billy grinned. 'Suffering's not so bad if you got a pretty blonde with nice legs to look after you.' He sighed. 'Jaworski never quite made the grade in that area – what do you think?'

Harden smiled. 'Bet he looks great in a dress.'

'Yeah, right.' Billy coughed and reached for a glass of water beside the bed. He lay back on the pillows. 'I was OK for a while. Knew things weren't getting any better, but I still thought the Army would look after me. They kept sending me to different doctors for different tests but none of them was the *right* test. I know that now. I was just the gesture for the media. That way they could claim to be doing something while all the time they weren't doing jack shit.'

'D'you know what you were exposed to?'

'Got a good idea. VX gas, probably. Made in the USA, then dumped by those B52s that came out of Diego Garcia. That's the worst of it. Getting screwed by your own side. Wouldn't have minded so much if it had been the Iraqis.'

'And then you started getting these allergies?'

'Each year it got worse. First it was just smell, then taste . . . started vomiting, breaking out in cold sweats. Then it was colours, bright colours. Couldn't tolerate even the sight of them after a while . . .' The voice seemed to drain away, like water down a sink.

Harden drew closer. 'I need a favour, Billy.'

'Tell me something I don't know.'

'I need Jaworski to fly us out of here, somewhere closer to Washington.'

'In this weather?'

'We've done worse.'

'I know that too. But not this time. Jaworski stays with me. For Chrissake, Harden, he's all I've got.'

'Listen to me.' Harden lowered himself in evident pain to the floor beside Billy's bed. 'There was a shoot-out tonight at my place. We got away – just. But they ain't far away . . .'

'Who's "they", Harden? All through the years you talked about "they" as if we were somehow supposed to know them. What are you talking about, man? Aliens from another planet?'

Harden opened his mouth to say something, but it was March who spoke first. 'Billy, if I can call you that, I'm Peter March, a British journalist. It'd take too long to tell you how I came to be here – I wish to hell I wasn't. I keep thinking that the last few hours never really happened and somehow I can go back to what I was twenty-four hours ago, just a reporter, trying to get few stories.'

'What's your point, friend?' The voice had sharpened like a blade.

'The point, I guess, is that if we don't get back to Washington people are going to die. Look, I killed someone tonight. I actually pulled a trigger and shot someone in the head.'

'Congratulations! You've finally been accepted into the club. Killing brings us so much closer together, don't you think? After all, it's what mankind does best.' Billy sipped from his glass of water.

March seemed to ignore him. 'There's a biological weapon. It's out there, stolen from an experimental plant. We have to get it back. The Government has other ideas for us.'

Billy clapped. 'Wonderful! Another doomsday scenario. And I was thinking the world had lost some of its fun.'

'I didn't say doomsday, I said some people were going to die.'

'So am I, Mr Brit.'

'Then you don't need Jaworski.' March froze even as he. said the words, horrified by his own glib, heartless logic. And suddenly there was silence in the room as they all looked at each other, knowing that a final corner had been turned.

For a moment Billy sat perfectly still, then removed his dark glasses. So unexpected was the move that all three of his visitors took a step back. Even in the dim light they could see that Billy's eyes were barely open and the skin around them was pale and hard, lined like stone.

'I'm sorry I said that.'

'Don't be. I like plain speaking. Never got that much of it in the military, everyone talking in codes the whole time. I just wanted to see what you looked like.'

'And now that you have?'

'You look damn scared to me, Mr March. And that's not a bad thing. I'm damn scared too, if you want to know. Maybe that's a strange thing for a soldier to say. I've been in plenty of wars, seen plenty of people dying right next to me. But that's different. You go into a battle hollerin' and screamin' and then someone shoots you dead. It's final but it's painless, OK? This is different. I die about thirty times a day in my mind, wondering and worrying. There's too much time. Maybe I should've done something about it a long time ago.'

'Billy, I'm really –'

'Sorry? I know you are. We're all sorry. Even Harden's sorry.' He pointed a finger and grinned. 'And he's been a sorry kinda guy for a long time. Anyway,' he sighed, 'take the lousy helicopter and get outa here. Besides, it still belongs to the military – just happened to get removed from one of their inventories one wet afternoon when we needed it for some damn-fool operation or other. And it always seemed too much trouble to give it back. Anyway, I need some sleep, 'stead of being bothered by folks like you all the time.' He replaced the dark glasses and lay back on his pillows. 'Send me a postcard when you get there.'

Jaworski went over to him and took his hand. 'I'll get 'em where they're going, Billy, then I'm coming back, OK?'

'No, it's not OK. You keep on flying, you hear me? Get the hell away, Jaworski, you understand?'

'No, Billy. I'm coming back.'

Billy turned on his side. 'Listen to me, there's something that these good people here haven't mentioned because it's not polite to talk about these things in nice company. But let me see if I can fill in the gaps.' He paused, and now his breathing was slow and laboured. 'By coming here this morning, these fellahs have left a trail. They didn't mean to. But they've done it. That tells me that in a very short space of time the people who're after them will be comin' up that road,' he pointed towards the window, 'wanting to ask some questions.' He shifted position and then relaxed. 'Better I answer them on my own.'

'No, Billy.'

'Yes, Billy. Now get the hell outa here, Jaworski. I'm getting tired of all this crap, and I need my sleep. You won't want to be around if I get into one of my moods.'

It took no more than thirty minutes to refuel the helicopter, drag away the tarpaulin and make all the external checks. By then the day had appeared grey and unhappy above the mountains.

March could feel the cold building like a wall around him, solid and immovable, as he watched Jaworski at work. The helicopter was his baby and he was the proud father. Touching it, talking to it, coaxing it to go out into the world and do its best. Brushing it down to keep away the ice and snow.

When he was ready, March knocked on the window of the Jeep. Harden had been lying slumped against the wheel with the engine and heater running. It was a few moments before he woke and remembered where he was. March had to help him out and almost carry him to the helicopter, as the main rotor began to turn, beating the thin cold air, breaking the peace of the morning.

Inside the cockpit, he put on the headset. Jaworski was already shouting to be heard. 'Where we heading?'

Harden adjusted his microphone. 'Into Washington.'

'You're crazy.'

'Rock Creek Park. There are plenty of clearings at the northern end in Maryland, close to Rockville. We can make it.'

'How? Air Traffic Control is gonna close us down the moment they spot us.'

'Christ, Jaworski, we used to do this all the time. You're working for a local TV station, you're up there to check on weather conditions, you gotta refer to your boss who's taking a piss and'll get back to them in a coupla minutes. You got a clearance for the flight.'

'And if they don't buy it?'

'You get pissed with them and start shouting, OK? Then they'll back off. Jesus Christ, this is America. The airways are supposed to be free. Anyway, by the time they come back to you, you've landed, got it?'

'That's just wonderful.'

As Jaworski lifted the Huey off the top of the mountain, March got a glimpse of a deeply unhappy man.

As for Harden, he was smiling ear to ear.

March reckoned the flight reminded him of something that had once gone right.

# Chapter twenty-two

'It's bad, Mr President.'

'Bad, Louis?'

'We're talking leaks. Leaks from one of the special chemical plants.'

'I try not to think about some of the things those guys are doing.' The President shut his eyes. 'This stuff should have stopped in nineteen seventy, for Chrissake, when Nixon signed the presidential directive.'

'It didn't. Just went out of sight. They farmed it all out to tiny research institutes in little universities no one had heard of.'

'For Chrissake, how am I supposed to keep my eye on all the balls?'

'I told you, Mr President, when you first came into office –'

'At least two hundred people tell me things every day.'

'You approved this one.'

'The CIA told me they had destroyed the stockpiles, everything except what was needed for peaceful research. I only approved the research.'

'They lied.'

The President's eyes opened again. 'That new director we appointed, Gatz, he comes in and gives me my intelligence briefing and I always say to him, "What are you not telling me, Ray?" And he smiles that stupid smile of his and replies, "It's all there, Mr President."'

Piedmont lit a cigarette with two gold rings around the filter. 'Gatz is just a puppet. He's not the heart of the beast.'

'Then who is, Louis? You've been around long enough.

You've dealt with all this stuff.' The President's eyes stared over his bifocals and held his visitor's gaze.

Piedmont sat back in his chair. The President could play innocent when he chose to, but you didn't want to turn your back on him in the same room. Plenty of others had made that mistake and been left counting the multiple stab wounds once they reached home.

'I know some of them,' he said quietly.

'You know most of them, Louis.'

Piedmont rubbed his eyes. 'They're rich sons of bitches. The Texas crowd, people like Baker, Reston – big shareholders in Lockheed, General Dynamics, Grumman. They buy the law-makers they need on Capitol Hill and that gets them the laws they want.' He chuckled. 'Never changes, does it?'

'Go on, Louis.'

'Well, then it gets serious, doesn't it? These guys are all tied in with their customers in the intelligence community. They make the weapons to order – weapons or chemicals.'

'And the CIA goes out and tests them, right?'

'CIA, DIA, National Security Agency and a whole damn clutch of others no one's ever heard of.' Piedmont looked hard at the President. 'Not even you.'

'I said go on.'

'The banks are in it, too. They've got to move the money that funds all this crap, move it around the world and out of sight, get it to whatever dirty little dictator or country or dealer needs to kill some people. Usually in large quantities.'

The President put his hands to his face as if he was praying. 'I'm not strong enough to stand up to them. You know that, Louis. They've got too much on me. Too much from the old days in Kansas. You know what I'm talking about, Louis?'

'I know, Mr President.'

'Nothing that all the others weren't doing . . . all of them. We did favours to people who did favours back. That's America. That's politics. Where would we be without it? You gotta do favours – that's what these fucking congressional committees and

163

special prosecutors don't seem to understand. All Republicans, all of them, you know that, don't you?'

'I know, Mr President.'

'I'm glad of your friendship, Louis, but get this stuff put back in the bottle, you hear me? Whatever it is that's leaked I don't want to know – you understand? Just put it back and bury it, Louis. You know how we do these things in Washington.'

'I understand perfectly, Mr President.'

'Time someone did round here.'

# Chapter twenty-three

Even at a distance Leah Killeen could see that the car was trouble. She had woken early, cold and stiff, instantly aware that the power had failed. The house was too quiet, no hum from the clocks, timers and machines central to daily life. Everything was dead. When she looked out of the window, the car seemed somehow responsible. A grey Saturn with a driver inside. Too cheap for the area, too anonymous, out of place among the Jags, the LeBarons and the Lincolns. Not a chauffeured car, not even a town runabout for one of the prissy Capitol Hill wives. Just sitting there with the engine running and the exhaust spouting into the chill morning air.

Just trouble.

She picked up the phone, half expecting the line to be dead but the dialling tone was loud, insistent. Normal. She called the electricity company, but the line was busy. Dammit – the capital of the Western world and every time there was a heavy snowfall the power went out.

Upstairs in the bedroom she dressed rapidly, pulling on jeans and a sweater, taking a thick sheepskin jacket from the wardrobe. She had no doubt that the offices were still closed. It was Friday and the radio was declaring an early weekend. Washington was cold *and* lazy. Business would have to wait till Monday.

But the car unsettled her.

In the kitchen she ate a slice of dry bread and wondered for the twentieth time that morning what had happened to Peter March. From her own contacts around town she knew he was making waves. After all, she'd helped him enough, offering leads and sources, going well beyond the remit of a Senate investigator. Now she needed him. Needed his strength and calm. Something was badly wrong.

Leah picked up the phone and dialled his mobile number. A recorded voice transferred her to an answering service, but she slammed down the receiver without leaving a message.

*Peter, please call, please . . .*

On impulse she stood up and went to the window, checking that the car was still there. As she pulled back the blind she gasped, seeing the silhouette of a second man in the front passenger seat. The engine was still running.

Leah reached for the phone again. For a moment her fingers wouldn't dial. She misdialled once, twice, then heard the deep 'hallo' as her next-door neighbour − a retired banker − lifted the receiver.

'Jim? It's Leah, sorry to disturb . . .'

'I've been disturbed for years, my dear. What is it?'

'You know the power outage we've got at the moment?'

'Power outage?' She could hear the puzzlement in his voice. 'You got a power outage? Everything's fine in here. Why don't you come on over? We're just cooking up some breakfast here, Mindy and me.'

'Thanks, Jim, I might do that.'

She hung up and paced the kitchen. Something, someone, seemed to be telling her to get out − and fast.

Fifty yards away, in the Saturn, Albright turned to his associate. The man had an open briefcase in his lap and an array of communications equipment.

'Well?'

The passenger removed his headphones. 'She called March's number but there was no reply. Then the power company, then a neighbour.'

'Clever bitch.' Albright took a sip of coffee from a flask. 'Now let's see what she does next. If she's as close to March as that NSA report suggests she'll wanna help him in some way.'

'Do I cut her phone? I've got a tap on the neighbour's as well – just in case.'

'Not yet.'

'What about March's wife?'

Albright replaced the lid on his coffee without offering it. 'Harries is doing that end of the deal. She's been flown here from Florida. They want her to contact March on his mobile, tell him something urgent's come up then get his ass over here. Let him worry about both the women in his life all at the same time.'

'Sounds like a caring kind of fellah.' The passenger smiled and replaced his headphones.

'Who gives a shit what he is?' Albright stared out of the window. 'Right now, he's the only lead we got.'

# Chapter twenty-four

Jaworski could have landed the helicopter on a chimney stack so the clearing in Rock Creek Park required little effort, even in the forty-mile-an-hour wind that swept Washington.

He let the Huey hover six feet from the ground, then shouted back to his passengers, 'This is it. If you're waiting for a red carpet, forget it. I've had enough trouble with Air Traffic Control. And now they've really pissed me off. I'm outa here.'

March jumped first, landing on his feet, ducking instinctively to avoid the rotor. But Harden fell badly and for a few seconds lay motionless in the snow. As the helicopter lifted away, his eyes were shut tight and his face contorted with pain.

'I can't move.' His feet scraped and kicked at the snow, but there was no strength in them.

March lifted him to a sitting position. 'You've got to stand. I can't carry you. And we need to find shelter.'

'I need a payphone. I have to check on Travis. There's a message system. A whole group . . .'

'OK, OK.' March pulled Harden to his feet. In the dawn light his face looked grey, the skin like crinkled paper. It was impossible to guess how much energy the last few hours had taken from him. By now he was running on reserve fuel only. March looked around: the trees were thick with snow, and the road was barely visible, but he could hear traffic nearby and guessed they were close to the Interstate. 'We'd better make for the main road.' He began to trudge slowly in the direction of the noise.

'You're crazy.' Harden caught up with him. 'Just keep out of sight.' He pointed to the road that snaked its way through the park and south into the city. 'Cars have been down this route in the last ten or fifteen minutes. Just wait. Leave the transport to me.'

He limped in evident pain to the side of the road, looking for cover.

'Are you up to this?' March examined him close to.

'No. Any other questions?' And then, without warning, he was moving with unexpected speed into the middle of the road, hearing the sound of a car, a full two seconds ahead of March. When it came round the corner, he raised his hands, caught like a scarecrow in the full beam of the headlights. A desperate figure, somehow quite divorced from the world around him.

The car slithered to a halt. Although he was just a few feet behind, March couldn't see what was happening. But suddenly the driver's door was opening and a figure in a black coat emerged into the grey cold morning, fear in his eyes, his hands quivering. 'Please, please . . .' he was murmuring, and only then did March see the gun in Harden's hand – the magic wand that he had always waved so effectively to get what he wanted.

Harden slid into the car and, as he did so, the driver made a break for it, tearing off through the snow, sliding and slipping, shouting to the trees, the fear inside him released in a giant, uncontainable explosion. March got into the passenger seat, but the vehicle was already moving forward, through the park, heading down towards Washington, Harden half slumped across the wheel.

I can't go back again, he thought. Old city, old friends, but nothing can ever be the same. I shall never sit in a café with a clear conscience, never sit through a movie, never stand on a cliff staring out at the sea, never stroll through a park . . . I shall never do anything without the knowledge that I have gained tonight. I killed a man and he will follow me all the way to my own grave – wherever it is, and whenever I reach it.

Harden glanced across at him, and read correctly the symptoms of a man interrogating his conscience.

'I need a payphone,' he said quietly. 'We gotta find out where we're going.'

Something more than the wind had woken Billy from a deep sleep. His temperature had risen sharply and he reached out for the water by his bed, drinking deeply, spilling it over his shirt. But he didn't mind. There were no appearances to maintain.

It was strange how easy the final decisions became. Once you've made up your mind to go, death is nothing more than an extra item on your timetable. You go to the cleaners, pick up your shirts, fill up the car – and then you kill yourself on Highway One, just past the fortieth intersection, at . . . let's say, six p.m. Write it in the diary so you don't forget. And someone else will tick it off for you when it's done.

Billy checked again that the Smith & Wesson .38 was lying by his right leg, like a faithful pet. He patted it, stroked it, laid his hand against the customised wooden grip. It was all there, comforting and dependable. A man and his gun. History of America.

He lay back on his pillows and waited till his mood improved. Lately, he had begun to enjoy playing out and imagining some of the scenarios after his death. Who would be upset? Who would even cry? Would that girl he'd met from Vermont, so many years back, get to read about it in one of the papers and cry her eyes out, wishing they'd 'done it' when they had the chance, instead of waiting for the marriage that had never happened? And then the mood would swing again, and he would rail at the injustice of it all and the pain – and when that happened the hatred would course through him, leaving him weak, frightened and exhausted.

The way he was now.

They were out there somewhere. He could sense the presence beyond his window. So what was the point of waiting? They would force their way in and make him talk, that was the reality, and if he waited too long he would lose the ability to end his own life the way he chose. But he wanted to see them first. And maybe take one with him. Just a glimpse, before he turned out the lights.

When they came, of course, it was not by stealth, not in the middle of the night, but in the grey hours of mid-morning with the sky locked solid in cloud. He heard the doors of at least three cars slamming. A few voices. No one in a hurry. They'd probably concluded he was in the helicopter that took off. So they weren't being careful.

And Billy found himself suddenly overtaken by the fun of it all – unable to stop himself laughing as he limped to the window, smashed the barrel of his gun through the pane and shot the first three he could see as they headed for the main door and long before they could reach for their own weapons.

And then came a dull thud as they opened up with some of the heavy stuff, blasting great chips of wood from the window-frame and forcing Billy on to the floor, more as an automatic reflex after all the years than a serious attempt to save himself.

God, it was fun to do a little soldiering again – just when he'd thought it was all over.

Only it was.

Away down the corridor, he heard, almost felt, the thud of the boots as they came tearing down the hallway, heading for his room.

So you don't wait around, Billy-boy, you hold the gun to your forehead and you give a little wave to anyone watching from Valhalla and you blow your head off before they do it for you. Recite after me, and carry out the instructions to the letter.

Billy was dead by the time they smashed in the door of his room – just about three seconds after his soul had departed, glad to be going.

# Chapter twenty-five

Harden replaced the phone and stood for several moments outside the 7-Eleven, trying to reclaim his breath. Around him the city had begun to move again. Cars and trucks were limping along, encrusted in snow and dirt. But he saw nothing.

*Facts first. The rest is emotion. You can come to that later. Cry later. Grieve later. Register the essentials and move on. Nothing else matters.*

The skypager message had been brief and simple enough to grasp first time.

Travis was dead. Angelo had retrieved the canisters and was waiting at Plaza 107. One other person had died and Washington was crawling with scum in grey suits and plenty of firepower in the pockets. The city was a shooting range. He was the target. No room for misunderstanding.

Harden lifted the receiver, dialled an 800 number and left a return voicemail. Plaza 107 was slang for the Defence Intelligence Agency's headquarters in Crystal City, right across the Potomac from downtown Washington. It was also slang for the safe house. At least Angelo had secured his position, but how long could he hold it together? How long before they followed his tracks?

As he stood in the grey morning light, Harden felt his breathing gradually return to normal and his pulse rate slow. None of this would have affected him in years gone by. He could take the risk of death, the way most commuters took delays on the trains. It was business. It was occupational hazard. But now there was a physical cost. Each setback resulted in a major expenditure of energy. Each wound was serious. Each one a little closer to the heart.

By the time he reached the car, March was outside leaning against it.

'We need to dump this one and get another. DC police will have the number by now.'

Harden forced a grin. 'You give 'em too much credit. They'll still be digging the cars out of the snow and whining about their back pain. Switchboard'll be jammed 'cos they're all calling in sick. We'll stay with this one.'

March shrugged and climbed into the driver's seat. 'What's the news?'

'News is lousy.' Harden stared straight ahead through the windscreen. 'News is always lousy.'

Angelo hung up and looked round at the faces. They were all tired, hostile and frightened. He allowed himself an audible sigh. 'Harden's on his way.'

They looked at each other in disbelief. And then a torrent of relief seemed to surge over them as the faces started to grin and a cheer went up, and they clapped each other on the back.

'Jesus, man, Vic Harden's gonna be here. Now we'll kick some ass. Damn, that's the best thing I heard in years.' Woike pushed himself forward, rocking on the balls of his feet to an imagined rhythm. Angelo knew the guy had served with Harden in the Gulf. In his twenties he had been fit, mean and carefree. Now he was fit, mean and nervous. If he lost control, the others would lose it too. He was the key.

'Vic's gonna be here inside the hour.' Angelo smiled as best he could. 'That's what he's telling me. So let's get a welcome for him and clean up this place, OK, guys?'

He looked down at the kit that littered the floor – sleeping bags were piled in a corner, along with rations, candy wrappers and newspaper. He clapped his hands together. 'Let's get a little order back in here, OK?'

The effect was immediate. As if with one movement, the men began to clear and tidy, laughing and chattering to themselves, fired up in the knowledge that the old commanding officer was on his way. With Harden around, things had always gone fine.

They'd always gone in with him and he'd always got them out again. Sure, there'd been people who'd died, but it had always been *other* people. Harden was pure gold. Harden was the main man. Harden would pull them through and out the other side. That much Angelo could read on all their faces. And that's what he wanted them to think.

No use telling them Harden was dying.

Louis Piedmont had been home for less than an hour when his daughter Jane rang the bell. He was not pleased to see her. Since her marriage to Lovett, his affection for her had waned dramatically. The little phone chats and visits had all but ceased. So had the presents for birthdays and Christmas. Only the sight of his grandson cheered the old man, and as he lifted the little boy from her he felt something he had never felt for Jane. The love of a man for his heir. The bonding of two males from the same bloodline. A tie that spanned generations. It was enough to bring tears to his eyes. As he hugged the child to his chest, he could almost feel the joy bursting through him. His grandson was no more or less, he told himself, than the continuation of the Piedmont line. A tough, rugged, ruthless fighter. A boy who would carry the family standard, reject his dysfunctional, incompetent father, and bring credit to his grandfather.

Piedmont took the child into the kitchen and sat him in his high chair, grinning and gurgling and making grotesque clucking noises with his tongue. He stopped for a moment and turned back to Jane. 'To what do I owe the pleasure?'

She unbuttoned her coat and hung it on the back of a chair. 'We were passing.'

'On a day like this?' Piedmont loved a lie, wherever it came from. So much more interesting, he always maintained, than a truth.

'I wanted to come earlier, but I wasn't sure . . .'

'One never is, my dear.' Piedmont grinned with pleasure. The day was looking up. 'Coffee?'

'Of course.'

'Decaf, no sugar, if I remember?'

'You always remember, Father. Always.'

They stared at each other without affection. Piedmont placed a toy car in front of the child and grinned with pleasure as he picked it up and threw it on the floor.

'I came because I'm worried about Dick.'

'We're all worried about Dick.' Piedmont avoided looking at her. 'Personally, I've been worried about Dick for years. In fact, now more than ever.'

'I know you never liked him.'

'"Like" didn't come into it, my dear.' Piedmont smirked at the child. 'I could have managed without liking him. My problem has been the utter contempt with which I have viewed him and his actions. My lack of appreciation for his ill-mannered behaviour and his incompetence . . .' He picked up the car from the floor and gave it back to the little boy. 'But,' he raised his hands in mock supplication, 'if I can help in any small way, you have only to ask.'

'I'm asking now, Father.' Jane took a deep breath. 'I believe he's involved in some kind of shady dealing.'

Piedmont raised his eyes and looked at his daughter with an expression of ill-disguised concern. 'That's a very serious charge against a man who is Speaker of the House.'

'I know that.'

'But what on earth is your evidence?' Piedmont's voice had risen to something approaching a squeak.

'I've listened to some of his phone calls. I know it's bad, but he's been going out at all hours and I was worried there was . . .' She blushed. 'I was worried there might have been another woman.' She dabbed at her eyes with a handkerchief. 'There, now, I've said it.'

Piedmont was silent as he weighed his choices. Then he said, 'What's been the nature of these phone calls?'

'It's hard to know, really.' Jane pouted, then shut her eyes. 'He's been talking to Vince a lot – Vince Albright. Well, he's the head of security for a company Dick's involved in and they're both very worried about some kind of chemical leak.' She put away her handkerchief. 'Sounds pretty far-fetched, doesn't it, especially when you say it like that. But they seem to be talking in some kind of code and I don't really understand what they mean, half the time.'

'I'm sure it's nothing, my dear.' Piedmont handed her a coffee cup and went back to making faces at the child in the high chair.

But Jane hadn't finished. 'That's what I thought, too, but then I'm certain they were talking about getting rid of someone. Oh, I know I'm stupid sometimes and don't listen, but I'm sure this was what they meant.' She stopped and suddenly the child was quiet too. 'I'm scared, Father, if you want to know. I think Dick's up to something very bad indeed and I didn't know what to do, except come to you.'

'You did the right thing, my dear. Leave it with me. I'll start making a few inquiries.'

Jane smiled a weak, watery smile and dabbed again with the handkerchief. 'I knew you'd help. If not for my sake then at least for the baby's. You do love him, don't you, Father?'

'You know I do.' Piedmont luxuriated in the knowledge that he'd told the full truth: it hadn't happened for a very long time. 'You go home now, look after my grandchild and don't worry about a thing, OK?'

'Will you let me know what happens?'

'Of course I will. I'll phone you before the weekend. Don't worry, my dear.' He kissed her cheek. She couldn't help registering that it was like being kissed by a brown-paper bag. 'Nothing's going to happen.' He winked reassuringly. 'Everything'll be all right.'

When she'd gone Piedmont buzzed for Charlie Richards, who bounded up the stairs, his heart straining madly and his breath coming in short jerks. Piedmont made him stand by the kitchen door, like a guard dog, refused permission to enter his master's domain.

'Well, did you hear what she said?'

'Yes, sir, I heard it all.'

Piedmont poured himself another cup of coffee and stared out of the window. 'No harm must come to my grandson, is that understood? He means everything to me.' The old man sighed. 'Everything.'

'I'm sorry, sir, I don't understand.'

'My instructions are from the highest quarters of the land, Richards. They are to clean up this mess, destroy whatever has leaked out.' He paused. 'As well as those who know about it. Do I make myself clear?'

'Mr Piedmont,' Richards was suddenly flustered, confused, his right hand held out in front of him shaking, as if it no longer belonged to him, 'you know I've never questioned anything you've said but, if I understand you correctly, we're talking here about your – your daughter, sir. Jane. I . . .'

'Yes, Richards?'

'But your daughter, sir.'

'She knows what's been going on – you heard what she said, she's listened to the phone calls. Don't you understand what that means? I know the girl. She's obstinate, headstrong, won't ever let it go. She's my flesh and blood, damn her. I know what she's like . . .' The voice died away, as if cut by a knife. Blood had filled Piedmont's cheeks giving them an almost crimson hue.

For a moment Charlie Richards considered drawing his gun and shooting the old man in the head. A quick, painless act, snuffing out the life of this grotesque creature – and saving the world some considerable trouble. A defining moment, he told himself. *Do it, man. Bury the bastard. Preserve a few more lives and give him what he finally deserves.*

But no sooner had he thought it than the opportunity had already passed, the way it had so many times before. The fact was, he had done too much for Piedmont across the years. Too much that was bad and dirty and would get him a short and very sharp stab in an electric chair. The moment to break away had come and gone a lifetime ago.

As he looked up, Piedmont was watching him, scooping the thoughts out of his head and reading them, a smirk spreading across his face.

'You have the people you need, Richards?'

'Yes, sir.'

'You've got twenty-four hours. My estimate is that the group with the poison canisters will attempt to use them at the Gulf War ceremony in the Pentagon. The target will probably be my son-in-law, Mr Lovett.' His mouth turned down at the edges.

'We'll stop them, sir. Whatever needs to be done.'

'The hell you will.' Piedmont's scrawny hand reached out and beckoned Richards to move further into the kitchen. 'They are to succeed, you understand me? Succeed! They can have Lovett, if they want him, and all the others as well. Minimum security,' he grinned, showing a mouthful of almost perfect teeth, 'maximum effect.'

'But it'll be a disaster! Scores of people could get killed!'

'I doubt it. I know what kind of stuff they were working on. It was for close-range attack. Nerve agents that act over a small area – very little collateral damage.'

'You have to be –'

'Let me tell you, Charlie, the day after this story has been flashed all over the world, and all the politicians and commentators have wept like babies, the day after all that happens I will have orders for that nerve agent flooding in – yes, flooding in – from every part of the globe. Everyone will want it – governments, armies, security services . . . This is the best advertisement we could ever wish for.'

'And Lovett?'

'Lovett will not survive. His factory will close. The President will deny all knowledge of this renegade operation. And I . . .' he smiled again '. . . I will open the factory somewhere else, just to keep all our new clients happy.' He rose to his feet, signalling that the meeting was over. 'Trust me, Richards, tomorrow will be a good day for our country.'

# Chapter twenty-six

Julie March was taken in a car with shaded windows to a house in Chevy Chase, just across the District line in Maryland. The journey had left her feeling nauseous, too tired to sleep, too hungry to eat. And, when she thought about it, too fearful to resist.

She knew she'd become a classic case – and they had softened her up by the book. By turns they had shouted at her, appealed to her, then scared her into compliance, leading her from one restricted zone to another, allowing her the appearance of freedom but in reality providing only the few choices they had pre-determined.

Harries had ushered her to a room on the first floor, bare except for a dusty bed and some old magazines on a table, and shut the door behind her. She had waited half an hour before trying the handle. But it opened easily enough and proved nothing more than her own weakness and vulnerability. They hadn't locked the door because they hadn't needed to: there was nowhere to go and no one to help her.

Whatever he had done, Peter had stirred the beast that lies at the heart of every government the world over, and once it was awakened, threatened and insecure, it wouldn't rest until there was blood. She could see it so clearly that she wanted to open the windows and shout it to the neighbourhood. But she knew it wasn't in her. She had worked so long for that beast, worked alongside it, that its actions no longer seemed strange or even indefensible. The beast was the dishonest core that acknowledged no laws or restrictions, that coated itself in respectability and tradition, that would do whatever it took to protect itself and perpetuate its power. Quietly, and below the surface, it had reduced democratic institutions and even the Government itself to the role of a local council, picking up the garbage and sweeping the streets, making sure the trains ran on time, but taking no part in the deals that mattered. And now the beast was angry and vengeful – and somehow the poison had seeped out of its body and entered her own.

She sat on the bed and tried to imagine who had occupied the room before her. It was clear that the house had been designed as a temporary refuge for America's 'unmentionables' – the new defectors, the troublemakers who had to disappear – a nameless, anonymous little place that they couldn't even afford to have dusted regularly.

Or was that also an element in the grand psychological game – the 'mindfuck' as they called it at the Agency's headquarters? Putting people in a cheap, tatty little room to emphasise their insignificance, to rob them of their pride and dignity. The whole process designed to manipulate a person's brain without drugs, surgery, or outside implements – then tear it apart.

She had read the classified reports and she knew how they operated. In a while Harries would come back and take her on to the next stage. By then they would have assessed her 'condition'. Was she co-operative, compliant? Where did they need to apply extra pressure? How far could they go?

She didn't even realise she had fallen asleep, but she awoke, cold and disoriented, to find Harries shaking her by the shoulder.

'Things are moving fast. We need you now.'

She pulled herself up, leaning against the wall. For some reason her head felt heavier than it should have done. She was opening her eyes as wide as they'd go but hardly any light was coming through. How long had she been there? Was it even the same day? 'I'll be right there. Two minutes.'

But Harries stayed where he was. 'My instructions are to bring you downstairs now, Mrs March.'

'Two lousy minutes.' She could hear her voice, as if from a

long way away, rising in tone. 'Now, get out of here while I make myself presentable, OK?'

And then, without warning, he had gripped her arm, pulling her from the bed, with no shoes on, her blouse half out of her skirt, dragging her through the door and on to the landing where the cold made her shudder. 'Fuck you, Harries, fuck you –' she kept shouting, but it made no difference. His hand had tightened like a clamp on her arm and she was being propelled down the stairs, stumbling, catching an ankle, crying out in pain and confusion. And still her eyes wouldn't let in the light, still the world was a series of shapes and shadows without colour or definition.

Later, much later, she remembered being sat at a long table, aware of other people, but unable to see them. She remembered a blinding light from above, she remembered stretching her head as far back as her neck would allow, and some cool drops inserted into her eyes. And then her vision cleared and she could see the piece of paper in front of her. Even with her pupils dilated she could read it – did read it, haltingly at first and then fluently as they made her practise again and again.

She was talking to Peter. A message to him. That was it. A message telling him she needed to meet urgently. An address on Capitol Hill. Whatever he was doing he had to drop it and go there immediately. It was a grave emergency and she'd explain when he got there. Please go there, Peter. Please do it now. If you ever felt anything for me . . . anything at all . . . do as I ask.

She sat back in the chair and closed her eyes, somehow exhausted by the effort. Harries leaned forward and turned off the recorder. A technician appeared and removed the tape.

Harries looked at the others in the room. There were nods of approval. The recording was OK. They could transmit it to March's mobile phone and wait for him to arrive. It was like throwing out a rope and hauling him in.

# Chapter twenty-seven

Dick Lovett sat at his desk on Capitol Hill, still hunched in his overcoat. He had been due to see the President at midday, right after his regular Saturday radio address, but the man had cancelled. Damn him. Some lowly aide from the Executive Office had left a curt message without any offer to reschedule. What was the matter? Too much snow in the West Wing? Had the President suddenly found the charms of the First Lady irresistible? That'd be a first. Or was he chewing the fat with a couple of rich drug dealers, who just happened to be major contributors to the Party?

Of course, as Washington well knew, Clinton had turned the White House into nothing more than a shady coffee shop where some of the world's most wanted men could meet, chat and deal with total impunity. Now his successor, older, more tedious and infinitely less charismatic, was simply continuing the tradition. But why should he, Dick Lovett, be surprised? All the presidents were the same, puffed up, over-preened crocodiles, who smiled only when they were hungry.

Damn the bastard.

An aide knocked on the door and brought him coffee. Lovett took the cup and gestured impatiently for the man to leave. It was clear that time was running out on all fronts. Unless the canisters were recovered, together with Harden and March, they were all under threat. Harden would attempt to disrupt the Gulf War veterans' ceremony at the Pentagon the next day. No doubt about that. He'd stage some kind of outrage, possibly threaten the use of the nerve gas. Unless Albright made some progress over the next few hours, he'd have no choice but to cancel the event. He picked up the phone and asked for the chairman of the joint chiefs.

The call was answered after the second ring by a political aide.

'I'm sorry, sir. The general's out of town but he's flying back specially for the veterans' ceremony tomorrow afternoon.'

'I need to talk to him about that.'

'I'm sorry, sir, that's out of the question.'

'This could be important – very important.'

'Unless it's a national emergency, sir, with fifty inbound Russian missiles closing on Alaska, I can't raise him. Are we talking crisis, Mr Speaker? We would need to be absolutely certain of our facts here.'

Lovett slammed down the phone. Dammit, he was a fool to have made the call in the first place. After all, facts were the one thing he couldn't give them. Now or at any time in the future.

Peter March had been searching his pockets for money when he found the mobile phone. He couldn't remember putting it there, couldn't remember turning it off. He took it out, expecting the battery to be dead from the cold. But it came to life and rang almost immediately, signalling that a message was waiting.

Harden took a hand off the steering wheel and snatched the phone from him. 'Christ, man, they can trace you with these fucking things in seconds, don't you know that? The Israelis have been killing the Pals for years like this – they lock on to your wavelength and then fire a missile along the target beam. What's the matter with you?' He snapped the battery off the phone casing, but March was too quick for him, grabbing it back, causing the car to swerve.

In the old days, he thought, Harden would have killed him with a single punch from the right hand, but now he hadn't the strength.

'There's a message there, for Chrissake. I'll only use it a second. Could be important.'

'You're a fucking idiot! You'll get us both killed.'

March slammed the battery back into place. 'Somehow that

doesn't feel as bad as it once did. If anybody's going to save our necks, it's more likely to be me.'

He dialled the message centre and then it seemed as if the world had frozen and stopped in its tracks as Julie's voice came unmistakably down the line. It wasn't so much the words. They were bad enough. It was the tone, and the timbre of the voice. The robotic delivery. The lack of emotion. The sheer distance between the Julie he knew and the one talking to him now. Christ Jesus, what had they done to her? What the hell had gone on in the last twenty-four hours? Even as he sat there, it was as if someone was running an ice-cold blade up his spine.

Harden grabbed his arm. 'Turn the fucking thing off, OK?'

March pushed him away. He needed ten seconds to think. He knew Julie was reading what they'd given her, knew she had had no choice, knew she would never sell him to the wolves unless she had to. Or would she? All the arguments they'd had, the bitter fighting, the trench warfare of a bad marriage . . . but would she really do this?

And what would he do? Stupid question. A lot more than he would have done a day ago. A day ago Peter March had been just a journalist, just a hack who went after the stories, a scribbler, a story-teller, no more and no less . . . and now he was a killer too.

*I want you to take down the address, Peter, please go there immediately. Please, please, please . . .*

And as he heard it, the fear hit him like a blast from a blizzard, straight in the face, cold, shocking and quite impossible to withstand.

The address of Leah Killeen.

'Take the next right,' he told Harden.

'What the hell . . .?'

'There's someone who's in great danger. I don't know what's going on but we have to get her out of there.'

'No fucking way. We got ourselves a rendezvous. We got the nerve gas. Nothing else matters. Nothing. You hear me? Not you. Not me. And certainly not any fucking bimbos. They're all in danger. Ever met a bimbo who wasn't?'

March calmly picked up Harden's gun from the floor where

he'd left it, and pointed it straight at his chest. 'You can die now or wait till your time comes naturally. Up to you. But we're taking a diversion. Do it.'

Harden glanced at him and shook his head. 'You learn fast, fellah, I'll say that for you.'

Albright took the call on his radio, nodded at the empty street, then turned to his associate. 'That was Harries. March has picked up the call. If he bites, he'll be on his way here any moment. Harries and the team should arrive before him.'

'What do we do?'

Albright removed a Smith & Wesson .38 from his coat, checked the magazine and screwed on a silencer. 'We keep our eyes open. You go round the back of the house. I'll stay here. With luck nothing'll happen until Harries moves in. But if it does, take it nice and easy, minimum of fuss and no shooting to kill. We need these people, but we need 'em alive and we need 'em to talk. Got it?'

Thirty yards behind Albright's car, Charlie Richards sat upright in the Ford truck and shut down his radio. From a contact in the National Security Agency, he had acquired transcripts of Albright's telephone conversations. He knew all about Harries and Lovett. By this time he had also located Julie in the safe house in Maryland just beyond the District line.

'Amateurs,' he muttered to himself. 'Lousy goddam amateurs, who couldn't investigate, couldn't follow up, couldn't mount an operation to save their dicks on a windy day.'

Under Piedmont's instructions, and with a clutch of classified phone numbers, Richards had the back-up and the knowledge that Lovett and Albright had never possessed. Of course, those two had fondly believed they'd reached the top of the system. They thought they knew everyone there was to know, that they'd covered all bases and all exits. But now they'd served their purpose and there were interests in play beyond their wildest imaginings.

The interests of Louis Piedmont. The interests of the real powers that kept America running.

Unhurriedly, and with no particular enthusiasm, Richards climbed out of the truck he had broken into three hours before, and walked down to Albright's car, leaning his back against the side door at the same moment as the passenger was trying to open it.

This move served two functions: it threw the occupants of the car into a rage, making them careless, and it gave him the opportunity to remove the silenced Heckler & Koch from inside his jacket.

The last things Albright and his colleague were to see was the bulk of Charlie Richards turning towards them, the kindest black face they had ever seen, stamped with an expression of genuine caring and regret, and the movement of the pistol as it came up to their level and fired twice.

It was, thought Charlie, an exercise in problem-solving of a high order. Quick and relatively painless, it saved such a lot of time and effort in the courts, saved the taxpayer, saved the prisons, saved the endless inquiries and committees and, at the end of the day, achieved the kind of result that the rest of America could be pleased with. If it ever found out. Piedmont's kind of logic. But the man had a point.

He stepped away from the car. No need to check that the men were dead. Charlie Richards hadn't missed a shot in twenty years and wasn't about to pick up bad habits.

Looking both ways, he checked that the street was still empty, the snow in thick drifts, the morning bad-tempered and ugly. Then he got back in his car and drove to meet Harries. On his scanner he could hear March, dialling his second call on the mobile phone, and he wondered if he'd make it.

# Chapter twenty-eight

'Leah?'

'Peter? Oh, my God I – I thought – Peter, please – where are you?'

'Listen to me, Leah. Get out of the house now. You hear me? Is there a neighbour next door?'

'Yes, yes –'

'Go there now, and wait – just wait, OK? Don't leave with anyone and don't answer the door unless you know who it is. Got it?'

'There are two men in a car outside.'

'Go, Leah, go – now!'

She didn't wait to be asked again, just slammed down the phone, reached for her coat and ran. Out of the back door, not bothering to shut it, across the snow-covered yard and on to the Ransoms' terrace, sliding, slipping, with the fear tearing at her chest. Thank God they were there in the conservatory, eating breakfast, a haven of normality, two seventy-year-olds, not knowing about the madness outside, Jim Ransom in his dressing gown, his fork raised to the mouth, stopping in mid-air, then faltering as he sees her knocking at the window.

'Oh, God, thank you, thank you!' as he heaves at the frozen door, sliding it open, standing aside, watching her stumble in with the cold morning air swirling around his feet.

'What is it, my dear?' Mindy Ransom, small and wizened and very determined. 'Sit down, have some coffee. It's all right, dear, whatever it is.'

'Mrs Ransom, please lock your front door and all the windows.

Immediately. Upstairs and downstairs. Don't leave anything open.'

The old lady turns to her husband and there's no nonsense because she knows it's serious. 'Jim, do as she says.'

Jim, still shaking his head, thinking that all the women of the world have gone crazy . . .

'Now, Jim!'

And he waits no longer, looking at his wife, the little firebrand, so frail and old, with the frontier spirit still running through her veins, the true-grit American woman who would have circled the wagons in days gone by and shot all comers.

'Sit down, my dear.' She holds out her hands and gestures Leah to the breakfast table, with the bacon all crispy and the home fries and the sausage links, brown and hard the way Jim likes them. 'You can tell me about this, if you want, but in any case just have some coffee. Jim'll be back in a second and then we'll see what's to be done.'

She reaches out and pours coffee from the silver flask – and Leah can see that her hand is a steady as a marksman's. Mrs Ransom means business.

'Two men outside is bad news.' Harden pulled at the steering wheel and headed round the circle beside Union Station. 'There has to be more. These guys don't move in twos, not with an operation like this, five, six, seven – they're badly trained and incompetent, so they don't like taking chances.'

'We have to get her out of there.'

'We don't have the firepower for it.'

Harden pulled up on the east side of the Capitol, two blocks from Leah's house. The street was already moving. People were leaving their houses, some sweeping the sidewalks in front of them, others attacking the drifts that surrounded their cars. America was digging itself out of winter.

March put the gun in his pocket. 'I'm going to take a look.'

'You're crazy.' Harden made a face. 'You don't know what you're looking for – and if you find it you won't know what to do.'

'And you're not up to it.'

'Even in this state I'm faster than you are. Now give me the gun.'

March took just a moment to decide.

Charlie Richards could always put on a show when he wanted. That was the beauty of working for Piedmont. Washington was controlled by less than a dozen men and all of them were in the old man's pocket. That meant two important things: facilities were supplied and questions weren't asked. As Charlie had told himself on so many occasions, it was a licence to swing the town by the tail and snap it off when you felt like it.

So his call to the chief of the DC police department resulted in six police motorcyclists waiting at the bottom of Whitehaven Parkway when Harries's limo drifted in from Maryland.

Charlie could speak to the lead officer by radio so he knew exactly their location. All the rest had been agreed in advance. As the car came down the ramp, the motorcyclists pulled in front of it and gestured to the driver to stop.

The glass was shaded but a window was lowered. The lead officer leaned in, his face covered by helmet and goggles. 'You're to follow us, gentlemen. There's a diversion ahead. I'd advise you not to make any sudden movements. My orders are quite clear on that.'

Harries leaned forward, a black leather pass in his hand. 'D'you know what this is?'

'Yes, sir.'

'Then back off and get out of here.'

The officer drew his sidearm, a Colt .38 police special and poked it through the window. 'D'you know what this is, Mr Harries?' There was a moment of silence. 'Now, follow me, and let's clear up this matter once and for all.'

They led the car back along M Street, through Georgetown and on to Macarthur Boulevard, two riders at the sides, front and rear. After a mile and a half they turned right across the four lanes and up among the small clapboard houses, past the larger colonials and down the frozen gravel track into Battery Kemble Park. A dark, silent convoy, winding its way slowly into the clearing, the motorcycles manoeuvring gingerly over the hard-packed snow.

Charlie Richards watched from behind the trees, moving out only at the last moment when the cars and the bikes had halted.

He opened the door on Harries's side and gestured him to get out. 'Albright's dead. I want you to know that. The operation's over.'

'Who the fuck are you and by what authority are you here?'

Richards grinned. 'The President of the United States.'

'I need more than that.'

Richards's smile widened perceptibly. 'Well, I'll be happy to give you more than that. Maybe I'll just order my men to shoot you dead and everyone else in the car alongside you. That satisfy you?' Charlie pointed to the sky. 'See that?'

Harries looked up. A black helicopter was hovering about five hundred feet above the park.

'They've got you in their sights too.' Charlie smiled amiably. 'Want a demonstration?'

Harries went over to him until his face was about six inches away. It was one of the most unpleasant sights Charlie had seen for a long time.

'You better be very sure of your ground here, fellah, 'cos I've got every federal authority in the book – and then some.' Harries turned away, then changed his mind and raised an index finger at Charlie. 'Don't leave your address anywhere I can find it, buddy, OK? I might just feel like paying you a call some night.'

As sick as he was, Harden could still play the professional. He had pulled on a woollen cap from his pocket and changed his walk, rolling a little from side to side, as if heavier and bigger than he really was. Look at him and you'd imagine a deliveryman, a taxi-driver, someone whose legs had bowed from a lifetime spent sitting on the job.

He could marvel at the street, not at the men and women shovelling the snow but at the small things they hadn't seen. Like the car with the half-frosted windows he passed, a few yards from the house of Leah Killeen. Two tiny holes in the glass, already encrusted with ice. Two holes that shouted out at him through the morning chill, set every nerve and muscle in his body on edge, and said not a single thing to anyone else. Two little holes that showed someone had been there first.

He stopped beside the car, bending as if to tie his shoe, peered through the glass and saw the bodies slumped against the seats. Albright, hugging the steering wheel, his own gun half out of his pocket, the passenger lying, mouth open, against him.

The professional in him told him more than he wanted to know, told him who had died first, told him the distance from target to gun, told him the speed at which it had all happened. And even as he stared in the professional couldn't refrain from saluting the one who'd done it. Killer's code. Killer's company. One dispatcher to another. Damn good job, son, did the business. Made the hit.

In that moment something deep inside Harden knew he should worry about the man who'd done this. Because it was quick and clean, and as good as he'd ever been, even in the old days back in Special Forces.

Harden ran back to the car. Now it no longer mattered if anyone saw him. There's a point that you reach in any operation where the stealth is gone, and you can shout out to hell and back again because it's time to go for it, any way you can.

'Get to the house, man, move it, move it!'

March swung the steering wheel, edging out into the first of the morning snow tracks, slamming his right foot down, feeling the tyres lose grip, not caring about the skidding and lurching. Past a mail van. Past a black Lincoln, quiet and still like a hearse. And into the street. March counting the numbers out loud. And now there's an unspoken code between them as Harden hands him the gun and he pulls himself from the driver's seat, no longer seeing the rest of the world, his blood up and his feet already on the Ransoms' steps.

He can't remember the sequence, but he heard his own voice shouting Leah's name, saw faces and shapes beyond the door, heard a shriek from within, seconds passing in front of him like endless days . . .

And then she's standing in front of him, half crying, half laughing, the two elderly people behind her, her arms outstretched, but he knows he shouldn't wait.

'Leah, quick. No time. Quick, quick!' March pulling her down the steps, the coat in her hand and a mouthful of breakfast, a stain spreading across the white blouse, where she spilt the coffee as he pounded the door. And Harden is urging them on, revving the engine – a terrible din, shattering the learned and dignified calm of Capitol Hill.

March lifts her, throws her into the back seat, tumbling in after, half on top of her, forcing her down in case someone starts shooting – but the car is already at the end of the street, turning, skidding again, leaving the house behind, moving out into the city.

Five minutes, ten, and Harden is circulating, making sure there's no tail, checking, rechecking the driver's mirrors. Leah is motionless, apart from her breathing, her eyes shut, her face pressed against March's chest. When he looked down, all he could see was the mass of her sleek black hair, all he could feel was the warmth of her body. He knew it was what he wanted, what he had wanted very badly, and yet his senses were numb. The hours of fear had wrenched him from his old life and dropped him into another. In his mind, he could still see the old Peter March, open, friendly, affectionate, standing far away in a different place at a different time. But as he looked up into the driving mirror he caught a glimpse of the new version – that he had never seen before. A startled, frightened face, unshaven, scratched, but with a brand new pair of eyes. Cold, unfriendly, unfeeling eyes. Eyes that would shut doors instead of opening them. Eyes that could no longer cry. The eyes of a killer.

Leah lifted her face and looked at him. 'Tell me what's going on, Peter. Tell me we're safe.'

His voice had changed too. 'I'm sorry, 'he said, 'I can't do that.'

The man in the Ford wagon watched them go but made no move to follow. He simply noted the car's registration number then switched on his high-frequency radio and called Charlie Richards.

'They're on their way.'

'Thanks for telling me. Why don't you stick around, see what happens?'

The man stayed for nearly half an hour before two local kids found the holes in the car window, then looked inside and saw the bodies of Albright and his associate. It was extraordinary how quickly things happened. He heard the boys scream, saw them run for their house, saw adults appear in the doorway. An elderly figure in a dressing gown, running out on to the snow, peering into the car, then running back.

The man packed up his radio, stuck it in a suitcase and got out of the car. The vehicle had been stolen the day before so it would be unclever to get found inside it. He wandered across the street, as if on his way to work, and stood among the growing crowd of onlookers. He didn't have long to wait. Within two minutes there were police sirens, the box-like ambulance, the unmarked cars with the flashing lights and mayhem throughout the street. Everyone came out. Even old Jim Ransom, with a piece of bacon in one hand and a roll in the other.

'Jesus Christ, Mindy,' he was heard to yell, 'whole fuckin' neighbourhood's going up in smoke!'

A moment later a little old woman appeared on the steps beside him. 'Don't you talk that way to me, Jim Ransom. Now get on with your breakfast before I wash your mouth out with soap.'

# Chapter twenty-nine

Dick Lovett got up from his chair and sat down again. The tenth time in five minutes. His calculation. But, then, he always kept an eye on himself, always checked his reactions, always held himself in control.

So he knew he was losing it.

He picked up the phone and called in his aide. 'What's the matter with the heating? Gone crazy all of a sudden. What do they want us to do – sit here in grass skirts, for Chrissake?'

'I'll see if we can turn it down, sir.'

'Jesus, you get better service at a drive-in.'

The aide hurried towards the door.

'And get me Vince Albright. Guy was supposed to call.'

'Right away, sir.'

Ten minutes later the aide returned. 'I'm sorry, sir, Mr Albright did call. I didn't see the note where the secretary put it till now. She's left early because of the snow.'

'What did he say?'

'Said everything was fine, sir. Problem had gone away. He was just tying some loose ends and he'd get back in touch as soon as he'd cleared it all up.'

Lovett slammed his fist on the desk. 'Get rid of that telephonist. I don't want her back any more and make sure Albright's put straight through when he calls again, OK?'

'Yes, sir, I'm very sorry.'

'Sorry isn't good enough. You'll be gone as well if it happens again. Understand?'

Lovett sat for a while in the rich leather chair, staring towards the rows of old books, the paintings and photographs of rituals and ceremonies long gone. On the face of it the message from Albright was comforting. He'd get a good night's sleep, make sure he was fresh for the morning at the Pentagon. For the first time in such a long time. He closed his eyes and thought about all the years he'd known Vince. First in the army, then as a fixer – bit of security work, bit of harmless intimidation, a few troublemakers sorted out, a few discreet pay-offs. The not-so-public side of American politics. Trouble was that in all the time he'd known him Vince had never once left him a message. If he'd had news he said it face to face. If it was good news or bad news he came in person. Always. No exceptions. Vince worked to his own routine. Sneaky but predictable. You wound him up and he went round and round till the cycle was finished. Never varied.

Lovett got up again but he knew there was nowhere to go. The message was wrong and he didn't believe a word of it.

Across town Vic Harden had the same feeling. Now that it was past he could play back the tape all soldiers run in their mind. You don't think about it when the operation's in progress. You blank out everything except what you need to stay alive. Only much later, when the stillness comes to you, in the grey hours of night, can you see it all return. You can see the men dying in terrible slow motion, you can hear their screams, look into their eyes, follow them down the road to death, then hand them over. All in colour and three dimensions. Because all your senses record – and sooner or later they all play back.

He could picture the scene outside Leah's house. The two bodies in the car. Then running back to March, drawing up outside the neighbours.

*Too easy, man. Too fucking easy.*

He'd been prepared to shoot her out of there. He'd checked the roofs for snipers, the other parked cars. Nothing in sight.

*Too easy.*

He'd known the risks they were running. A damn-fool, do-or-die number that you only undertake when you're blind and screaming and there's no other way.

*Too easy.*

They could have picked him off – March too – if they'd wanted. Nothing would have been simpler.

And then, as his mind took him back along the rows of parked cars, he could see the Ford truck. Something about it that he hadn't had time to check. A face inside, a body, a trace of breath on the windscreen. A thousand little things could have triggered his brain, but you never know.

Fact was, someone had been watching from that truck. Someone had let it all happen. Whichever way you cut it, that was the only version that worked.

She couldn't help the tears. No longer out of fear or anxiety but tears for the powerlessness. Tears for Peter. Tears for the way she had sold him for her job and the state she believed she was serving.

Julie March had watched in silence as Harries had been turned back in the park. She had observed the oversized but irrepressibly amiable figure of Charlie Richards without in any way knowing who he was, yet fearful of a man with such obvious power. If he could tug on Harries's chain and send him back to his basket then he was a man with awesome influence. And that only confirmed the gravity of it all.

When they returned to the house, Harries had said nothing. But the anger was easy to read on his face. Jaw clenched tight. Eyes screwed into tiny burning holes. He had simply pushed her into the room and shut the door. An hour ago, two hours? She no longer had a watch, no longer had a handle on time.

In the mid-afternoon she opened the door and went out to the bathroom, curious about the silence and the draught coming from downstairs.

Unsure what to do, she tiptoed into the hall, expecting to hear voices, but she could see through the open doors that no one was there. She hurried to the kitchen, where the wind was blowing in through a window no one had bothered to close. On the cabinet was a McDonald's wrapper, a half-eaten sandwich, a handful of drink cartons and no other sign that life of any kind had visited.

Her hands started to shake and she was suddenly aware of the cold. Running back upstairs she lifted a blanket from the bed and wrapped it around her shoulders. It made no difference. The cold was inside her. The sense of isolation and loneliness. She was like a prisoner turned loose into a bigger prison with no one to help her and no haven to take her in.

Of course she had to get out. They could come back at any minute. They or someone else. Perhaps they had forgotten about her, perhaps there was no decision on her fate. Or did they realise that they could find her whenever they chose – and then do whatever they wanted?

For a long time she sat in the corner of the room, draped in her blanket, as the day darkened around her.

# Chapter thirty

'You worry me, Louis.'

'I do, Mr President?'

'Yes, Louis.' The President kicked off his shoes and stretched out his feet on the sofa. 'You tell me everything'll be just fine, and all I hear about tells me it isn't fine at all.'

'I don't understand, sir.'

'Don't you, Louis? Let me enlighten you. I get a very angry national security adviser standing in the middle of the Oval Office telling me there's a fucking insurrection underway, that his own people are getting turned back on the streets of Washington by armed thugs in uniform, that two related bodies have just turned up in what used to be – until a few days ago – a nice neighbourhood on Capitol Hill. More than that, Louis, the canisters have still not been located.' The President shot a dangerous look at Piedmont, but the voice was barely above a whisper. 'Forgive me for being obtuse, my friend, but how could any of that be classified as "fine"?'

'May I ask you something, sir?'

The President drew breath in an attempt to calm himself and nodded.

'How much are you aware of Iraqi arms purchases?'

'Where is this leading, Louis? Which purchases? When?'

'I'm talking about current purchases, sir. Baghdad's arms-procurement network is up and running. We've known that for a long time. Russians have been supplying some of the up-rated SS20 missiles, Turkey has helped with high-technology requirements.'

'I told the Turkish foreign minister – they're our allies, for Chrissake!'

'If you'll let me finish, some of the weapons they're receiving come from companies that we set up ourselves. Front companies. Shell companies. Whatever you want to call them. Some are headquartered in Eastern Europe, some in South Africa, but they channel US and other arms to Iraq.'

The President stood up. He looked slightly comical without his shoes but there was no trace of amusement on his face. 'You tell me this on the eve of the Gulf veterans' ceremony? If it ever came out, Louis . . .'

'We'd deny it.'

'And if anyone ever proved it, that would be the end of this administration. I could never go to the people. I simply couldn't survive.'

'Exactly.' Piedmont sat down opposite the sofa the President had just vacated. It was, he reflected later, a defining moment. To sit while the head of state stands is a mark of deep disrespect. And yet there had been a subtle but distinct change of roles. Piedmont was no longer the supplicant, waiting for an audience at the ruler's table. He had the power – and now the President knew it.

'Let's get one or two things straight.' Piedmont's mouth turned down at the edges. 'If this affair isn't capped, it'll be more than nerve gas that leaks out. This production line is linked in with the rest of our supplies to Iraq. Not only are we giving them conventional arms but the shipments of chemical and biological weapons have also resumed. Iraqi military officers, carrying Jordanian passports, are back in this country on training exercises, as we speak.'

'Jesus Christ Almighty, Louis, what have you done?'

'What have I done? What have I always done?' Piedmont's cheeks had turned bright red. 'I've spent my life trying to assure the stability and security of this country and its presidency. Do you realise that in five years' time, Iraq is likely to be the world's second largest arms buyer? Do you realise what we can sell them? Do you realise what this will do for our defence industries, for employment in this country, for our technology base, for the health and competitiveness of our industries?'

'The Iraqis have violated just about every human right in the book.'

'Tell it to your congressman, Mr President.'

'You overreach yourself, Louis.'

'And you are dangerously naïve for a man in this most sacred office.'

There was silence in the room as the grey daylight flickered through the blinds and the lunch-time traffic ground past in the snow. Piedmont reached for his coat and gloves. 'I told you that this matter would be settled – and it will be. What's more, there will be more bodies before we've finished. More bodies – and one or two in high places.'

'Are you threatening me, Louis?'

'On the contrary, sir. In order to safeguard the presidency and the security of this country, I'm prepared to make some of the biggest sacrifices of my life so don't talk to me about a couple of stiffs on Capitol Hill or some federal noses out of joint. This town needs straightening out, and we have to start acting like the greatest power in the world – instead of like some lapdog, jumping up to lick everyone's face. You can't do it, I can see that now. But I damn well will.'

# Chapter thirty-one

The men had fêted Harden when he arrived. But the greetings hadn't lasted long. March stood aside as they threw their arms around their former commander, then recoiled in horror and bewilderment as they looked into his face. In the last hours he had got used to the gaunt, grey complexion, to the lines of tiredness that spread outwards from Harden's eyes. But the men were seeing them for the first time. Lines that wouldn't simply go away after a good night's sleep. They were like a railtrack, leading inexorably to death. Harden had a few more stops to go along the route, but he was nearing his destination.

In solemn procession the men led them into a small storeroom, no more than ten feet square, and switched on the light. In the centre of the room were the two canisters Travis had stolen from the factory. Leah clung tightly to March's arm, then pulled him away into the corridor.

'I can't look at this. I can't take it all in.'

'Then don't.'

He tried a couple of doors before finding one that opened. It had once been a windowless office but was empty except for a sofa and some typists' chairs pushed against the wall. She watched him quizzically as he pulled her inside, then wedged the sofa against the door.

'What are you doing, Peter?'

'I need to talk to you. I need to tell you what's been going on. We have to make some pretty quick decisions.'

'I think I've guessed some of it. These guys have stolen the monster's toys and now he's getting angry and wants them back.'

'More than that, these were toys he isn't supposed to have. He can't let anyone find out he had them.'

'What are they going to do?'

'Present the canisters in public at the Gulf War vets' day tomorrow. Maximum shock, maximum impact. All the cameras will be at the Pentagon. For Chrissake, I was supposed to cover the thing myself.'

'Then you should get quite a story.'

'I think I've gone beyond stories, Leah.'

She beckoned him to sit next to her on the sofa and it was as if he was seeing her for the first time. The eyes drew him in. Dark, all-seeing eyes, shrouded by the black hair that curled across her face. They were eyes that could tempt and challenge. An entire language of their own, stared, not spoken. She unbuttoned her coat and he was immediately aware of her body. The tight white sweater over her breasts, the long neck, the olive skin. Suddenly there were colours and smells that seemed to engulf him as her arms reached for him, pulling him forward.

He knew what it was. The hours had wrenched away his inhibitions, leaving him with raw desires, and the urgency of fear. There was no time to woo, no time for the slow lovers' dance. His hands were already grasping beneath the sweater, his tongue exploring her mouth, crying out for the warmth and softness of her body. She moved against him with the same intensity, lifting her hands in the air, as he pulled the sweater over her head, unclipping her bra, smothering her nipples in kisses.

And then she turned away, kneeling on the sofa, her hips already writhing, urging him to pull down her sweat pants. As she looked behind he could read design and even impudence in her expression. The ultimate challenge. The licence to proceed.

His clothes had already fallen on the floor. And with his hands on her buttocks he found himself already inside her, expecting to meet resistance, but encountering only warmth and wetness – the body of Leah Killeen unwrapped and opened for him alone, a gift of breathtaking enormity.

For a few minutes he could forget the hours that had passed. He wanted to touch her and cherish her at the same time. He wanted the moment – and he wanted a lifetime. Over and over again he said her name, as if somehow he might possess her more fully. Her mind and her body. Her strength and her love.

He lay for a while, across her, his face pressed against her cheek, listening to her pulse and her breathing.

'Leah, I must talk to you – Leah –'

'What is it?'

'Please look at me. Here, sit up – I need to tell you this.'

'What, Peter?'

'I don't know what time we'll have. This thing is moving so fast and it's out of control. I never knew anything like this. It's outside my world, Leah – you have to understand this – outside everything I've ever known.'

'I hear you.'

'I was betrayed tonight. Julie left me, you have to know that, but she called me on the mobile phone. Told me to meet her at your house. It was a trap. Two bodies outside your window – and I was to be the next. I know that. Something happened and we got away with this but I'm certain she betrayed me. She hated my work – even hated me at the end.'

'I understand, Peter.'

'Leah . . .'

'Get some sleep, my love. We'll talk in a few hours. Please, there's nothing more you can do tonight. I'll do whatever has to be done. Count on it, my dear. Count on it.' The voice was soothing, hypnotic, and March was beyond tiredness. So he no longer saw the eyes of Leah Killeen, didn't see the anger that had begun to burn inside them. Didn't see the set of her jaw. Couldn't follow the tortuous route her mind had begun to take.

By the time he was asleep, she had it all worked out. The past was settled and the future had been mapped. There was just a fleeting moment – in between – that needed handling.

She turned out the light and sat in the darkness, waiting.

Angelo handed Harden a beer and sat back in the chair. 'You look lousy, Vic.'

'That supposed to make me feel better?'

Angelo grinned. 'We always told it like it was. That was the way we did things, remember? If we couldn't move a guy, we told him, "Hey, soldier, you're too bad to move, so we're gonna give you a choice. We leave you a pistol or we'll shoot you before we go." Basic options, Harden. You know that. Guess we never learned the nice way to say things.'

'Wanna know what I think?'

Angelo nodded.

'Last fucking thing I want is you with a bedside manner. You got about as much charm as a pig's dick on a bright summer's night.' He grinned. 'Just gimme the details about tomorrow and let's get on with it. I gotta tell you something – I'm ready to turn out the lights. Believe me, it's time.'

Angelo took out a notebook and leafed through the pages. The handwriting was abysmal. No one would ever be able to read it.

'OK, this is the plan. You, me and two of the others go in. The boys have called in a few favours so the security passes are cleared. No sweat. Just at the time when the Speaker's gonna make the presentation and the defence secretary's standing there, we step up smartly to the podium and we make our little announcement. Press releases are printed, details where the canisters were taken from, what's inside and what it can do. Fact after fact, man. Everything that the papers can check out. So that when we get taken away, the reporters got something to get their teeth into.' He took a beer bottle by the neck and swung it towards his mouth. 'Till then we guard the canisters. Mazer's on first watch. Woike does second.' He took a long gulp. 'What d'you think?'

'Don't ask me that, OK?' Harden shook his head. 'It sounds lousy. All these plans always sound lousy.' He shut his eyes. 'And most of them are.'

# Chapter thirty-two

It was close to four a.m. when she got up but her mind was fully awake. She hadn't even dozed. The anger was close at hand, almost tangible, the memories white hot in front of her eyes. Leah Killeen didn't have to ask herself why she'd do it. The past held all the answers.

On the floor beside her Peter March was asleep, half covered by his parka, fists clenched tight. No easy sleep. God only knew what had happened to him in the last few hours. There was a rawness, a new sharp edge, a coldness she had never seen before. In the past he would never have taken her the way he had – and maybe she would never have offered herself. But they had both seized the moment, hungry for warmth, all inhibition gone, knowing it wouldn't come again.

Of course, they had both been betrayed, he by Julie and she by Lovett, who had taken her all those years ago, dumped her and lied, so this day would be as much for Peter as for herself. A little justice, well away from the Washington courts and committees, from the chat-show capital, from the pompous empty words that sounded so good and achieved so little.

Today would see a rare and spectacular marriage of time and circumstance – the talk of the town for years to come.

Merv Woike had only ever had two things on his mind, not that he was ashamed of it. Besides, they weren't always the same two things, so the version he told in public depended on who was there to listen. But, boiled down to their essentials, he was interested in sex and cars. Soldiering paid the bills and killing even had its moments – depending on the target. But it was the smell of a woman and the burning of tyres on tarmac that got his blood moving.

For a while he had played with his gun, stripping it in the dark to its component parts, then snapping it back together again, though even that had palled. Once you could do it with your eyes closed you had nothing left to prove. He took out the throwing knife, balancing the stiletto point on his index finger, tossing it and catching it – soldiers' games with soldiers' toys. Time he grew up and got a real job. But he knew he never would.

After a while, he stood up and leaned against the wall. Beside him was the door to the storeroom and inside were the canisters. But he didn't want to think about that.

*Too much for me, man. Left all that shit behind years ago. Woike wants a quiet life now with the sun and the babes . . .*

He shut his eyes. Give it a couple of days and he'd get out of DC and go south to Florida, pick up a plane to Central America – Honduras, maybe, or Belize – somewhere where they were lazy and corrupt and the girls would show you a good time for dollars. There were still plenty of places like that. Less than there had been. But he'd find 'em. Yessir, he'd find 'em, OK.

He must have drifted off because he never heard her, never saw her, until she was right up close.

Harden had heard something, but when he tried to sit up his body wouldn't let him. There was no feeling in his arms and he began to shiver, lying on his back on the concrete floor, his muscles ignoring all commands. He tried to cry out, to wake Angelo, who was sleeping next to him, but no sound escaped. Perhaps, he thought, I'm already dead. Perhaps you have to wait a while before they come and take you away. To hell, of course. To Valhalla. So that you can relive your sins and atone.

He wasn't sure that atonement was his thing. He didn't know what to say or how to act. Should he call them all sir and confess to anything they wanted? Or should he tough it out and go in all guns blazing?

And then, for a brief moment, he knew it was madness, knew

he was losing it, knew he was falling from a mountain top with no ground to brake him. If he carried on, he felt sure he'd pass right through the world and come out the other side . . .

But even as the thought formed in his mind, he was unconscious.

'Woike.'

'Yes, ma'am. What the hell are you doing here?'

'I can't sleep.'

Woike smiled and shook his head. How many movies had he seen? How many lines had he heard? Had he ever imagined that one day in the middle of the night . . .? 'I don't believe this,' he muttered.

'I want a drink.'

He looked again. He had noticed her when she'd arrived with Harden and the Brit. They'd all noticed her. Miss Killeen. Leah. The name itself was sex. Sex in a tight white package, bursting to get out. Now here in front of him.

'What kind of drink?'

'Whisky.'

'We ain't got any.'

Even in the semi-darkness, he could see her smile. 'Find some.'

He was back within seconds. Mazer's bottle – he'd kill him when he found out – and a couple of paper cups.

*Jesus Christ, Woike, get a grip, man . . .*

She took a mouthful, swilled it around with her tongue, then swallowed it. 'Let's go inside.' She pointed to the room.

'No way. D'you know what's in there?'

'Sure.' She seemed to sway in front of him. 'Turns me on.'

'Yeah, right.' Woike's grin dried up. He didn't want to be taken for a sucker, didn't want some snot-nosed bimbo hanging him out to dry. Not after what he'd been through these last few days. Jesus, he'd give her something to take home to her fucking –

Leah turned away, moving off down the corridor, but he wasn't going to let that happen. He grabbed her hair, spun her round and pulled her mouth on to his, tasting the whisky even as she began to struggle. He wasn't going to stop now, not once she'd got him going, not once he could feel the hardening in his pants, her breasts in his hands and every sense inside him, yelling out to take her.

He pulled her to the ground – and suddenly the struggling had stopped. He looked down at her face, his rhythm broken, the chase somehow over. And while he tried to read her expression, he failed spectacularly to see the stiletto in her right hand, the one she had pulled from his belt, the one he had played with to while away the time.

He was still trying to work her out, when the anger in her eyes seemed to burst with a terrible flash, as the stiletto streaked out across his throat. There was a second when he felt nothing – and then he fell back, mesmerised by the shock and the speed of what had happened and the sight of the blade in her hand.

Even as he died, Merv Woike was trying to understand why she had done this, why she was looking through him with such rage – and so little compassion.

# Chapter thirty-three

Dick Lovett spent the night in the spare room, but he didn't sleep. It was, in fact, one of four spare rooms in the grand, gaunt house in Potomac, near Washington. As he lay there the television pictures flickered endlessly in front of him, and the telephone, to which his hand appeared cemented, stayed silent.

He had watched the news over and over again, but it left him with more questions than answers. Two bodies – no identification – had been found in a car on Capitol Hill. Not a rarity in Washington but rare when no one came forward to claim them, and no descriptions were released. Now, nearly twenty-four hours later, the victims were still nameless and Lovett's anxiety was growing fast.

In other circumstances he could have telephoned the DC police, kicked ass, called in some favours. But he didn't want his calls logged, didn't want any congressional investigators beating a path to his door long after the whole affair had ended. In Washington you had to cover your tracks, even as you made the journey. Everywhere you looked there were busybody committees, special prosecutors or snoops from the General Accounting Office, against whom no one was safe. Not unless they'd paid off the right people.

That was what Washington was *really* about. Finding the right people, then buying them.

By five he was dressed, fumbling for his cufflinks, finding, to his horror, that his hand was too unsteady to fasten them. He took a quick look into the master bedroom. Jane had stretched right across the giant king size, her nightdress apart, a bare thigh and buttock on show to anyone who cared to look.

Lovett didn't. He drew the cover across her, not as a gesture of affection but because the sight appalled him. He didn't love her. Didn't care for her. And if he had known it was the last time he would see her alive he would have done exactly the same.

Twenty minutes later he stood on the doorstep of Albright's house and waited for the man's wife to emerge. As she opened the door Lovett took in the pale, sweaty face, robbed of its sleep and its security, and he could smell the whisky on her breath.

'He left a message . . .' The voice was slurred, eyes all over the place.

'What message?'

'Said he'd see you later today at the Pentagon.'

'You heard his voice?'

'I guess so . . . was a pretty crackly line . . . one of those mobile things . . .'

'But it was him? You're sure?'

Her eyes opened wide, as if she hadn't quite understood the question, and her lips quivered from the cold. 'I gotta tell you, mister, these last days have been a little difficult for Vince and me. I ain't too sure of anything right now.'

Julie March pushed open the front door of the house on King Place and stood in the doorway listening. It didn't feel like home any more. It had stopped being home the day she had decided to leave Peter – back in another life, her other life, just a week ago. There didn't seem any point in running or hiding. Besides, where would she have gone? They had shown her their power and their reach, and there was nothing she could do to stop them.

Ironically, it was only Peter who could do that. Peter, the brave man she had thrown away because he had wanted to ask questions in a free society. And she hadn't liked that.

Worse, she had gone along with betraying him. Done what they'd asked. Recorded the message they'd sent him.

And in so doing she had forfeited her right to see him or hear from him ever again.

She went upstairs and lay between the sheets, hearing the snippets of old conversations, the laughter of days long past. She tried to remember how he'd looked at her the first time he'd said, 'I love you.' But the image had disappeared, wiped from her memory.

Even in the early hours of the morning the hotel staff were amazed at how well she looked, how composed, how sure. Not like the usual late arrivals, drunk and bleary-eyed and loud. Or the young secretaries with their bosses, giggling and blushing, or the ones in suits, who paid everything cash up front. Didn't want any credit-card receipts, no questions asked, no explanations to be given.

But Leah Killeen didn't fit that group. True, she didn't have much in the way of luggage, just a pair of small parcels in a carrier bag. But she looked, in the eyes of the night receptionist, 'classy', 'well-groomed', one of the Washington power set, in short, a lady of substance.

Upstairs, she undressed, went into the bathroom naked and stepped under the shower. By the time she came out, it was as if the rest of the night had never happened. She felt calm and determined. She felt that right was on her side. She slept well until the alarm woke her at eight thirty and she went downstairs for breakfast. In the dining room she acknowledged the greetings and the glances and chatted a little to the Filipino waitress who brought her coffee. But to anyone who knew her, she was changed. The eyes seemed locked and badly focused, strangely devoid of the humour and serenity that had marked her out among her peers. She saw only the mission in hand. The goal — and the means to achieve it.

After breakfast she took a packet to the reception desk, and asked them to post it. It lay there for almost an hour, until the bell-hop took it to the post office and brought back a receipt. No one thought about it until much later. By then it was far too late to get it back.

Charlie Richards stared over his coffee cup at Piedmont and

wondered for the hundredth time whether he ever slept. The man was fresh and shaved at any hour of the day or night. Now, standing in his kitchen with the early-morning sun bleaching the snow outside, he looked relaxed and composed, like an old monument freshly polished for the day ahead.

'All the passes were issued to the veterans?'

Richards nodded. 'They took the lot. My people are set to take over the security detail tomorrow but we couldn't get to the Secret Service in time. Anyway, it'll be good for the old boys to have a real fight. Been a while for most of them.'

'And once they've had their little demonstration and released the gas?'

'Our guys will dispose of them in the line of duty. They've had the antidote shots so they'll be OK. I envisage a short exchange of gunfire – none of the others will survive.'

Piedmont turned away and sat at the table. 'Don't kill them all, my friend. Never kill them all.'

'Why d'you say that?' Richards looked puzzled.

'Always leave some alive. That way we can follow any loose leads if we need to. No one talks much in a graveyard. Finish it at a later date – if we have to.'

'We've never done that before.'

'I have an odd feeling about this one.' Piedmont poured himself a cup of coffee but didn't drink it. 'It's different from the others.'

# Chapter thirty-four

March heard the shouting from a distance but decided to ignore it. Wasn't for him, wasn't in his life. Somewhere, some time, you had to take a decision what to filter out – and this was it. All he wanted was sleep. He wanted a warm morning and a sunny beach – and he wanted to go back to a time when he hadn't killed anyone and didn't know a man called Harden.

And then someone was pulling away his parka and the cold flooded on to his bare skin and his face was being slapped hard.

'Wake up, fucker, wake up.'

He crawled to his knees. Angelo dragged him upright, pulling his arm along the corridor, past the men standing silent and hostile against the walls. He stopped at the storeroom and March stood his ground, the anger rising fast in his throat. No fear. Just the sudden, intuitive realisation that he would have to fight again to survive.

'What's going on?' He shook himself free.

Angelo flung open the door, and March stared into the room, unable to make sense of the sight there. He could see the pool of blood, and the body that had released it; he could see scraps of paper and shards of glass; he could see the old chest that had housed the poison canisters, upturned and empty. But the images seemed to come at him isolated and unconnected. He should have been shocked by the sight, but he knew he wasn't. Some time, over the last twenty-four hours, death had lost its bite, its drama. He could gaze at a body, dispatched in violence, and feel no sadness, no horror or pity.

*You're cold*, he thought. *Your heart slipped out during the night and didn't come home. I don't know who you are, Mr March. You're a stranger, carrying my name.*

'I don't understand.' He stared blankly at the faces. 'What, in God's name, happened?'

Angelo came up close to him, his face just an inch from March's cheek. 'The bimbo you were with. Right? You came here with her, right? Some time in the middle of the night she walks in here, all lovey with Woike I guess, slits his stupid throat and takes the fucking canisters, right?' His head jerked back and his hand grabbed at March's throat. 'This is the woman you brought here, OK?' The voice was close to a scream. 'Now where the fuck d'you suppose she's gone?'

Angelo's hand never reached its destination: March caught it in mid-flight, and twisted it. The man cried out in pain.

'Hold it there.' His own voice surprised him. A sharper edge, more authority. 'I don't know what happened here last night – and nor do you. But if I was part of it, d'you think I'd be waiting around this morning to meet you people?' His eyes fixed on Angelo, as he released the man's arm. 'Where's Harden?'

'That's another lousy story. Harden's in a coma. Hasn't woken up. Mazer's done the medical course, doesn't know if he's gonna pull through. He's very weak. We gave him a shot to increase his pulse rate but it's not helping.' He shook his head. 'As of now, we don't have a mission. No canisters to produce. No Harden. Just a body.'

'Wait a moment.' March clenched his fists. 'Something she said to me last night . . .'

'What, for Chrissake?'

March shut his eyes. Outside on the street a burglar alarm had gone off, filling the air with its shrill warning. '"I'll do whatever needs doing," that's what she said, something like that. "Count on it. I'll do whatever has to be done."'

'Jesus, man . . .'

'I think she's gonna go for it by herself.'

Angelo took a step back, his face registering disbelief. 'You mean the Pentagon?'

'I think she intends to use the gas.' There was silence in the room as they stared at him. 'What I don't know is why.'

At exactly nine fifteen Jane Lovett left the house in Potomac and slid behind the wheel of her LeBaron coupé. The time was logged in a notebook because such things are done with thoroughness and precision. The client might want to know even the tiniest details – and, after all, the client was paying.

She had left the baby boy with Elizabeth Seton, nanny to the rich and famous of Washington, who had long since assured her relatives back in England that she wouldn't look after anyone whose father didn't have a title. And while Dick Lovett didn't have a drop of blue blood in his veins, or a 'Sir', 'Count' or 'Lord' in front of his name, he was at least Speaker of the House of Representatives, which in a 'young' country like America, *had* to count for something. So that was all right.

But today she woke with thoughts of moving on. After all, she preferred to be in a 'happy' household, and whatever else it was, this one wasn't that. Of course, all families had bad blood but at least they talked to each other, or threw things at each other or had some form of meaningful communication. But not here. Not in this empty palace, not in this neighbourhood where money trickled from the trees. It was all too sad for words.

She sighed deeply to herself and dressed the little boy in his warm winter coat with the dark blue leggings. Since the morning was fine, she had decided to take the young heir in a push-chair through the snow and try to get him to sing. Perhaps a lullaby or two, or a folk song – something to evoke the joys of nature and the glorious winter countryside.

Jane Lovett turned left out of the drive and headed for Interstate 95 – the Beltway into Washington. On her way she'd pick up some cleaning, buy some cookies at Mrs Field's and perhaps book a manicure. If all else failed, and she got depressed or anxious, there were always the store cards to help her through. She never spent excessively. Of course not. That would be uncouth. But a few hundred dollars, littered here and there, were wonderful for morale.

The highway exit was about three miles, reached along a winding road across open fields. In normal times, it would have taken her about five minutes but the snow had yet to be cleared so she was forced to go more slowly.

She saw the truck in her rear-view mirror when it was still a hundred yards away, and even then she knew it was going too fast. It was a giant articulated monster with burnished chrome, sitting high as a house, adorned by aeriels, horns and coloured stripes. The whole edifice had 'attitude' written all over it and Jane decided she'd pull over at the first opportunity.

About half a mile further, she sighed and slowed down. The road widened into four lanes and she eased the LeBaron over to the far right to let the truck pass.

For a second or two, she looked over to the passenger seat, searching for her powder compact, thinking she'd stop and check her face before she went into town. But when she looked back into the mirror, the sight made her scream in the grip of paralysing fear. The truck had pulled to within an arm's length of the back of her car and impact was a second away.

She knew in that single moment – knew with extraordinary clarity – that she had reached the end of her life, and that there was nothing to save her. Even then she waited what seemed like an age before the truck hit her, splintering the boot like a matchbox, slicing its way through the back seat and into her body, smashing, compressing and destroying, with truly industrial brutality.

Jane Lovett died in a pile of twisted metal, from which it became impossible to extract her body in any recognisable form. No truck had been sighted along that stretch of road at the time of the incident, and no witnesses ever came forward.

# Chapter thirty-five

Leah Killeen turned left out of the Four Seasons Hotel and made her way up M Street towards Wisconsin Avenue. A few of the boutiques were already open, but she passed two or three before she saw what she wanted in the window. Something elegant and colourful, not too young-looking, not a fashion statement.

After careful consideration, she chose a dark grey coat, a tailored jacket in navy and a matching skirt. Then she bought a hat with a veil, and approached the checkout. The lady behind the counter was old enough to be her mother. 'Oh dear,' she announced, 'I do hate it when people wear the veils. Is it a funeral, child? I'm so very sorry.' Leah smiled and snuffled a little, paid in cash and returned to the hotel. By nine a.m. she had completed her makeup and faced the mirror for a final assessment. She was pleased with what she saw: a face with its features clearly defined, eyes wide open and focused, her stance full of purpose. And so it should be. It was a day for settling old scores. A day to redress a serious wrong. A day when she would avenge some very old injustices. This was for her and for Peter. Nothing else mattered.

Leah opened her bag and touched a single canister, fashioned like a hair-spray. The metal felt smooth and cold. Satisfied, she snapped on the black plastic cap, left the hotel and covered six blocks on foot to the nearest metro. She could have taken a taxi, but she wanted the walk and the cold air to keep her sharp.

The men had put on their old Army uniforms and stood ready for Angelo to inspect them. Even March had been given a clean shirt and jacket. He couldn't help admiring the discipline. The men might have been old soldiers from a rag-bag unit, but they had thought of everything. Each was given his pass to attend the ceremony, the tickets obtained with a standard application. Each had fought in the Gulf War. Each had a right to be there.

And then, as they stood waiting to leave, a figure shambled into view, leaning against the doorway, barely able to stand. There was a quite audible gasp from the group, and then the shock seemed to diminish. Vic Harden had managed his pants and shoes, but his shirt hung out and his hair stood in spikes like a gorse bush. But it was the face that had changed. The life had gone out of it. So had the strength and the last vestiges of colour. Harden's body was shutting down and saying goodnight, even if he wasn't.

'I'm coming with you, guys.'

They had to strain to catch the words.

'What did you say?' Angelo moved closer and bent his ear close to Harden's mouth.

'I said I'm coming with you.'

After a moment or two, Mazer helped him dress, tied his tie, fastened his laces, brushed his hair. Then Harden grinned at March, who took his arm and led him out of the building into the frozen street at the head of a small procession.

They travelled in two cars. Several of the men were unarmed for the first time in their adult lives.

Charlie Richards had reached the Pentagon well ahead of time. He knew the place a lot better than most, knew the reinforced concrete bunkers, the secret conference rooms and the tunnels that led beneath the Potomac. At eight thirty a.m. he strode in Air Force uniform through the grand pillared entrance, accompanied by a ten-man team, dressed as military police. They were met by the head of the Pentagon's internal security department, Bill Myers, and taken to a holding room on the ground floor.

There, Richards produced a sealed envelope and handed it to Myers to open and read. It took him less than thirty seconds. 'Your documents are impeccable as ever, Charlie. I don't think the Angel Gabriel could ask for much more authority than that.'

He handed back the papers. 'I'm out of here. So are the men at the gate. You know what to do.'

Richards smiled and shook his hand. 'Won't be so painful, Bill. By the time you come back it'll all be cleaned up.'

'It's good to know you're on the side of the angels.' He turned away, then back as the afterthought struck him. 'Are you, Charlie? Are you with the angels?'

But by this time Charlie Richards was transferring a Colt .38 police special from his pocket to his waistband, and the question seemed academic.


Piedmont's house contained sixteen rooms but he only ever worked in the kitchen. He liked the closeness of everything, the warmth, the smells of food and spices and drinks. But he didn't like them today.

When the news came to him he had almost shed a tear. He had put a finger to his eyes to see if they were moist, but they weren't. He couldn't remember the last time they had been.

Strangely enough, he reflected, Jane was more of a presence in death than she had ever been in life. He recalled her as a child, how noisy she'd been, how frivolous, how unlike her mother. She had no dress sense, no grace or innocent appeal. Worse, she had always shunned him, spurned his kisses, refused his kindnesses and he had always been disappointed, wondering when that special bond would develop between father and daughter. But it never had.

Now, he decided, he almost missed her. Almost wished the whole thing had gone wrong and that she would flounce through the kitchen door, and he would make her coffee and everything would be all right.

But even as his heart threw up the scenario, his mind tossed it out. Ever since he could remember, life had been about the mission in hand. And she had been a threat. So why was he even questioning the thing?

Maybe, after all, he was getting tired of the killing.

# Chapter thirty-six

The Pentagon press room was so full that they had to clear out the chairs and insist on standing room only. By the time March went in, the network camera teams had already set up and were making their final adjustments.

His White House press pass had been sufficient to get him access but he didn't want to be recognised and pushed to the side of the room, avoiding the eyes of any fellow journalists.

'Hey, Peter.' Eliot Ray from CNN slapped him on the back. 'God, you look terrible. Wher've you been?'

'Skiing – bit of an accident. What are doing here?'

Ray made a face. 'Nobody cares about the Gulf War but we're doing a piece on the cut in veterans' benefit so this is good footage to run alongside it. That's why there are so many people here.'

But March was already looking round. No sign of Harden or Angelo, and yet they had been close behind him. Dammit – where the hell were they? They'd all made it through Security. Now they should have been searching for Leah, searching for the canisters. How the hell –? He began to shove his way angrily towards the door, but his way was suddenly barred by security men. In that moment the secretary for defence marched through the door, with Speaker Dick Lovett by his side.

'Would you men step this way, please?'

Angelo and his team turned in their tracks and stared back down the corridor into the unmistakable barrel of an MP5 pistol.

One soldier was holding it. Three more were resting their hands on their holsters.

'What's the problem, fellahs?'

The soldier's arm was outstretched and perfectly steady. 'No sudden movements, please, gentlemen.'

'I don't understand.'

'We didn't get the serial numbers from your invitations. If you'd all just come along with us for a moment, we can sort this out quite quickly.' The voice was as young as the face. But it was the gun that held the authority. Always the gun. Angelo stared at his men, then shrugged his shoulders. Far behind them he saw Vic Harden stop some way down the corridor, then turn around and reverse his steps. It was the figure of a frail old man, bent double in pain, barely recognisable from the night before.

Angelo put his hands in his pockets and said a short prayer – for all of them.

The defence secretary speaks first. A face covered by spectacles and moles. He had somehow missed the course on charisma and never caught up. But March isn't listening, his eyes scanning the audience, adjusting to the darkness. The veterans' families are in the first two rows, then the serving officers and the press, but it's all so normal. Another Washington event, spun for propaganda. An uncaring and devious administration, trying to appear benign . . .

And then he catches sight of the woman in a veil, a young boy beside her, a whole group of children, and a little way along come the wounded, men who've lost their legs and won only a wheelchair in return, their uniforms sewn up at the knee, heads held high, eyes fixed and unblinking.

*Wait a minute, what's this veil?*

He shifts position to get a better look. Just a woman in a veil. The only one in the room. But it doesn't add up. All the other veterans' families are there, but no veils. All those years since the war had ended. No one went into mourning for that long. Not even the most –

And then he knows. It isn't suspicion. Isn't even fear. Just a pure and simple fact, delivered free of charge to the brain – and beyond question. He knows it's Leah. Knows exactly what she'll do.

Across the room he can see her opening her handbag, a movement so practised and unhurried that he's unable to react.

A white handkerchief emerges, makes its way beneath the veil, returns to the bag. But she doesn't close it.

There are seconds in time but March can hear only his heartbeat.

With terrible slowness she removes a metallic canister, fashioned like a hairspray, same shape, same size, not a big object but round and compact and built, you'd feel sure, for the most normal of all things.

And March has the sense that he lived this moment thirty years before, watching in horror as his mother stood furious in the kitchen, holding his china pig, threatening that if he ever did what he'd done again she'd drop it on the floor and it would smash into a thousand pieces. And then he had watched in horror as it fell from her hand, had frozen the split second with his eyes, unable to reach out only to watch as the unthinkable turned real and the pig tumbled over and over, falling from far above him . . .

*Please, God . . .*

A prayer in silence.

The canister is still in her hand. No one's looking. No one senses the danger. She's left it out there for all to see and get accustomed to. And, as he watches, he can see her remove the black plastic cap . . .

'Leah, don't do it!' Faces turning now. 'Leah!' People murmuring. The secretary falters in his speech but carries on. And March knows it's too late, pushing through the crowd, yelling and gesturing – and yet, just for a moment, she turns. Just as the security men get ready to bring him down. He's tall enough to see her, the head held high and straight, some twenty feet away, her body poised to spring like a cat. 'Oh, God, *stop her*!' but it isn't going to happen. She's already throwing herself at the podium, the canister outstretched and pointing straight at Dick Lovett.

★　★　★

He could only hear the screaming, only see darkness, only feel pain. They didn't let him up until the room had been cleared, forced him to lie face down, his legs spreadeagled, the weight of three bodies crushing the breath out of him. And when they dragged him to his feet, he couldn't help gasping in shock at the sight of them – the faces invisible behind full chemical-warfare suits and masks. When they spoke, their voices came from tiny loudspeakers in their chest. Above them all an orange emergency light burned in the ceiling and there was the acrid smell of something he couldn't place.

He was taken to a room with high ceilings and bare walls and examined by a man in a white coat with a boil burning brightly on his chin, who claimed he was a doctor – but wouldn't answer questions, wouldn't say what had happened. For a while he peered into March's throat, listened to his chest, took his pulse and his blood pressure. When he had finished, his face showed no expression. Only the boil seemed angry and impatient. He wrote notes on a piece of paper, then stuffed it into his trouser pocket and left the room abruptly, locking it from the outside.

March didn't want to think. Didn't want the time or the silence. Didn't want to open the gates to the wave of questions and fears waiting outside.

When he shut his eyes, he tried to imagine a different scenario. What if he'd received Harden's letter and walked away? Forgotten about it? Cut it into pieces and burned it? Life would surely have gone on much the same. He would have written his stories and collected his pay cheque, and gone back home twice a year to his parents' cottage in Sussex – and told his mind that none of it had mattered.

Some time, somewhere, he'd have read of Harden's death – and thought nothing of it. Sources came and went. So did stories and fashions – and maybe his kind of investigative work was no longer much in vogue.

But he was a digger, a scavenger, a forager by nature. Always had been. Couldn't leave it alone. And sooner or later another Harden would have come along, with tales of unspeakable behaviour by another so-called civilised government, and he would have been back there in the middle of another intrigue, facing another letter, and another series of choices.

At some time, very early in your life, he thought, you get assigned to a particular star and you never stop following it – a few deviations, a few distractions, but your course is set. It doesn't matter who set it.

In the end he would have encountered the same people with other names and done the same kind of thing. The outcome was inevitable.

When the door opened again, it was a very different style of man who entered. His eau-de-Cologne came first, then his meaningless smile, then finally the uniform of an Army captain – and a dry piece of board, held outstretched for a handshake.

'I'm sorry about the doc,' said the smile. 'Doesn't speak much, does he?'

March nodded.

The Captain sat down and grimaced. 'We have a mess here, Mr March.' The smile seemed to duck behind a cloud.

'That's an understatement.'

'This is what I propose, in the first instance, and then we can get to filling in the details over time. Anyway, in order to get you out of meeting your colleagues from the press and having to answer questions – at least for now – you let us take you to a hotel for tonight and then we'll meet again in the morning.'

*Too friendly, fellah.* March can feel the tiny hairs rising on the back of his neck.

'I don't think so, thank you.'

'I don't understand.'

'It's a kind offer but no thanks.'

The smile tried coming back. 'I really think it's in your best interest, sir.'

'The answer's the same, Captain. Thank you but no.'

The man shrugged and stood up from the table. 'In that case, Mr March, you're free to go. We'll have to talk to you at some stage about what happened but we know pretty much most of the details. What happened tonight had been planned for some time. Of course, if we'd known earlier, the defence secretary –'

'What happened to him?'

'He's in a critical condition, in an isolation hospital. So is Speaker Dick Lovett. Lovett's worse off. They were attacked by a lady with a very poisonous substance – but I guess you knew that.' He shrugged again. 'By the way, sir, what you did back there was a very brave thing – and I want to thank you and apologise for the way you were handled. The security people had no choice but to consider you a suspect.'

March's mind had begun racing. 'I need to talk to that lady.'

'It would be highly irregular, sir.'

'Other lives may be at stake.'

'Please wait here.' The Captain got up and left the room. March stared at the ceiling. He had to see Leah. Had to find out. Had to look into her eyes and tell her . . .

But what would he tell her? How could she have done something like that? Who was she, after all?

In less than a minute the Captain was back. 'If you think you can help the investigation, then I'm authorised to allow you access to the lady. But only on that condition. And only for a few minutes.'

March nodded, obscuring his surprise. As they left the room, he turned to the officer, a single eyebrow raised. 'As a matter of fact, how come the chemical team was on the scene so quickly?'

'We were damn lucky, sir.' The eyes held him tight. 'The guys were conducting practice trials on the floor below. Normally, we don't have teams like that on standby.'

March nodded. It was only then that he knew it for certain: everything he'd been told was a lie.

Charlie Richards caught up with Harden just as he was about to go through Security. 'Excuse me, sir.'

The grey face turned and looked at him.

'Vic Harden?'

'Who cares?'

Charlie smiled. 'A hell of a lot of people used to care in this building, Major. You know that.'

'I think you got the wrong guy.' It was just a reflex. Harden himself was past caring.

Charlie offered his hand. 'Why don't we go get a cup of coffee and talk?'

'Long as you're paying.'

They went down two floors into the basement, Charlie leading as Harden shuffled behind. It was funny, thought Harden, when you really get to the end, there's no fear, no fuss, just take your ticket and go. All it is is a journey somewhere else.

Charlie took out a key and opened the door to a windowless office. Grey metal table, two chairs, a pot of coffee and two cups.

After he'd poured, he drew his chair close to Harden and stared straight into his face. 'You're dying, aren't you, Major?'

'Good of you to ask. But you can use your eyes.'

'I'm asking myself how long you've got, Vic – can I call you Vic? – I'm asking because there are people who don't want you around too long.'

'So what's new?'

'Tell me something . . .'

Harden smiled. 'Anything, darling.'

Richards smiled back. 'Tell me you're going to crawl away somewhere and die and not talk about anything you've seen or heard. Tell me that.'

Harden sighed and leaned back in the chair. 'I can't do that.' He shook his head. 'And you know something? Who the hell are you to tell me what to say or not say?'

'Doesn't matter who I am, Vic. I'm a soldier one day, messenger the next. Priest one day, sinner the next. I'm whatever you want me to be.'

'But on contract to the faceless few, huh?'

Charlie grinned again.

'Oh, I've met a few of your people over the years.' Harden winked. 'One or two of them I laid gently into their graves.'

'That's nice.'

'Well, sometimes these things have to be done.'

'I hear you perfectly.' Charlie put his hand in his jacket pocket, drew out a small revolver and screwed on the silencer. It was such

226

an ordinary, matter-of-fact gesture that he might as well have been lighting a cigarette. Neither man seemed to think it worth comment. After all, it was simply the kind of thing two guys get up to when they're having a little chat. Nothing special. Nothing remotely out of line.

Charlie put the gun on the table between them. 'Tell me I don't need to do this, Vic, and we'll both walk away, and tomorrow or the next day or the day after I'll go light a candle for you in the cathedral and read the notices in the *Washington Post*.'

Harden laughed. 'Fuck you, man. Fuck you to hell.'

# Chapter thirty-seven

When they let him into the cell she was curled up on the mattress. Place was wired, he knew that, but at this point, it made no difference. He had to see her face to face. Nothing else mattered.

He shook her arm, aware immediately that it was the old Leah who opened her eyes. Soft dark eyes that he had loved for a single hour, on a single night.

'Peter. How did you get here?'

'Doesn't matter. I had to see you . . . had to talk to you.'

She propped herself up on her elbows. 'I'm so sorry, my dear.'

'Leah, why did you do this? Why?' And he could feel the control slipping away, the hours of panic and fear wearing down his defences, the pain almost tangible before his eyes. I must have loved you, he thought. These last weeks and months, even as his marriage was failing, he had felt her filling his thoughts, infusing them with life and hope. Now it was gone. 'You have to tell me, you owe me that. I've been all the way to hell . . . I have to know.'

And as she stretches out her hand to him he can see she's calm. Whatever had driven her to kill at the safe-house and attack at the Pentagon has gone, as if it never existed. For a few hours she had stepped outside her normal world and now she was back again. The madness was over. The dragons slain. Leah Killeen had found peace.

He recalled his father telling him about the calmness of the murderers he had defended in court, and now, years later, the memory was like the cold blade of a dagger sliding down his spine. 'They were some of the nicest people you could hope to meet,' the old man had said. 'They'd just killed the one person in the world they couldn't stand so, after that, everything was fine. They were pleasant, plausible and back to their happy old selves. Quite oblivious of the consequences.'

And so it was with Leah.

He took her hand. 'Talk to me. Please, God. Talk to me, Leah.'

'I need to sleep. I'm ill, my dear. I've been ill for a long time. Only now I'm beginning to feel it.'

'But why the Pentagon? Why you?'

Her eyes were closing. 'It wasn't the Pentagon. It was Lovett. Lovett and what he did to me. Years ago now, my dear. And the rest . . .' She yawned. 'The rest was for you. Just for you.'

'How do you mean? What rest? Leah!'

But she had already fallen back on to the bed – and now the eyes were tight shut. He knew she would say no more. Perhaps it was the shock or the fatigue, but she had fallen suddenly into a deep sleep – halfway, he guessed, between slumber and coma.

As they locked the cell door behind him, he couldn't help the tears begin to fall, tears for what could have been – and never would be.

The officer in plain clothes drove him to the Marryat in Crystal City. The night was clear and freezing and the snow rock hard underfoot. The clearers had been out in force during the day: the traffic was flowing again. Back on show was the American pioneer spirit. Whatever the climate threw at them, they'd handle it in the end.

He had suggested going home, but the officer hadn't recommended it. 'I think you'll find your wife is back in the house, sir – you may not want to . . . Of course, it's not a matter for us.'

March had been too tired to argue. For now they were giving him some space. No doubt they'd move in closer when they felt like it. But his first duty was to tell the story, get the facts and get them out – the old phrase tripping off the tongue.

And then he stopped for a moment – and he didn't like the taste in his mouth.

The story was one thing but he had killed a man himself – shot him at a distance of three feet, seen the blood gush forth from his forehead – and that was something else. That was a life-changing moment.

Was he going to write his confession and go to jail for what he'd done? Was he about to construct an elaborate funeral pyre and then climb on top of it himself? No wonder they'd let him go away to think about it. And what if he didn't go public? Was he destined to slink shamefully around Washington, terrified that somebody would leak the story one day and expose him? In all conscience could he simply forget about what he'd done and lie low?

Christ Almighty, he was a murderer not a journalist.

*Wake up to the new world, Peter March. The other one's gone for good.*

He awoke with the sun streaming in through the blinds – and the sure and shocking knowledge of what Leah Killeen had told him. And done. For a split second he could see her sitting in front of him at the end of the bed.

'The rest was for you, just for you.'

Bolt upright, he dialled his home number – but the line was disconnected.

*Oh, God, oh, God, oh, God. Julie, get out of there. For God's sake, get out of the house.*

He didn't wait to dress, simply pulled on shirt and trousers and ran down four flights of stairs.

Across the foyer yelling for a taxi. A bearded madman, rampaging in a hotel. Someone shouted at him to stop. A young receptionist called the police.

But March was already in the cab, urging it down the street, through the snow and slush, across Key Bridge.

Please hurry.

*I know what she did.*

*Please, God . . . no.*

*When she opened the handbag there was only one canister.*

*One more missing.*

*I know what she did with it.*

Along Macarthur Boulevard, parallel to the river. Past the frozen reservoir, the little cinema and the Safeway supermarket.

*Please, God . . .*

Right here, man.

Left up the hill.

But the taxi is old and the tyres are worn and the beast can't make it up the icy slope.

So he's out now, shirt flailing behind him, shoes half tied, falling, staggering, falling again, his heart screaming pain, legs driving forward, eyes seeing nothing but the little house, half buried in snow.

Her car's in the drive. Door's locked. Curtains pulled.

*Thank Christ, she's out.*

And he's banging on the door and shouting, knowing that it isn't true, knowing that she always pulled the curtains first thing, always let in the light, loved the light and the sunshine and the fresh morning air . . .

On the third charge the door splinters inwards, the frame shattered, and he stands in the tiny hallway, unable to take it in. It's as if the world is sending signals but the brain has stopped receiving. When the life you have known is so brutally inverted the pictures make no sense and cannot be comprehended. When your ordered little house is wrecked and shabby, when there is water overflowing the bathroom, surging down into the den, and when the woman you married lies motionless on the floor, her eyes wide open with fear and her heart stopped dead, there is nothing to recognise, nothing to hold on to, no piece of the old world to connect to the new.

For now, he kneels calmly beside her, lifting her head, knowing that she's gone, the pain seeping slowly into his mind.

On the floor is the package, addressed by Leah Killeen, and the little chemical pods, like tea-bags, open where she would have torn them, allowing the poison to invade her system.

Something macabre about a woman doing that to another. Though he doesn't know why.

Maybe it was ten minutes, maybe fifteen before the neighbours found him, another thirty before the sirens could be heard, the police cars thrashing about on the hill, the ambulance, jerking and gurgling through the snow. And all the people now out of their houses, coats over their pyjamas, orange juice in their hands, for that old American ritual of watching the blood.

He'd once written about their fascination with death. 'They all think it's optional,' he'd said. 'They all believe in their heart of hearts that no one has to go if they don't want to. They refuse to accept it's a matter of timing. That's why they watch with such total surprise and disbelief when someone they know makes the journey.'

In the end, when they've taken her away, Peter March gets up and walks out of the house. He's answered their questions, he's refused their help. He'll come in and make any statement, tell any story, once he's got his thoughts together, rung his parents, been supported by his friends. And they look at him, as if he, too, is from another world. Surely he should be screaming and yelling. Surely he should be on a stretcher. Surely he should be drugged to the eyeballs and down again, counselled, sedated and packaged as yet another casualty to be cared for – and sent a bill.

By this time his old faithful taxi has limped up the road and slithered down to the house. And he tells the driver, quite calmly, to take him to the airport and get him on the morning flight to London.

'Mr President.'

'Ah, Louis. Come in. You look tired. A little pale.'

'Perhaps I'm getting a cold. Weather's terrible.'

They sat in silence for a moment at the coffee table before the President leaned forward. 'You saw the broadcast, I trust?'

Piedmont nodded. 'I thought you looked very concerned and sincere . . . What were the words? "A most dreadful tragedy at the Pentagon . . . two of my closest friends, both with a lifetime in public service . . . chemical nightmare become reality . . . need for tighter controls . . . full investigation . . ." I think you covered all the bases.'

'You're too kind, Louis.'

Piedmont paused to allow time for effect. 'I might add that, despite the tragic nature of the circumstances, certain of our friends were highly impressed with the demonstration.'

'Which friends?'

'Does it matter?'

The President stared up at the ceiling. 'Apparently it doesn't – until the press finds out about it. I trust these friends have brought along their credit cards and are in a mood to spend.' The head turned down to the desk, as if the President were searching for some papers. 'By the way, Louis, people are telling me the death rate has gone up pretty dramatically around town in recent days.'

'Always happens in cold weather, I'm afraid.'

'That so?'

'It was necessary to wash up some very dirty dishes.'

'And that is what you've done, my friend? All washed and dried? We can't have this cold snap lasting indefinitely.'

'As you know, Mr President, I like to leave some of my cases open – but we can foreclose on them at any time, if it should prove necessary. I prefer to leave certain options open.'

'I quite understand, Louis. There's really no need to explain.'

The President sat in his chair long after Piedmont had left, his mind racing back to old snapshots and other conversations. Sometimes it was hard to remember what was secret and what was already in the public domain. Had he heard such things or merely dreamed them? Were they facts or imaginings?

At six he flipped on the Channel Four local news and stared at the screen without blinking. The unidentified woman who had staged the Pentagon attack had been on her way to court in Arlington to be arraigned – but she had never made it. In what the Virginia gas company described as a freak million-to-one tragedy, the prison truck had been blown up by an exploding gas main. No one had survived. Not the woman, the guards or any of the others in the truck, believed to have been accomplices. Police and civil engineers were investigating. There was talk of criminal negligence. The inquiry was expected to be a long one.

233

When the bulletin had finished, he got up and shivered as the draught seemed to catch him from an open window.

It was colder than he'd realised.

# Chapter thirty-eight

The London plane was delayed for more than an hour, sitting, battered by winds, on Washington's Dulles airport runway, while the pilot blamed a freak storm over the Chesapeake Bay. March had hoped to get two seats to himself and was annoyed to hear that the plane was full. Just before they left the gate an elderly man sank down next to him, coughing and blowing his nose, apologising profusely for the disturbance.

He was expensively dressed. The suit was of the finest merino wool, the tie by Donna Karan, cufflinks courtesy of Georg Jensen. Someone had shopped for him, and done it with care. Not the usual passenger in economy. More at home on a corporate jet or in the pampered confines of first class. But perhaps this was the only seat he could get.

As they took off, March could feel the tiredness pressing down on him, forcing his eyelids shut. His mind was refusing to return home – there was a vacancy, an emptiness about everything he saw, everything he heard. Some vital part of the set had disconnected: there were flashes from the past, like lightning in a darkened sky. But no coherent picture. He was suspended between isolated moments that seemed to have no connection. There was Julie and Leah, Harden, Billy, a jumble of faces and sounds that came in and out of the darkness. There was a gun and a crowd of people. There was a woman he loved, curled up in a prison cell. There was a run through the snow, to a house half buried. A siren and then a plane to board. Deep gaps, deep pain to fill them.

Sleep came suddenly, like an anaesthetic pumped into his arm.

He awoke with no sense that time had passed. And yet, looking at his watch, nearly four hours had gone by, wrenched out of his life, on a plane across the Atlantic. Darkness had been replaced by a grey, discordant dawn.

Beside him, the old man appeared to be dozing – and for a moment March imagined the words had been spoken by someone else.

'You seem very tired, my young friend, but then, that's not surprising.' The eyes were still closed. 'You've been busy this last day or so.'

March felt the coldness in the plane. It was the same feeling he'd had that night in Lost River, when the man had come up silently behind him, a jolt of terror, now familiar, almost expected.

'Who are you?'

'Does it matter?'

'Probably not.'

'Then think of me as a kind of guardian.' The man opened his eyes and March could see they were clear and dry. 'You and I have a close relationship, even though you don't know it.'

'How's that?'

'We protect each other, Peter. You protect me and I protect you. What could be closer than that?'

March bit hard into his lower lip. 'I don't believe you people . . .'

'Yes, you do. You believe it because you've seen it. And that puts you in a unique position. Let me make it even clearer. The uniqueness of your position is that you are still alive – not an insignificant achievement after all the things that have happened.'

March turned in his seat and faced the man. 'Do you have any idea what I do?'

'You're a reporter, Peter. And a very good one. But people change jobs. Why, I've even known reporters go into politics and –'

'I'm going to London to write a story.'

'Of course you are.' The old man tapped his arm affectionately. 'I shall look forward to reading it.'

'Why did you come here? Why did you get on this plane?'

'I wanted to meet you. And also, as I said to someone in Washington yesterday . . .' He sighed a little. 'Maybe I'm getting tired of what I do.'

They didn't speak again. On landing, the old man simply got up and walked away. March caught a glimpse of him, standing in line at Immigration. But they didn't look at each other. No sign passed between them.

# Chapter thirty-nine

'Bloody hard to get a table here, Peter. But we managed. Sorry it's in the bar, old chap. But if you will turn up unannounced . . .'

March stared round the the restaurant, recalling some of the familiar media faces. A few stared back. He opened his mouth, but the editor, Max Stewart, had got up to talk to someone else.

'Two thousand words, Harry, OK? Not the usual six. We'll only have to sub the bloody thing down.' He sat down again and turned to March. 'Sorry about that – old tosser Harry Dillon, you probably never met him, writes crap, but it's quite engaging crap.' He shrugged. 'Anyway, you must be starving. Drink?'

They didn't speak until the gin arrived.

'Cheers, Peter.'

'Max.' March took a sip and put the glass down.

The editor sat back and examined him thoughtfully. 'You feeling better, old chap?'

'What d'you mean?'

'We got the fax you sent about being sick – flu, wasn't it? Lousy time to be ill with all that stuff going on at the Pentagon.'

March shivered. Same feeling from the plane, from the forest in Virginia. 'What fax? I never sent a fax.'

'Well, that's bloody odd. It said you were sick and in bed with a high temperature and the next thing you're on the phone saying you're in London and need to talk.' The chin jutted forward. 'Happy to see you, of course, as ever – but a bit puzzled, mm?'

'Julie's dead, Max. Died yesterday at home.'

Stewart's face seemed to fall apart, as if the bolts that held it in place had been pulled. 'My dear chap, I'm so very sorry, I had no idea . . . God that's awful.' And his face went a deep red and the hands gesticulated with embarrassment and suddenly he was acting like a schoolboy and saying schoolboy things, like 'rotten luck' and 'too awful for words'.

March held up a hand to stop him. 'I can't begin to tell you what's been happening this last day or two. But it's the most unbelievable thing of my life. The story –'

'Look, bugger the story, Peter. It's you I'm concerned about. And Julie. I can't tell you how sorry I am. Is there anything we can do, anything? I'm so bloody flabbergasted I don't know what to say. I mean, how did it happen?'

'She was poisoned.'

'I don't – I can't believe it.'

March took another sip of the gin. 'I have to get out of here for a few days.'

'Yes, anything – goes without saying. Take as long –'

'I'm going to get my thoughts together and write you the story of what's been happening. The most extraordinary story I've ever been involved in.'

'Peter, I don't care about the story.'

March slammed the drink down. The crack of glass was unmistakable. Stewart's tumbler hit the table on its side, rolled off and splintered on the floor. Everyone around them stopped talking.

And he knew he'd lost it. But somehow it didn't matter any more. When you have something to do, you do it. Doesn't matter about glass or hurt feelings. Not when there are bodies all around America – and you've helped dispatch them. Makes ordering lunch a little trivial, he thought. Shall I have the rack of lamb – or go out and shoot someone? Those were the choices – and, Christ only knew, he'd made his.

He stood up. Stewart was towelling his knees with the napkin, looking about five years old and muttering soothing noises. 'What I meant to say was – look – the story can wait. You've got to have some time to yourself. Sort things out. You're upset. Only natural. Course it is.'

'I'm sorry, Max. I'd better pass on lunch.'

'My dear fellow. Quite understand. Bloody tactless of me.'

They stumbled out into the street, Stewart still dabbing at his trousers. A taxi pulled up beside them and he opened the door with one hand and took March's arm with the other. 'Don't worry, old son. Write the story in your own time and we'll print it the moment it's finished. You're our star, you know that. Open access to the pages. Anything you want to say. OK?'

'Thanks, Max.'

'For nothing. Give me a call when you're ready and we'll do lunch properly, OK? And, Peter . . .' the voice trailed away theatrically '. . . awfully sorry about Julie. Look after yourself, mate. God bless.'

He slammed the door and watched as the taxi nosed its way into the traffic. 'Bloody bollocks,' he muttered to himself. 'Fellah's gone completely barmy.'

March caught a train to see his parents in Sussex, but he didn't stay with them. He booked himself into a guest-house in Brighton, full of silent Turkish students learning English, and noisy Italian girls slamming doors and studying sex – and he began to think about what he'd write. But he couldn't think for long. The first night he fell asleep at around seven in the evening and didn't wake up till midday. As he arrived in the hall, a burly American, in baseball cap and with a totally irrepressible smile, was checking in.

He turned conspiratorially to March. 'What's the place like?'

'You like noise?'

The man grinned. 'I grew up with eleven other kids – you think I notice noise?' He held out his hand. 'By the way I'm Charlie Richards.'

March smiled. 'Have a good stay, Charlie.'

'Oh, I will.' Charlie's grin widened. 'I always do.'

Two days later, Max Stewart received two visitors at *The Times*. Josh Stevens, the deputy editor, came first, bringing his long face with him and his own particular brand of world weariness that made people tired just to look at him.

'There's an American to see you.'

'Haven't time,' said Stewart. 'Tell him to piss off. Better still, you deal with him.'

'Tried that, knowing how much you like our brethren from overseas.'

'Who is he?'

'White House aide.'

'Bollocks! They don't just turn up like that.'

'This one has. Checked his identity. Embassy confirms he's who he says he is.'

'What's he want?'

'Says it's just a chat.'

'Well, tell him to come back this evening. I've got a bloody paper to put out.'

'He's in the outer office.'

'Christ!' Stewart put his head in his hands. 'Give him ten minutes, then come and tell me there's an emergency, OK?'

Stevens nodded, and thirty seconds later ushered in a man who walked like a forty-year-old, but with a face that said seventy and eyes that said a hundred.

'Louis Piedmont, Mr Stewart. Good of you to see me.'

Stewart threw a meaningful glance at his colleague and held out his hand to the American. 'Pleasure, Louis. Now what can I do to help?'

When Josh Stevens returned ten minutes later, the door was locked. He tried the intercom, but all calls had been barred. In desperation he went out into the atrium and peered through the blinds: the two men were talking. At least Piedmont was talking and Stewart was listening. He gave up and left them to it.

It turned out to be a busy afternoon. Just before five thirty an eight-thousand-word story arrived by fax from Peter March. He'd intended to read it later but he scanned the first paragraph and then, as so rarely happens in journalism, he couldn't put it down.

He arrived at the editorial meeting in a high stage of excitement.

'Max, I've got to show you this piece March has just sent in.

It's bloody amazing stuff. We need to clear the whole lot off the decks and start again.'

'Just leave it with me, OK?' Stewart held up a hand. 'We'll talk after the meeting. I don't want to get into all that now.'

'I'm sorry, Max, this is something incredible. I've just read it straight through.'

Stewart glowered from the head of the table. 'I said, we'll look at it in a minute, Josh, OK? English suddenly a bit of a problem for you?'

When everyone had left, Stewart shut the door and turned to his deputy. 'Give me the stuff from March.'

'Listen, this is about the best, most staggering piece of journalism I've read in thirty years. It's got prizes written all over it.'

'Forget it, Josh.'

'You're kidding me. You haven't even read it.'

'I don't need to.'

'Then you're a fucking idiot and I resign.' Stevens got to his feet. 'You'll never read a better piece. So why not close down the bloody paper now and have done with it?'

'Josh, wait a minute. Let me explain.'

Stevens halted, half-way between the table and the door.

'This fellow who came to see me today, Louis Piedmont, told me all about March. It's a terrible story. Awful story. But it's not the one he's written down, I guarantee it.'

'What d'you mean?'

'March's wife died during a scientific experiment. She was working on classified programmes, top-secret stuff – hence the reason a bloody White House aide comes to see me. Turns out March and she hadn't been getting along lately and he'd flipped. Went off to see a counsellor and then chucked that in because he couldn't take it. Things came to a head last week when Julie found drugs in a briefcase he kept at home. He immediately went storming out of the house, high as a kite, and didn't come back. She had to go back to work the next day – and died tragically in this accident. Well, we all know what happens next. Three days later March shows up here and starts ranting like a maniac. Don't

242

you see, man? He's off his head. We couldn't print this stuff of his — we'd be laughed off the newsstands all the way to Abu Dhabi and back again.'

'Just read it, Max.'

Stewart came round and put a hand on his shoulder. 'Of course I'll read it, Josh. Promise. But you see what I'm saying? March has gone off with the fairies. Bloody sad, but it happens. We both know that, mm?'

Charlie Richards took the prearranged call that night from the payphone in the hall of the boarding-house. Old voice, old cadences. But not the message he'd expected.

'Pack your bags and go home, Charlie.'

'What about the consignment?'

'Leave it where it is. No danger to anyone, as far as I can tell.'

'Just like that, huh?'

'Just like that, Charlie. The world's a surprising place some-times. See you back in Washington.'

Charlie went up to his room, a little lighter than when he'd come down. He broke the MP5 down to its component parts and loaded it in different parts of the rucksack. He'd drop it off at the embassy when he passed through London.

And then he sat on the bed and listened to the slamming doors and the shouts of the Italian girls. He almost felt like knocking on March's door and telling him the good news. *Hey, buddy, you're gonna be OK. Charlie ain't gonna waste you, after all.*

For now, he'd go out on the town and get himself some beers. Long time since he'd had anything to celebrate.

Three days went by before Peter March got the letter. It came, oddly enough, the day after Dick Lovett died in hospital. The story had run on the *Nine o'Clock News* and there'd been a picture of him, and a few quotes from a distraught President, standing, tears close, in the White House press room.

Something about a 'dear and esteemed colleague — a friend and a confidant'.

March had turned it off and gone out for a walk to think about the letter. But that wouldn't take long. 'Thanks for the piece, running it by the legal people, come up and talk next week. Need to clear up a few things . . .'

It was obvious they weren't going to run it. Obvious that the fix was in.

In a couple of days, he'd return to Washington, pack up the few things that remained and come back to Britain for good.

He'd try the other papers with his story – but he already knew the response. If *The Times* wasn't buying from its own man the rest would shy away. It was always the same. Once the health warning was out on the street you were already dead.

Tired and angry, he rang up an old friend in publishing and invited him to dinner.

Two hours into the story, the friend drained his glass for the tenth time that evening and asked the waiter to call a taxi. 'Before I'm too drunk to know what I'm saying, let me give you one piece of advice.' He got up and reached for his coat. 'You've frightened me, Peter, and that's good on one level and bad on another. What you told me is a book. But write it as fiction. If you sell it straight off as fact, people might have a hard time believing you, although in a strange way, when it comes out as a novel, they'll know it's true.'

'What's the bad part?' March leaned back in his chair.

'It's bad because if what you've told me is true, I'm very much afraid you may not live long enough to write it.' He shook March's hand and hurried off into the night.

Three months later, this was the book Peter March delivered to his office.